As he slowly remove [barcode: T0009141] **she took a sharp inta** ~~as the~~ **man's face came into view.**

"I am Destin, Your Highness. Bodyguard to the Byzantine emperor, a commander of his Royal Guard."

For a moment, she felt off-balance, dazed by his striking looks. Despite his swarthy skin being ravaged by silvery scars, he was darkly attractive. With a slash of thick eyebrows, a wide jaw covered in unkempt stubble and a dynamic, broad frame, he was a man in his prime. He had a dominant air of confidence about him, and when she looked into his sharp ebony eyes, she felt a lurch of awareness. They were deep—almost black. Hard and forbidding.

She had recognized his uniform of the Varangian Guard—she had seen the burgundy cloak and dragon emblem before, when she had visited Constantinople. Her father had explained that most of the emperor's men were hired mercenaries with barbaric reputations... Was this man a pagan from the north? It would certainly explain his rough exterior. And she was well-educated. She had studied enough languages to know his tongue had a Norse influence.

Author Note

In Viking times, it was often the case that babies who weren't born "perfect" would be put out to die. It's such an atrocious thought, that a child might have been abandoned if it was thought they wouldn't be able to help the settlement, or that they might bring shame upon the family, and it sparked the idea for the hero in my story...

Destin was born paralyzed on his upper left side and was abandoned as a child. However, he was saved by a wanderer and raised to fight. His prospects had always been limited, so he made his way to Constantinople and joined the Byzantine emperor's Varangian Guard.

Now he has been tasked with fetching the sovereign's runaway bride from Saxony and delivering her to Constantinople for the wedding. The only thing is, Princess Livia doesn't want to get married! And when the two meet, sparks fly. Destin has pledged an oath of fealty and must do his duty and return her, pure and unharmed, to receive his reward. But the closer they become on their journey, the harder it is for him to hand her over... What will win out, his duty or desire?

I hope you enjoy this story as much as I enjoyed writing it. I fell in love with my hero, Destin—but I'm happy to share him with you.

SARAH RODI

The Viking and the Runaway Empress

HARLEQUIN®
HISTORICAL™

Recycling programs
for this product may
not exist in your area.

ISBN-13: 978-1-335-59605-5

The Viking and the Runaway Empress

Harlequin Enterprises ULC
22 Adelaide St. West, 41st Floor
Toronto, Ontario M5H 4E3, Canada
www.Harlequin.com

Printed in U.S.A.

Sarah Rodi has always been a hopeless romantic. She grew up watching old romantic movies recommended by her granddad or devouring love stories from the local library. Sarah lives in the village of Cookham in Berkshire, where she enjoys walking along the River Thames with her husband, her two daughters and their dog. She has been a magazine journalist for over twenty years, but it has been her lifelong dream to write romance for Harlequin. Sarah believes everyone deserves to find their happy-ever-after. You can contact her via @sarahrodiedits or sarahrodiedits@gmail.com. Or visit her website at sarahrodi.com.

Books by Sarah Rodi

Harlequin Historical

One Night with Her Viking Warrior
Claimed by the Viking Chief
Second Chance with His Viking Wife
"Chosen as the Warrior's Wife"
in *Convenient Vows with a Viking*
The Viking and the Runaway Empress

Rise of the Ivarssons

The Viking's Stolen Princess
Escaping with Her Saxon Enemy

Visit the Author Profile page
at Harlequin.com.

For Jackie & Mark and Zoe & Phil
friends who have become family

Chapter One

Harzburg Castle, Saxony,
Twelfth Century

'You Highness, you must now come with us.'

Oh, God, no. No! She had thought she would have longer…

Princess Livia watched the armoured men stride up the aisle of the hall towards her and felt her heart submerge in despair. She had known the Byzantine emperor might one day send for her. Her father had warned her this would happen. And yet, she had been living in denial, hoping it would never come to pass.

'His Royal Sovereign Emperor, Alexios Brasilenius demands that you honour the agreement your father made and join him in Constantinople as his bride,' the leader of the men said, from behind the cold steel covering of his helmet.

So, Alexios had sent his entourage all this way, along the river road and through the Alps to do his bidding. If he was that enamoured with her, why hadn't he come himself? And instead of sending ambassadors, armed with coercive words of love and affection, he had sent his military, armed with weapons—soldiers to seize her and force her into doing her duty. Livia could have wept.

King of the Romans, her father had presented her to the Byzantine emperor at his bride show in Constantinople four winters before. The Great City had been resistant to her father's claim to emperorship in the West and his incursions into the south of Italy, so he had attempted to win them over by offering her hand.

She remembered the cool breeze from the ocean, the majesty of the imperial white palace rising before her—and the swirling sickness in her stomach as she'd been trussed up and put on display for the young emperor's pleasure. She hadn't wanted to disappoint her father, but she had desperately hoped Alexios wouldn't glance her way.

But he had, and her fate had been sealed.

She shivered at the memory of his blue eyes running brutally over her body, making her skin crawl. He had chosen her as his bride and she had felt her life—her freedom—slipping away. Panicked, she'd had no other choice but to flee, then plead for extra time from afar…

Her father had brokered a deal for four winters' grace, until she and Alexios had matured, and she had sought sanctuary at her late mother's castle in Harzburg, hoping this day would never catch up with her. Now she was eighteen winters old, it seemed she had finally been hunted and tracked down.

She knew she was more fortunate than most, to have had this time for herself. And she knew her only role—

her duty—was to make a good marriage alliance, one that would help her family and her empire. But still, she couldn't come to terms with the fact that she had to leave her home. That she had to be a wife to a man she barely knew.

'My father made that agreement when I was just a child,' she said, boldly attempting to stand up to the uniformed men. She wondered if the king would have made the same deal now. After all, during the years that had passed, his firstborn—her brother, Otto—had died, making her the king's sole heir. Whereas previously her hand in marriage had been a gesture of goodwill, if she were to be elected as queen now, it would mean a union of two great empires. It would place a foreigner on the throne of the Holy Roman Empire.

'It has been four winters. More than enough time for you to get used to the idea.'

She didn't think any amount of time would be long enough for her to come to terms with it. Who was this man dressed in head-to-toe leather and chain-mail, who was so unfeeling, so unsympathetic?

'Are you going back on the agreement, Your Highness? I would hate to return to the emperor and have to tell him the word of your king cannot be trusted.'

Her heart jammed in her chest.

'No…my father's word still stands,' she said stoically. 'I'm merely saying he has raised me to follow my own counsel—and I have questions before I agree to leave the safety of my home with someone who hasn't even had the courtesy to introduce themselves,' she clipped.

Slowly removing his polished helmet, shaking out

his full head of outrageously long hair, she took a sharp intake of breath as the man's face came into view. 'I am Destin, Your Highness. Bodyguard to the Byzantine emperor, a commander of his Royal Guard.'

For a moment, she felt off balance, blinded by his striking looks. Despite his swarthy skin being ravaged by silvery scars, he was darkly attractive. With a slash of thick eyebrows and a wide jaw, covered in unkempt stubble, and a dynamic, broad frame, he was a man in his prime. He had a dominant air of confidence about him and when she looked into his sharp, ebony eyes, she felt a lurch of awareness. They were deep—almost black. Hard and forbidding.

She had recognised his uniform of the Varangian Guard—she had seen the burgundy cloak and dragon emblem before, when she had visited Constantinople. Her father had explained that most of the emperor's men were hired mercenaries with barbaric reputations... Was this man a pagan from the north? It would certainly explain his rough exterior. And she was well-educated. She had studied enough languages to know his tongue had a Norse influence.

He was taller, more muscular, more formidable than any other man in the hall. More *everything* than any other man she'd ever come into contact with. And his powerful body had a peculiar impact on her own, as if she had suddenly been shaken awake.

She tried desperately not to stare at the prominent, ragged marks etched into his face and wonder how his left arm was out of use—bent at the elbow, covered in a splint and strapped tightly across his chest. Were they all battle wounds he had suffered?

The tall, dark warrior appeared to have caused a stir in her hall, too, exciting whispers from the lords and ladies about his arm, his fierceness, but the man was unflinching, showing no signs of hearing them. Instead, his cold, assessing eyes remained trained on hers and her heart began to pound out an erratic beat.

His men were like a body of troops in close ranks— like the phalanx of their infantry, surrounding her. It was as if they were planning to lead her away to her execution, not her wedding... But she was not about to be pressured into going anywhere, despite their intimidation tactics—at least not without knowing it was still her father's wish that she did this.

'Speaking of my father... Did Emperor Alexios receive word from our king before he sent you?' she asked, giving a defiant thrust of her chin.

'I met with your father just seven days ago, Your Highness. In fact, he was the one who told me where to find you.'

Her hope all but left her, and she couldn't shake the feeling of being pursued, stalked by a predator, of being trapped.

'Now that I have, it is imperative I speak with you. *Alone.*'

She frowned, her skin prickling with anticipation. She couldn't be left alone with this man—he was the embodiment of danger!

'Commander?' she queried, her eyes drifting to his arm again. Could he ride, fight and defend with such an injury? 'You can say whatever you need to say to me here.'

'What I need to say must be said in private, between the two of us, Princess Livia,' he urged, lowering his tone. And she had the feeling he never gave in. That he was unable to compromise.

She pressed her lips together, her chest tightening. She didn't *have* to speak with him. She could say no. And yet a curious part of her was telling her to listen to him. He had piqued her interest, making her wonder why she needed to hear what he was going to say, away from the prying eyes and ears of the court. Perhaps he had a message from her father…and perhaps it would make it easier to oppose his demands to take her away without an audience.

Her eyes darted around, wondering for a moment if she could even escape, make a run for it if she sent the nobles and his men away. But she was older now, her days of running away were behind her. Besides, she could see her unwelcome visitor had soldiers guarding each of the doors and he would no doubt give chase.

She was aware he was waiting for an answer and she forced her mouth to move.

'Very well,' she said, rising out of her chair and drawing herself up to full height, giving the commander a challenging stare. 'Leave us,' she commanded her court.

Gasps and mutterings echoed around the room.

'Your Highness—' her chief advisor protested. 'Are you sure?'

'Yes.' She nodded. 'Leave us,' she said again, sterner than before. And her advisor bowed and began to retreat at once, and the rest of the lords and ladies in the hall began to move too.

The commander held her in his gaze until the last of the people filtered out of the room, all whispering and muttering, finally closing the door behind them, and the silence stretched. She was excruciatingly aware of him. She had never seen such an imposing man.

'Well?' she said curtly. 'What is it that you want to say to me, Commander? This had better be good.'

He took a dominating step towards her. 'I have come to tell you your position here is precarious, Your Highness. You must leave with me immediately.'

'The life of a royal *is* precarious,' she said. 'You tell me nothing I don't already know.'

'I'm not finished!' he bit out. 'What I am about to say may come as a shock…you may want to sit down,' he said, gesturing to her seat.

She shook her head stubbornly.

'All right,' he said slowly, as if he was trying to find the right words. 'It's your father, Highness… I am sorry to be the one to have to tell you this, but the king is dying.'

It took a moment for the words to hit home.

'What?' she gasped, her hand coming across her chest. Of all the things she'd been expecting him to say, it hadn't been that. She felt herself sway slightly, and he reached out to grip her arm. But his long fingers curling around her elbow did nothing to reassure her—instead, his touch sent unsettling heat rippling across her skin.

'You were sent word he was injured in battle in his campaign into southern Italy, yes?'

She nodded. 'Yes, but we were told it wasn't serious.'

'Your father and his council didn't want to cast doubt or cause unrest among his people. Not until your safety has been secured. Only a handful of people know. His wound is infected. He is in excruciating pain.'

Her throat closed in fear and she cast off his hand, lowering herself back down into her seat, her legs feeling weak. 'Are you certain?' she muttered.

'I saw it for myself. I'm sorry, Your Highness.'

'But is there not a possibility he might yet recover?' she said.

She wasn't ready to hear of her father's passing—or of her possible ascension to the throne. Despite the years of preparation, she wondered if she would ever be ready for either. She had lost her mother when she was a girl; she did not want to be parted from her father too. And to be queen at such a young age...

And yet she knew that on the death of a king, succession was not hereditary. This would throw the empire into chaos. The next Holy Roman Emperor would have to be elected by an Electoral College. If Otto had been alive, he would no doubt have had the greater claim than anyone to secure the crown, but she was a woman, and she knew she was at risk of losing the title to a man. But who?

'The healers are doing all that they can. But the infection is spreading. Word will slowly get out and it will cause instability among the people. I have come to escort you to Constantinople quickly and safely...'

Safely? With *him*? If the situation hadn't been so

fraught, she might have laughed. There was nothing safe about this man…

'Surely I am needed in Rome, my *own* empire, not Constantinople right now? I need to be there, at my father's side. To be there for our people.'

'It is not safe for you here,' he said, cutting her off. 'We have heard of a plot to remove you from the line to the throne. We must secure your marriage to the Byzantine emperor before that can happen.'

The room began to spin. Her father was dying. And now there were rumours of an assassination attempt on her life?

'A plot by whom?'

'Your uncle, Prince Lothair, Your Highness.'

'No!' she said, aghast. 'He wouldn't—' she said, shaking her head fiercely.

'He has. He is. Prince Lothair was at the palace at the same time I was. He was privy to learning of your father's pain. He left swiftly after, and we believe he may have tried to rally support among some of the nobles. You must know many dislike the thought of a woman, and one of your age, petitioning the Electoral College and coming to power when your father dies… We think he intends to fight you for the crown, and stop any chance, no matter how slim, of you coming to power.'

No matter how slim…

'You give your opinion rather freely, Commander. If my chances are so small at being successful, why does my uncle see me as a threat? Why is he so determined to remove me?'

'It is easier to prevent something from happening in the first place...'

'Than have to go up against me later...' she finished for him.

'Your Highness, we need to get you to Emperor Alexios immediately. A husband and an ally might help to secure your position.'

'You think so?' she bit out.

So this was why the emperor had sent for her after all this time. If word had reached him of her father's possible demise, now he knew that if something were to happen to her and the Roman king he was at risk of losing all the lands and wealth she would have brought with her to the marriage.

Oh, God, she hoped her dear father would survive...

'I wonder, is the emperor interested in me, or instead all that he is set to inherit through our marriage?'

'I would not assume to know the emperor's feelings on the matter. But if you are to petition to be queen, many believe you need a man to help you rule here.'

'I do not!' she said, launching herself out of her seat once more. His patronising words sent a shaft of anger through her blood. 'Perhaps my people do not wish to see my marriage take place, for fear of a foreigner ascending our throne... Perhaps the emperor should take note and find another bride...'

The commander's reprimanding gaze narrowed on her. 'Your people might see an ally in Constantinople. What is it, Princess? Your father is agreeable to the match, why aren't you? Do you not wish to marry?'

No! She did not wish to marry Alexios, she thought

miserably... And she did not want to lose authority to a man. Someone who would use her as a puppet, for power—to claim her lands for himself.

'That is none of *your* concern!'

It was interesting Alexios had only sent for her now that her father was dying. Now that he realised what was at stake. If they wed before her father died, the terms would still stand. If she became queen afterwards, then the prize would be great indeed. Alexios would be ruler of not one but two empires. And yet she did not want to lose her throne to her uncle either. But she wasn't about to share any of that with this man. A stranger...

'Isn't it? Seems it is as I've been sent all this way to fetch you and take you to Constantinople. Perhaps I would understand your reservations about coming with me if you explained.'

He had such a commanding presence, she had to will her legs to stop trembling. She had to force herself to stand up to him.

'I do not have to explain myself to you! And I don't believe my father sent you... I would have heard directly from the palace. He would have sent his own men to fetch his heir, not a foreign convoy.'

He reached inside his leather vest, behind his armoured sling, and pulled out a delicate piece of material. 'He said you wouldn't believe me. He told me to give you this.'

Her fingers reached out to curl over the square of embroidery. It had belonged to her mother, a long time ago, and Livia had slept with it when she was a child, to give her comfort. She felt a sob rise in her throat, the tears burning behind her eyes, and forced them away. She would never let this man see her torment.

'I was sent to Rome to find you, but met with your father instead. He agreed it would be safer for you in Constantinople right now. He welcomed Alexios's support in protecting you. He thought my men might be less sought out than his on this mission.' He stepped towards her. 'Let us not argue the details any more—or forget that we *both* have a duty that we need to fulfil.'

She swallowed. *Duty.* It always came back to that, didn't it? She felt it like a weight strapped to her feet, pulling her down, deeper and deeper. She knew she couldn't escape the agreement that had been made four winters before to link their empires through marriage. She knew she had been given longer than she ever hoped for. And she knew she couldn't break her father's word.

'You are very insistent. I wonder, Commander, what's in it for you? What do you get as a reward for taking me there? You are a hired mercenary, yes? Is coin your motivation?'

'One of them.'

'And if you return empty-handed?'

'Then neither of us will have fulfilled our promise. You should know I live by three rules, Your Highness— courage, conduct and fealty—and I will not be moved on any of them. If you deny Emperor Alexios, he will see it as an affront and you will lose your own honour and respect, as well as an ally at a time when it seems you need one the most.'

'Is that a threat?' she asked, her eyes narrowing on him.

'It is advice, Your Highness. Let the emperor try to help secure your throne. It would be far better for Alexios to govern your people alongside you, peacefully, than to lose your crown entirely.'

I have no choice, she thought, shaking her head.

'He must think a lot of you to send you. To *trust* you.'

'Yes,' he said, giving nothing else away.

'All right, Commander, I will come with you,' she said, tipping her face up to look at him, accepting her fate. 'But I do have one condition of my own.'

He stepped towards her, and his large, intimidating body was just a breath away from hers. A muscle flickered in his cheek. 'I don't make concessions.'

No, she believed that.

'Do not forget that *if* I marry your leader, you will bend the knee to me also, will you not?' she asked.

His right hand tightened around the hilt of his sword.

'I will go with you to Constantinople,' she continued. 'But you will take me to see my father in Rome on the way. We need to pass through there anyway, do we not?' She needed to see her father, to see if all this man was saying was true. She needed to look the king in the eyes to verify whether this marriage alliance was what he still wanted for her—that there was no way out. And if he was as ill as the commander was saying, she wanted to say her goodbyes.

The man gave a short, sharp nod. 'Very well. We leave at first light. But I will determine the route we take. And it will be just you, no entourage—'

'But…'

He held up his hand to silence her. 'We will be more

conspicuous if you bring a convoy. We can send for your maids and advisors after we have reached Constantinople.'

Could she really travel alone with this man and his soldiers?

'Then you and your men are staying for this evening's meal—and for the night?'

'Yes.' He nodded, moving away from her. 'I will make sure we won't cause you any trouble.'

She watched his broad frame and tall legs move as he stalked towards the door. Trouble...he had been here less than an hour and she already felt her whole world had been turned upside down.

Destin was impressed. He had expected tears. He had expected Princess Livia to try to run. But he hadn't expected to come up against this stoic—and stunning—woman.

Looking around the small hall, decorated simply with wall hangings and a few shields, the people talking jovially, she had created a well-run home here. But it was rather modest for a princess, the daughter of the Roman king. She must know she had an even grander home waiting for her in Constantinople—that she was destined for greater things. He wondered why she had hidden herself away here, amid the rugged countryside in the mountains, far away from her father's grand and glamorous court in Rome. A woman of her age and status usually wanted to be seen. And yet she had bloomed in such harsh conditions, like the alpine flowers he'd seen on his way here, springing up from the barren landscape of the mountains, their vibrancy taking you by surprise.

Tucking into his meal of meat and vegetables, he stole a glance at her, watching her push her food around her bowl with her spoon, barely eating. She had grown up since the last time he'd seen her, when she had participated in Alexios's bride show. Back then, she had been a plain, graceless girl, holding herself awkwardly. But in the winters that had passed she had blossomed into a beautiful maiden. The emperor would be pleased. Perhaps it would ease Alexios's own reservations about marriage.

She had smooth olive skin; high, sculpted cheekbones and sparkling jewel-like golden-brown eyes. Her hair was silky black—like the colour of the figs on the trees in Constantinople, and just like them, she was carefully cultivated, with a delicate, ornamental quality about her. She wore a simple blue silk tunic, and a dark stola pinned over the top with brooches, yet her slender body beneath made him think of that ripe, pink flesh of the sweet fruit…

Helvete!

His response to her was instinctive. He had felt the bolt of awareness, like an arrow shot from a crossbow. His body had unexpectedly hardened, reacting to hers. It was most inconvenient. The last thing he needed was to be attracted to the emperor's bride. He was oathbound to fetch the sovereign's runaway empress from Saxony and deliver her to Constantinople for their wedding. He had accepted the task with a great sense of duty—and he could be condemned to death just for thinking about her like this. She was forbidden and he must never forget it.

Her eyes had widened as he'd removed his helmet. They'd flickered over the ugly scars on his face, before drifting down to his arm strapped across his chest. He was used to it, of course he was—the curiosity, the stares and the whispers—but it never made it any easier. And he was certain it was one of the reasons he'd been chosen for this task. Yes, he was one of the emperor's commanders, and he had proved himself in battle time and time again. But he felt sure he had been chosen not just because of his prowess on the battlefield, so that he would be able to keep her safe, but because of the way he looked. If anyone was going to spend days travelling in close proximity to the emperor's bride-to-be, it made sense for it to be him—a man no woman could ever find attractive.

Princess Livia looked lost in thought, and he felt the prickle of guilt that he was the cause of her melancholy—a dark stranger descending on her peace and happiness, bringing her distressing news of her father's failing health and her uncle's deceit. He had been forceful in his demands that she leave with him, and he hadn't missed the tension in her body, the way her arms had protectively wrapped around her waist. He had sensed her reluctance—to leave this place and be wed. But he was just the messenger, sent to fetch her—she was the one who had agreed to this marriage! She and her father were the ones who were responsible for the union. And this alliance would still make her empress of an empire, if she wasn't successful in securing her own crown here. He couldn't understand her objections. Most women would aspire to make such an advantageous marriage. To live a life of exceptional privilege.

All of a sudden some of the men he'd sent out on a scouting party burst through the doors, causing a commotion. 'They're here, Commander!'

He launched himself out of his chair, his right hand instinctively reaching for his sword, and he felt Princess Livia's eyes swing to look at him across the room.

He beckoned the men to approach, but eager to hear what they had to say, he met them halfway, his long legs carrying him quickly across the hall. 'We scoured the surrounding forests and fields. All was quiet. We had just begun our return journey when we saw a convoy of men approaching from the east. They will be upon the gates before this feast has ended.'

'How many?'

'Forty. Maybe fifty.'

The princess's delicate, floral scent drifted under his nose, alerting Destin to the fact that she had crossed the distance between them and reached his side, before she even spoke. 'Who is it?' she asked. 'What's wrong?'

'There are men approaching the fortress,' he informed her.

'They fly the banners of the phoenix, Commander,' his man said.

'My uncle...' she whispered, her hand coming up to her lips.

'Man the walls. Prepare all the men for battle,' Destin said.

She gasped. 'No! There will be no fighting here.

I don't want anyone to get hurt because of me. I will speak with my uncle, try to appeal to—'

'No,' he said, cutting her off. 'That is honourable, Your Highness, but we cannot risk Prince Lothair and his men seeing you. We don't know what they're prepared to do, how far they're prepared to go to secure his claim to the crown. They must be told you're not here. We must leave now.'

Her beautiful golden eyes were round and wide. 'Surely it would be better to stay? The castle is impregnable. We are safer here, where we can defend ourselves should we need to. My men will protect me, I will stay hidden…'

He shook his head unwaveringly, staring down at her. 'They might decide to lay siege—hold you captive while they make arrangements for your uncle to ascend the throne. We must get you away from here.'

'But I haven't had time to gather my belongings… And what about my people?'

'I fear you will put them in more danger by being here. It gives your uncle's men a reason to stay. No,' he said, determined, consulting no one. 'I must get you to Constantinople.'

He turned to his men. 'Ready the horses. Tell the guards on the gate to be on alert. They are to inform these visitors that the princess departed days ago.'

They instantly moved into action, not questioning his command. He released his hand on his sword to take the princess by the arm. 'Let's get what you need for the journey and go.'

The impact of their skin touching was disturbing.

He had felt it earlier, when he'd told her of her father's failing health. It had been the only time during their interaction that she had faltered. Now he felt the frisson of heat again in his fingertips.

He led her out of the hall, but as soon as they reached the corridor, she swung out of his grasp.

'I can walk by myself!' she spat. 'And I don't appreciate being ordered about. I am in charge here.'

'It's for your own good, Highness.'

'Is it?'

She strode down the corridor and he tried to keep pace with her. When she finally reached a doorway and halted, his body collided with hers—and the reaction in his lower body was instant. He drew in a sharp breath.

'Do you mind?' she bit out.

She pushed open the door and stepped inside, before looking back at him, hesitant.

'This is your room?' he asked, scanning the corridor, before ducking his head inside the chamber to check it was safe.

'Yes.'

He took in the huge bed in the centre, scattered with furs, and the trunks overflowing with clothes and trinkets. Silk tunics and an array of stolas lay abandoned on the floor, where she'd undressed and discarded them.

'You're not coming in. You can wait there,' she demanded.

'It doesn't look like there's any room to move in there anyway.' He smirked.

Her eyes narrowed on him and she opened her mouth to bite back a retort when there was the sound of an almighty commotion outside, followed by shouts and screams coming from the hall. They shared a look.

'Inside. Now.'

He backed her into the room and closed the door behind him.

'What are you doing?' she screeched. 'You can't be in here!'

'That's the least of your concerns at the moment, Highness. Now grab what you need so we can get going. Bring as many layers as you can.'

As many layers as she could wear would be good if only to cover her gentle curves and put as much material between them as possible. His body was still responding to the impact of colliding with her out in the corridor, and being in this confined space, her opulent bed standing between them, her scent wrapping around him... What was the matter with him? He needed to get himself together.

'We'll be taking the Via Imperii and the mountain pass through the Alps to Rome. It's a dangerous path. And it's going to be cold where we're heading. Despite the fact we're coming into summer, there will still be snowfields...'

'I *have* made the journey before,' she informed him.

'By horse?'

'And cart.'

'Ah,' he said.

'What was that noise? What do you think's going on?' she said, rummaging around in her trunks, pulling out a cloak and a satchel, and beginning to stuff it with clothes. He noticed her slender fingers were trembling.

'I don't know. It sounds like your uncle's men aren't wasting any time. Perhaps they don't believe you're not here.' He looked at the handful of silk in her hand and frowned. 'Bring something…less arresting. We will want to go unnoticed. You'll want to blend in.'

If that was even possible. She was stunningly beautiful. She had been born to be looked at for all the right reasons, unlike him. He had always been stared at because of his arm, for being different.

Still on alert, he checked the corridor again. It went against every bone in his body not to go outside and help his men, to find out what was happening, but he also didn't trust anyone but himself with the princess's safety. He had to get her out of here. It was what he'd been ordered to do. It was his task and his alone.

Turning around, he saw Princess Livia was sitting on the bed, tugging on a pair of long boots and he caught a flash of pale, creamy skin at her ankle. His mouth dried.

'Hurry up,' he whispered.

Finally, she appeared beside him, wrapping her cloak around her.

'Ready?' he asked.

'If I have to be.'

He took the satchel from her and slowly opened the door and checked the corridor again.

The sound of metal clashing and men roaring sent a chill down his spine. He could hear the release of arrows and the pelting sound of bodies being hit. This was worse than he'd thought. He had hoped Prince Lothair might want to just keep her prisoner while he tried to usurp the throne, but he was clearly willing to do anything to remove Princess Livia from her position.

'At least my men are here to help your guards put up some resistance. It will allow for a distraction for us to get out of here. Is there another way out, apart from the main gate?'

'Your men aren't coming with us? It's just us?' she asked, panicked.

'Looks like it, for now. They'll have to catch up with us when it's safe to do so.'

She nodded slowly, reluctantly accepting what he'd said. 'There's the well and a secret passage. It leads us out into the forest at the bottom of the mountains.'

He nodded. 'Then that's what we'll do.'

'But what about the horses? We can't make the journey to Rome on foot.'

'Getting you out of here unseen is my main concern right now. We'll worry about finding some horses later. Which way?'

She gestured with her head, and he took her upper arm again and propelled her forward.

She immediately shrugged him off. 'Don't touch me!'

A group of soldiers ran past them in the corridor. 'Man the gates. Get the women and children to safety. Don't give up the princess's whereabouts,' he barked out to them, and they nodded, heeding his command.

He followed her along the corridor to some winding steps which led them down and down, deeper into the basement of the castle.

She kept glancing back behind her, as noises of the skirmish carried on above them.

'Do not fear. You have my sword and protection, Highness.'

She looked back at him. 'Can you even fight like that?' she said tautly.

His eyes narrowed on her in the darkness, as he took two steps at once. 'Like what?'

'I'm just wondering why the emperor and my father thought you were the best person to fetch and protect me. How can you fight if one of your arms has already been injured?'

An old anger roared through him. He hated that she was doubting him and his ability, making assumptions… He had always despised being judged as weak or incapable. And yet, why wouldn't she think that? She thought he had been temporarily wounded in battle. He knew he should correct her, but what was the point? He didn't want her pity—or to see the repulsion on her face. And it would destroy what little confidence she had in him even further if she knew the truth.

'I don't need both my arms to fight, do I?'

'I don't know, do you?'

'No.'

He'd spent his adult life strengthening the rest of his body to compensate for the failings of his upper left side. Born without the use of it, he knew it was the reason he'd been abandoned by his family. Perhaps he had brought shame upon them, or they'd felt he wouldn't be able to contribute to their settlement, but whatever the reason, it had been unbearably tough growing up knowing he'd been unwanted. Rejected. As a boy he'd always felt like he'd been a disappointment to others and he'd loathed his own body for letting him down.

It had been a hard existence, a childhood spent being mocked, as he'd learned to get by with the use of just one arm, his other hanging lifeless and loose. As soon as he'd been old enough, he'd learned how to fight, building up his strength, never wanting to feel weak or incapable, wanting to prove himself to silence the critics. It was why he had left Norway and headed to Constantinople, determined to make a name for himself in the emperor's army. And he'd thrived on the glory of winning, finally beginning to receive the praise and recognition he'd always longed for.

Coming to a stop at a solid wooden door, Princess Livia tried to open it, but it wouldn't budge.

'Move out of the way,' he barked. And using the frustration surging through him, the anger at being judged by her, he pressed his full weight against the wood and pushed it open.

The door led to a long narrow tunnel, but they could barely see further than a few feet ahead, as it was thrown into darkness. They could have done with the light of a fire, but it was too late now.

'I'll go first,' he said.

It smelt dank and musty in the tunnel, and he felt along the wall with his hand, unable to see the way, treading slowly. Water splashed beneath their feet and he thought it was a good thing she couldn't see what they were wading through.

'How long does this go on for?' he asked.

'A mile, perhaps.'

'Does your uncle know about this?'

'I don't think so…'

'Good.'

The tunnel felt endless, so much further than it probably was. And everything was heightened in the dark—the awful battle noises from above, her delicate footsteps pattering behind him and the sound of her rapid breathing. He was so aware of her. She stumbled a few times and he stopped to steady her, their hands colliding awkwardly. Eventually, he gave up and took her hand and placed it on his shoulder. To his surprise, she didn't object. Her slender fingers felt warm as they curled around him and on the occasions when he slowed, her body was crushed against his back, making him tense. He wanted to reach the end just so he could get out of her proximity. If he'd known what torture this would be, he might have risked another way out. He didn't want to be attracted to her—he disliked himself for being so. It went against everything he believed in. It threatened his loyalty and everything he prided himself in being.

'We must be nearly at the end now,' he said.

Finally, they reached a stone staircase that wound its way upwards towards the daylight. He pushed open the trapdoor at the top, relieved to breathe in the fresh night air, and clambered out into the clearing, before holding out his hand to help her up. Stubbornly, she refused his assistance. She was fiercely independent, he realised, rejecting help, despite being in need. But he could relate to that.

He sighed, raking his hand over his hair and waiting for his eyes to readjust to the evening light.

And then he heard her strangled cry, saw her reel in shock. He turned to look at what she was staring at, and nothing could have prepared him for the sight before them. Looking back at the castle, built on a high escarpment into the mountains, flickering flames engulfed the rampart walls and the terrible sound of screams and wailing carried across to them on the wind. People were scurrying around the battlements like ants, and the violent sounds of men fighting and clashing metal thundered in the sky.

'We must go back!' she gasped.

'No! There's nothing you can do for them now.'

'There is. We can't just leave them,' she said, horrified. 'We must try!'

'No, look at the lengths your uncle is prepared to go to. He's burning down one of your father's castles to get to you. See reason! If we go back there, he'll try to kill you.'

'But they're my people. They rely on me,' she wailed. 'And I've just abandoned them!'

'Yes, they're you're people. Which means they are prepared to die for you.'

'Please,' she begged suddenly, gripping his arm. 'There are women and children inside. We must help them.'

He regarded her silently for a few moments, and looked down at her fingers on his body. 'We can't. We need to carry on. We need to get you away from here and keep you safe. That is the best thing we can do for your empire right now.'

'The king won't like it if we don't help them.'

'The emperor won't like it if you get hurt.'

'Coward!' she threw at him.

A muscle flickered in his jaw, his brows knitting together. 'What did you call me?'

She planted her hands on her hips. 'A coward,' she said again.

He had been called a weakling, a freak—you name it—over the winters that had passed. He'd been told he should never have been born. But he'd never been called a coward before.

He took a step towards her. 'I've been called many things in my time, but never that. I'm not one to shy away from a fight, Princess. Believe me, I don't like it. If I thought it would make a difference if I went back there, I would go. But I can't risk you being found. You are my priority. If Lothair is determined to stop you getting to Rome and to the Emperor, I am intent to hinder his plans. My duty is to keep you safe.'

'So you're prepared to die for me too, are you?'

He held her gaze. 'Yes.'

She flicked her hair over her shoulder. 'Why would you do that?' she said, her voice sounding strained, shaking her head. 'You don't even know me.'

'It is what I've been sent to do.' His face betrayed nothing. 'And I trust my men to do all they can to help the women and children of your castle escape.'

And yet as she stared up at him, her hands on her hips, fire in her golden eyes, he wondered if she was right. For the first time ever, was he afraid? Not of fighting. Never. But afraid of the traitorous feelings rushing through him… He didn't like the thoughts he was having about her, the way his body was responding to her… He was finding he wanted to get this journey over with, because the sooner he got her to Constantinople, out of his sight, out of his mind, the safer he would be.

'This isn't how I wanted us to start our journey, already under attack, being pursued by your uncle's men.' He took one last look at the burning castle. 'But we stick to the plan. Right now, I need to get you as far away from here as possible.'

As far away from himself as possible.

'Let's go.'

Chapter Two

'Do you have any nearby allies? We'll need to borrow some horses. The journey should take no longer than a week on horseback, but walking…'

A week! She didn't want to be alone with this man for a week! He was hateful—and intrusive! He'd demanded she leave with him, giving her no choice. And she'd seen the way he'd looked around her room, judging her. She could tell he didn't miss anything, not the slightest detail, and it unnerved her. She felt as if she couldn't flinch, or make a sound, without him noticing.

You are my priority,' he had said.

It should have reassured her, but she wasn't sure she wanted to be the focus of his attention. There was nowhere to hide.

'Is there somewhere your uncle wouldn't think of heading? A small settlement or lone farm perhaps?' he asked.

She nodded, pleased he was at least asking for her advice. 'Yes, I know a place…'

'Which way?'

She pointed to the south. 'Through the forest and down the valley.'

'How far?'

'A few miles.'

'Let's make that our aim for tonight then.'

Why did it have to be him who had come for her? Someone a little less hostile might have been good... Someone a little less intense, who didn't look at her with irritation in his brittle black eyes and stony face.

She lingered, still reluctant to leave, looking back at the blazing fortress. 'It was my mother's castle,' she said, shaking her head sadly. 'I cannot believe my uncle would do this. How could he harm innocent people?'

'It's amazing what people will do in their pursuit of power, Highness.'

'But my father hasn't even passed. He may live yet...' she said, hopeful. 'Why would my uncle risk being hanged for treason?'

'Come away now,' the commander said.

And she realised his lack of an answer, his absence of words, conveyed just how sick her father was. She shivered, the reality dawning on her. Her uncle would only risk this if her father's death was imminent.

She fought against her desire to sit down on the rock at her feet, put her head in her hands and sob. To cry for her father and her people. Instead, she ran her hands over her face and drew in a breath as they began their descent through the wooded valley. She focused on following the commander's broad back, watching where he placed his feet. She noticed he was vigilant, on alert.

'Why did you choose to come here, after leaving

Constantinople, instead of going to Rome?' he asked her over his shoulder. 'Of all the palaces… This doesn't strike me as the place a princess would want to live.' He unsheathed his sword and began to use it to hack down some of the brambly undergrowth to make it easier for them to get through.

'Because it's my mother's castle. Because she's buried here. It made me feel closer to her,' she said, wading through the weeds behind him. 'I spent many happy times here as a child. It felt more like home to me than my father's palace in Rome.'

He nodded. 'What happened to your mother?' he asked.

'She died. In childbirth, when I was just eight winters old,' she said, catching her skirt on some nettles and stopping briefly to untangle herself. 'The baby too.'

'I'm sorry.'

'She would hate to have seen her home in the state it is in tonight.'

He halted on the path he was carving out of the brambles and turned to look at her in the moonlight. 'She wouldn't care about the stone walls, she would care that you were safe.'

She nodded, accepting what he said, and she was surprised it did give her a little comfort. 'Where are you from, Commander?'

He hacked down a few more branches. 'You know, it might be better to lose the formalities in case we encounter anyone on our journey. You can call me Destin. And I don't want to draw attention to the fact I have

the Roman princess in my midst, so if you don't mind,
I will call you Livia.'

She nodded. 'Very well… Destin,' she said, trying
out his name on her tongue. 'Are you from the north?'

He gave her a glance, as if he was wary of her question. 'Yes. Norway.'

'Constantinople is a long way from your home and
family. Do they still live there?'

She noticed he tensed, gripping his sword tighter.

'What? You get to ask me questions, but I'm not allowed to ask you anything? I'm meant to just follow you
willingly, not knowing anything about you?'

She heard him sigh and he relented. 'Like your
mother, my family is also not around any more.'

'Then I'm sorry too.' He obviously didn't want to talk
about it, so she tried to change the subject. 'What brought
you to Constantinople and the Emperor's Guard?'

He sighed. 'You know, we can walk in silence. You
don't have to ask me questions just to be polite.'

'I'm not being polite. I merely want to know a little
about the man who arrived at my home and demanded I
leave with him, before bringing a whole load of trouble
to my door when he promised he wouldn't!'

He paused again, slanting her a look. 'I didn't bring
the trouble, your uncle did,' he said, correcting her.

'I was jesting…' she said.

He didn't break a smile and she rolled her eyes. This
was surely going to be the longest week in the world!

They carried on battling through the undergrowth
for a while, and he tried to help her with climbing over
nettles, holding out his hand to assist her, but each time

she ignored him, wary of how his touch made her feel, sending a prickle of awareness and ripples of heat along her skin.

'I came to the Great City wanting to make a name for myself—and my fortune,' he said, relenting. 'Constantinople is an impressive place. You will like it there...'

'I *have* visited once before...'

'I remember. And yet you don't seem in any hurry to go back.'

'I am happy here. Or was...'

She hadn't wanted to leave, but would there be anything left of her home once the night was over?

They both fell into silence as they walked on, with only the moonlight dappling through the trees to guide them. It felt good to be putting as many miles between them and her uncle as possible, yet her thoughts kept wandering back to her people, hoping they would survive the ordeal.

Her situation had changed so fast.

One moment, she'd been surrounded by her closest friends and advisors at the castle. She'd spent the day walking and riding, and now, she had left all that behind.

She noticed the commander kept a tight grip of his sword, constantly glancing around, surveying their surroundings—like a wolf ready to pounce. He had an extraordinarily strong body despite his injury, and she couldn't believe she was out here, all alone with this man. She was certain this wasn't what her father or the emperor would have had in mind. And yet what could she do about it? She had no choice but to place her trust in him.

She was pleased when finally, the small, familiar farmstead came into view.

'There it is,' she said, rushing forward, out of the forest and into the field. 'I can go and explain—'

Destin gripped her arm, hard, tugging her back, pulling her down to the hedge line. 'No, we need to make sure it's safe,' he said in hushed tones.

'There's no one out here!' she said.

'We don't know that. And we don't want to compromise your friends, do we?' he said, still holding her, his long fingers curled around her arm.

She swallowed. 'No,' she relented, shaking her head.

As if satisfied she wasn't going to make a run for it, he loosened his grip on her. 'Where are the stables?' he whispered.

'Round the back. Do you intend to take the horses without asking?' she said, incredulous.

'We're just going to borrow them... I'm sure if they're your friends they would loan them willingly if they knew what danger you were in. Yes?'

She thought about it, then nodded.

'All right. Keep low and follow me.'

She was glad when he released her and they began to push through the fields of barley, trying not to make a sound. Her friend, Theodosia, would find it absurd if she could see her creeping though her field. But if the commander thought their being here would put Theo and her husband at risk, she would do as she was told.

They headed round to the back of the building, keeping low, and finding the stables, they slipped inside. The horses began to whinny at having visitors so late at night, but as Livia stroked their noses, they calmed, recognising her.

'These horses know you.'

'The owner is one of my closest friends. We ride together often,' she said.

Destin nodded. 'Take one you feel comfortable riding for a long distance then,' he said.

She watched as he made his way around the animals, assessing them, approaching a dark stallion.

'I would advise against that one,' she said. 'He's lame. He's been limping these past few days and no one is sure what's wrong. My friend Theodosia is worried they may have to put him down.'

His eyes narrowed, studying the horse's gait. The animal shifted from one leg to the other. His left leg was definitely sore. 'They would put him down for having an injured limb?'

'I guess if he can't ride or work…' She shrugged.

'Then he doesn't deserve to live?'

'It's not my decision,' she sighed. 'I'm just saying you shouldn't ride him.'

But he didn't seem to be listening. He stroked his large hand down the horse's nose, calmly, gaining his trust. Then he stooped to run his fingers over the horse's bent leg, inspecting it, checking for any signs of injury. The horse nickered. Destin crouched down and lifted the hoof and ran his thumb around it, clearing it of debris. One single sharp stone seemed to be wedged in. He asked Livia to hold the horse's hoof steady and he reached for a small knife in his belt. He used the tip of the blade to coax the stone out of the crevice, and as it fell free, she couldn't believe it, almost instantly the horse shuffled back and put weight on his hoof again. The lameness had been instantly cured.

'I think I'll ride him after all,' Destin said, looking up at her, his eyes defiantly blazing into hers.

'You know about animals?' she asked, surprised.

'Only that they don't deserve to be killed for having a bad limb,' he said. 'He deserves a chance just like the rest of us.'

She sensed he was cross with her and she couldn't understand it. 'For a man who says he doesn't shy away from fighting, who has presumably been in many battles, I'm shocked you care about the feelings of a horse,' she said, crossing her hands over her chest. 'You don't seem to care about anyone else's feelings!' she said angrily.

'You're talking of your people back at the castle, I suppose. Or yourself. I told you, I did what I did to keep you safe,' he said, rising to his feet, pushing his hand through his hair. 'Look, we're both tired. How about we rest here for a while and leave at first light?'

She nodded, her face brightening just a little. 'My friend would happily make up some beds for us.'

He shook his head. 'We can't risk letting them know we're here. I'm afraid it's going to be a bed of straw for you tonight.'

Livia sighed. She didn't have the energy to argue. Her legs were weary from the long walk and she slumped down onto a bundle of hay, at least safe in the knowledge her friends were nearby. And she felt reassured the horses were here. If anything were to happen, if he was to try anything, she could call out…

Destin sat down opposite her, guarding the door. 'Get some rest now, Highness.'

She studied him. Did he really think she would just fall asleep on his command? That she wouldn't be worried about being alone with him and his intentions? He must know a woman of her stature would never have been in this situation before.

'Livia,' she corrected him. 'You said we were going to use our names.'

'Livia,' he whispered, and her skin erupted in goose bumps.

She leaned back against the wall of the stables, glad to rest her aching muscles. And her thoughts wandered to how he had looked after the horse, stubbornly helping the animal when she'd told him it was lame. Perhaps he did have an ounce of compassion in him, after all, although she hadn't seen much of it so far. But still, she didn't think he would harm her. No, he took his duty much too seriously. *'Courage, conduct, and fealty,'* were the rules he lived by, he had said. Or he simply wanted a reward for taking her to the emperor safely. She could probably drift off and yet every time she allowed herself to close her eyes, sleep eluded her…

'He doesn't deserve to be killed for having a bad limb. He deserves a chance just like the rest of us.'

Destin's angry words came back to her. Did he liken himself to the animal? she wondered.

'What happened to your arm?' she asked, surprising herself.

He looked up sharply, his brittle black eyes boring into her across the dark space.

'What did you do to it?' she said.

He cleared his throat. 'Actually, I was born like this.'

She drew in a sharp breath. 'Oh. I'm sorry... I thought...'

The silence stretched.

'What's...wrong with it?'

'Do you always pry this much?' he asked.

'If you don't want to answer...'

He sighed. 'I can't move it...use it, from the shoulder down. I can't feel anything on that side of my upper body.'

'Nothing?'

'No.'

'That must be hard...'

'I get by.'

Her brow furrowed, thinking over what he'd told her. Wondering what impact an impairment like that must have had on his life. And yet, it didn't make him any less attractive. Any less formidable. It was just surprising that he had become a great warrior, a soldier of fortune, with such an ailment. And before she could stop herself, she'd outed the words she'd been thinking. 'How is it that you came to be a commander in the Emperor's Guard, what with...?'

His eyes widened, as if incredulous. 'How did I get here?' he asked, giving a bitter laugh. 'You're unbelievable.' And she instantly realised she'd asked the wrong thing. That she'd offended him. 'Despite what you might think, I'm a good fighter,' he said, his voice deadly. He got to his feet and paced to the door. 'Perhaps I've learned I have to try harder, be better, more committed, than anyone else.'

She swallowed. She could believe that; he seemed very determined.

'How did *you* get here?' he threw back at her. 'If we're on the subject of asking personal questions, how is it that you came to be the emperor's bride, when you don't even want to be?'

Her eyes narrowed on him. 'I *told* you. I'm being held to an agreement my father made when I was too young to make the choice for myself.'

'You did not have a say in it?' he asked, crossing his arm over his chest, gripping his other elbow.

'No,' she said, through gritted teeth.

'Surely you must see the advantages?' he said, coming off the wall towards her. 'Most women want to marry the emperor, why don't you?'

'Is it so strange that I might want to stay here, even rule here on my own, without a man to govern me?' she said, staring up at him. She didn't wait for his answer—she already knew his feelings on the matter—he thought she'd be safer married, with an ally. She knew he wouldn't see her point of view—she knew where his loyalties lay. 'I'm like that saint in the myth, only without the beard,' she said miserably.

'What saint?' he asked, giving a little shake of his head.

'Have you not heard the story of the female saint who was promised in marriage by her father to a king?'

'I don't follow your religion.'

'To stop the wedding going ahead, the saint prayed to our God to be made repulsive. When she woke up the following morning, she had grown a beard.'

He raised his eyebrow.

'Her future husband was so reviled he broke off the engagement...'

He dropped his arm. 'I've never heard of such a thing. But don't you think about going to such extremes, Livia.' He lowered his voice. 'It would be a shame to ruin such beauty...'

Her breath stalled. Was he mocking her? Or did he really think she was beautiful? It was hard to tell with him. 'What is he like anyway?' she asked, flustered, waiting to change the topic, quickly. 'Emperor Alexios?'

'He is a good man,' he said, his voice clipped. He gathered up his long hair with his hand and wrapped it up into a bun. She thought how his unkempt locks were at odds with the orderly, uniformed look of the rest of him. 'I wouldn't be able to serve him, swear to lay down my life for him, if he wasn't worthy. He's young. Rich—you'll want for nothing.'

'But is he kind?'

'Men of power have to be ruthless, but I have seen him be compassionate on occasion, yes.'

'Are *you* married?' she asked suddenly, her thoughts and eyes returning to him, taking in the sheer breadth of his body, his defined jawline covered in unruly short, dark hair, and his mysterious mouth that she hadn't yet seen curve upwards into a smile.

He frowned. 'No.' He ran his hand around the back of

his neck. And she knew she'd probably overstepped the mark—personal topics seemed to be off-limits. 'Look, if we're not going to get any sleep, perhaps we should just get on our way, yes?'

Destin gripped her elbow to help her up onto the mare she'd chosen, but she cast him off. She swung her leg over the horse and his eyes widened.

'You do not ride side-saddle?'

She pulled a face. 'It is more comfortable like this. And my father hasn't been around to chastise me,' she said.

'Perhaps you've been left alone out here too long,' he mused, frowning, yet he waited till she was safely settled before he moved over to the black stallion.

He felt her watching him with interest as he pulled himself onto his own animal. It wasn't easy to do with one arm as he was unable to stabilise the horse or himself, but he had mastered the technique over the years. He was used to being studied and he knew when people looked at him, they just saw what was different, but he'd tried to learn not to let it bother him. Only her scrutiny felt different… He found it maddening.

He pressed his ankles into the horse's sides and he led them quietly out of the stables and out across the fields. When they were a fair distance away, he looked back, and there was no sign of any disturbance at the farm. Good. He hoped they hadn't put her friends in any danger.

He picked up the pace, traversing over undulating hills, and he was glad Livia was able to keep up. He kept glancing behind him, checking they weren't being followed, and each time he looked, he was relieved all he could see was farmland and forests.

He couldn't believe she'd openly admitted she didn't want to marry the emperor. If Alexios had heard her say that! Although he had a feeling her thoughts weren't too dissimilar from his leader's. They both seemed to like their freedom, not wanting to be tied down in marriage.

Perhaps Livia's critics were wrong, maybe she didn't need a man to rule her... She'd certainly kept him alert since he'd met her. She was stronger than most women and yet she was still vulnerable. He knew she needed his protection, even if she didn't want it.

He took a sideways glance at her, a faraway look in her eyes. She was riding well. She certainly had the ability to surprise. And the kind of beauty that made you look twice. Or in his case, never want to look away... But she seemed tired and cold, and he felt a pang of guilt. He was taking her away from her home, to somewhere she didn't want to go. But it was an arrangement made between two emperors—she didn't have the power to get herself out of it, and neither did he.

He couldn't believe she'd asked whether he was married in return. What did that have to do with anything? He'd realised a long time ago he would never be able to have what other people had. He knew no one would ever want to be with someone like him. Choosing to be alone was far better than chancing rejection, so he'd thrown himself into his fighting and proving his worth in other ways. He'd learned there was value in what he could contribute and his men and the emperor now needed him. That counted for a lot.

Her personal questioning disturbed him. People rarely asked about his life—and that's how he liked it. He chose to keep people at a safe distance. When she'd asked about his family and he'd said they weren't around, it wasn't exactly a lie, but it was the quickest and easiest way of letting her know his parents and his siblings weren't in his life. She didn't need to know that he had no clue where he'd come from, or what blood ran through his veins.

A burden to his family, he had been put out to die. It shocked him when he thought of it, even now. He was found in the woods by a ranger, just before the wolves had reached him. Taking pity on him, the man and his wife had brought him into their home. He knew how fortunate he was. If it hadn't been for Áki and Gerdur, he would never have survived. He owed the couple his life.

But it had been a miserable existence for a while. Gerdur had died when he was four, and after that, he and Áki had lived a nomadic existence, wandering the fjords and mountains, Áki not being able to settle to anything. But Destin had preferred the solitary existence to when they chanced upon a village or market, for when he encountered new people, he was mocked and taunted for his limp arm. He had never fit in. Yet out in the wild, Áki had shown him how to forage and fish, hunt and make fire, and the man had taught him how to fight. He'd learned he didn't need anyone else to get by.

It had felt good that first time, when, after he'd been mocked in a square, pushed about by a group of older boys, he'd finally had the strength and skills to stand up for himself. He'd raced back to Áki, bloodied and bruised but elated, having won the fight.

He'd got a taste for it after that. He'd realised he could get noticed for something else other than his impairment, so he'd honed his skills, and his body and confidence had grown.

When the old man had died, he'd been bereft. He'd lost the one person who had accepted him and cared for him despite his flaws. He'd wallowed in his grief for a while, until new lands had beckoned. Seeing a ship in the harbour one day, looking for a crew and preparing to leave for Constantinople, the city of great riches, where fortunes were made, he'd decided to join them. So, he'd left his homeland behind, following the Silk Road from Norway.

But arriving in Constantinople, things had been the same. The people had whispered about him, mocked him, those first few months, and he had felt his difference to them in every bone of his body. He'd felt alone, locking himself away. It was only when a rebellion broke out in the capital one day, and he'd single-handedly saved the emperor, that he had been offered a reward. When Destin had told Alexios he wanted to be part of his Royal Guard, the emperor had laughed at first. But when he'd seen he was serious, his face had changed and he'd said Destin could train with the men.

He hadn't looked back since. The men had respected him after that, and he had become one of them. He'd since proved himself over and over again, earning the men's and the emperor's trust, finally receiving the rewards and recognition he'd always longed for. He had made a name and a fortune for himself, and proved his impairment hadn't limited him.

The emperor had now set him this task, telling him if he was successful in bringing his bride to Byzantium, he would make him his chief commander and right-hand man. It was more than he had ever dreamed of achieving.

He turned to look behind him again, and this time, his blood froze. He saw soldiers on horses charging out of the trees. Without hesitation, he urged Livia to ride harder, encouraging their horses to gallop faster.

'We're being pursued!' he said, kicking his ankles into the black stallion.

'How will we lose them?' she cried out, and he heard the fear in her tone, saw her eyes widen in her ashen face.

'We'll head to the next settlement. It's not too far from here. We'll try to lose them there. Don't look behind you. Keep going.'

'How did they find us?' she asked, breathless.

'Lothair probably has scouts all over the place.'

As they bore down upon the next village, he didn't dare slow the horses. But he knew as they came over the brow of the hill and down, it was their one fleeting moment of being out of sight from the riders behind them. They had to use it to their advantage.

Thundering along the road, he led them into a barn. 'Get down, quickly. We need to leave the horses,' he said reluctantly. 'We'll go through the village on foot. It'll be easier to stay unseen that way.'

He leapt off his stallion first, before helping Livia down, and for once, she accepted his hand, placing her trembling fingers in his. He didn't let go as he led them out through the back of the barn, tugging her with him. They waited as they heard the riders tear down the path, not stopping as they raced past the barn, continuing into the village.

'They'll search the settlement. They'll try to prevent us from getting to the mountain pass. We need to find somewhere to hide,' he whispered.

They kept low, creeping from building to building, until they came to a small chapel. 'Look,' he said. 'Let's take sanctuary here for a while.'

Inside the tranquil church, all was quiet. It was functional, not elaborately decorated, and monks were gathering at the altar—perhaps saying their prayers before setting out on their pilgrimage to see the Pope in Rome. Destin and Livia stalked around the pews, keeping within the shadows of the recesses, and Livia finally slipped her hand out of his and he let her go. Dark and watchful, Destin kept an eye on the monks and the door.

It was serene in here and he watched as she looked around, standing still for a moment, her expressive eyes taking it all in. He was aware he probably looked out of place. And he felt restless.

'How is it that the emperor is more willing to place his trust in mercenaries, men of a different religion, to his own native soldiers?' she asked. 'I take it you worship the pagan gods...'

'Perhaps his own people are more of a threat to his power,' he said. 'Like your uncle is to you.'

'And why would you take an oath to serve him?'

She was distracting him from his thoughts.

'You would die for the emperor...but I'm guessing you wouldn't convert to Christianity for him?' she said, running her hand over the tops of the pews.

'Never.'

He wondered why she was analysing him, or perhaps it was the emperor she was trying to better understand.

A feeling of unease spread through him as two soldiers suddenly entered. Livia tensed, and Destin immediately reached for his sword. He stepped in front of her, putting himself between her and the enemy.

'You can't spill blood in here,' she warned him.

'You forget, I don't believe in your God,' he said. 'And surely he would want me to protect you?'

The soldiers came around the pews, bearing down on them, surrounding them, and Destin gently pushed Livia back into the confessional. 'Stay inside,' he ordered. 'Don't come out until I say so.'

'We've been looking for you,' the men sneered.

Destin stood his ground.

Instantly, the men lunged, and Destin took them both on, his sword clashing against theirs.

He managed to duck one blow while slicing his own blade through the air. He slammed one of them against a pillar, while the other stabbed and jabbed, sending wooden beams splintering. It was unfortunate this had to happen in here. He didn't want to cause any damage.

Two of the monks approached, shouting at them to

stop, begging them to take their fight outside, and Destin was shocked when the largest soldier swung his sword, brutally and unnecessarily killing one of the holy men. He reeled. He saw no honour in killing a man who was unable to defend himself. A man of the cloth.

He heard a gasp from behind him. Livia. She raced forward from behind the curtain, putting herself between the soldiers and the other monk. 'No!' she cried out. 'Please, stop this. Don't hurt them.'

For a moment, he was stunned. He couldn't believe her instinctive courage, her recklessness and total lack of regard for her own security—and her blatant disobedience of his orders.

The soldiers moved towards her, getting to her first, shoving her out of the way with force, causing her to fall back into the pews, while they plunged their blades into the heart of the other monk.

Their arrogance sent a shot of rage through him, and Destin's fierce need to protect her made him even more determined. He turned on the men with lethal precision, disposing of one, then the other efficiently, causing them both to slump to the floor.

The other monks began to back away, wailing in outrage, trying to get out the door in wild panic, and he knew it wouldn't be long before more of Lothair's soldiers came rushing in. He moved over to Livia and gripped her arm, pulling her up. 'Are you hurt?'

'No,' she said, shaking her head. But she was trembling. Her face white.

'I told you to stay hidden!' he bit out, turning her around, roughly checking her over for any injuries, disturbed by her behaviour. She was the Roman princess. Did she not care for her safety?

'I didn't want them to hurt those men. They'd done nothing wrong,' she said, appalled at what had just happened, her eyes scanning the scene of the bloodied bodies before her.

'I know that. But it was foolish of you to get involved,' he said, shaking her elbow, reprimanding her.

'Well, I'm sorry—perhaps I'm not as cold and unfeeling as you. I had to do *something*!' she spat, tugging herself out of his grasp.

Unfeeling? Ridiculously, he felt wounded. But he prided himself on never showing his emotions, it was what made him strong. And he didn't know why her comment bothered him.

'Are you sure you're not hurt?' he asked, his brow furrowing.

'No! I just…can't believe they killed them,' she said, angrily swiping a tear away from her eye. 'I feel responsible… Those soldiers were after me, not the monks. If we hadn't come in here to hide…'

'I made that decision.'

'They were only trying to help. They didn't deserve to die.'

'It's not your fault, Livia.'

She slumped down into a pew, shaking her head. 'Then why does it feel like it is?' she sniffed. 'Where did you learn to fight like that anyway?'

He shrugged. 'Ours is a warrior culture in Norway.'

And he had never thought he would fit in. He'd never

thought he'd be able to fulfil his dreams. But he was glad he had, if only to protect her today.

'The monks should have stayed out of it,' he said, crouching down, running his hand over their faces to close their eyelids. 'But their deaths won't be in vain. They may have helped us more than they had thought they could… I think I have an idea to get us out of here,' he said.

Chapter Three

They emerged from the church a while later dressed in monks robes, and they fell in line with another group of priests making their way through the village, towards the start of the meandering mountain pass.

Prince Lothair's soldiers were manning a perimeter around the settlement, but they were letting the monks through, uninterested in the holy men, instead tasked with finding a Varangian soldier and a Roman princess. Destin's plan might just work.

'Pull your hood up,' he whispered, as they neared the soldiers.

They had found the robes in the back of the church and had thrown them on, to see if the disguise would work. It covered them almost completely.

Still, she was tense as they passed the armed men, keeping the basic, roughened material of the cowl around her hair and face, hoping they wouldn't be recognised in their disguise. Only when they had safely passed the blockade and started up the winding path, through the valley, did she allow herself to release the breath she was holding.

She was still trembling, shocked by what had happened in the church. She'd been horrified that those soldiers had killed the holy men in cold blood, for no reason at all. Was that what her uncle's rule would be like? It was becoming increasingly clear she could not let him lead their empire. She would have to do something to stop him.

When she'd seen the soldiers' bodies collapse to the floor, she had actually felt relieved, momentarily pleased they were dead. They had got what they deserved. And suddenly, she was glad Destin was the one who was protecting her. She couldn't believe she'd ever doubted him—he was a sight to behold as he'd fought. She couldn't bear to watch the stabbing of each sword, and yet she hadn't been able to look away either. She had been in awe of his prowess. It had soon become clear the men were no match for his powerful strength. He'd seemed almost indestructible, his impairment not hindering him at all.

They followed the monks for a way, through the hills, the views of the snow-capped mountains dominating them on either side and in front of them. And she thought he was a little like the mountains—cold and rugged, imposing, lethal. When they came to a rocky outcrop, they broke away from the group to rest, allowing the entourage of holy men to carry on in silence without them.

'We can probably take these off now,' Destin said, nodding to the robes. 'You know, I think this is the closest to your God I'll ever get,' he said wryly, his lips twisting.

She smiled. But she was glad to be rid of the garment, discarding it on a rock. She was surprised when Destin began to remove his maroon Varangian cloak too and ripped the dragon emblem from his tunic.

'Probably best to obscure this for now,' he said. 'Are you going to be all right walking for a while? It gets pretty steep and narrow further up.'

'Are we really going to attempt it without horses?' she asked, wary.

'Let's aim for the hospice near the top, where I imagine these monks are heading. We could see if they'll allow us to rest there for the night.'

She knew the stark, block-like building he was talking about. She had passed the place on the few occasions she had come through this way, vaguely being aware that it was a place where travellers could seek sanctuary. She just never thought she'd be one of them.

'We might be able to borrow some animals, or a cart…' he added.

'Borrow…or steal?' she asked, raising her eyebrow, referring to how he'd suggested they borrow her friend Theo's horses—and then abandoned them.

He grinned at her then, and she felt her stomach flip. It took her by breathless surprise. It was the first time she'd seen him smile—and she thought her heart had stopped for just a second. He was incredible.

'Hopefully your friends will soon be reunited with their animals. My stallion seemed pretty astute—they might even find their way back to the farm.'

When they started walking again, her legs felt shaky and she wasn't sure whether it was to do with the fight, the long journey and lack of sleep, or the man beside her, making her feel a whole jumble of emotions. She just couldn't work him out.

'You've gone quiet. Are you sure you weren't hurt back there?' he asked, peering at her closely.

She shook her head. 'No,' she said. 'Just bruised. How do you think my father is faring with his wound? Do you know how he was injured—and what he was doing fighting in the first place?'

'He has been trying to expand into the south of Italy for years, much to Alexios's despair. Much of the land he'd been fighting near belongs to the Byzantine Empire. I believe he was shot with an arrow in this recent battle. He has a wound just above his hip. It's deep.'

She nodded grimly. 'Do you think we'll make it back in time for me to see him?'

'I'll do my best, Livia. Are you…very close?'

'Yes, although since coming here, I don't see him as often as I should like… At first, he insisted I return to Frankfurt, then Rome, but I think he thought I was safer out here, out of the way of his expeditions in Italy. And out of the way of other men at his court, after he'd secured my marriage alliance with the emperor. He always thinks he knows what's best for me.'

'And he doesn't?'

'No. And I don't know why he insists on this Italian campaign. I think perhaps it filled a void after my mother died. But after my brother, Otto, was killed during one of those very battles, you'd think he might have stopped. It's become all-consuming. Is Emperor Alexios the same? Does he thrive on war and expansion too? Does he fight himself?'

'Alexios doesn't need to fight—he has a great army of six thousand men to fight for him, in whatever campaign he wishes them to. But all men have goals greater than what they have currently, don't they?'

'What are yours?'

He frowned. 'I have achieved mine. It was to make a name for myself, to earn respect.' He shrugged. 'My greatest one is to die with honour.'

'You don't want more?' she asked, surprised, pausing on the path. 'A wife. A family?'

'No.'

She went quiet for a moment, letting that information sink in. 'My mother and father cared for each other very much. They met at court and fell in love. There was certainly no bride show, no arranged marriage. I bet my father wouldn't have dreamed of marrying a woman he didn't even know...' she said bitterly. 'Don't *you* want what your mother and father had?'

He bristled. 'No.'

'I should have liked a baby brother. Otto was much older than me and we weren't that close. He was always my father's focus, of course, being his son and likely heir. A younger brother would have been someone to talk to, to confide in, and have fun with. Do you have siblings?'

'No.'

'No?' She stopped dead on the path, infuriated. 'Is that all you can say? Here I am, wittering on, trying to make conversation after you tell me I'm quiet, but all you can say is no! Do you not have anything else to add? Anything else to contribute?' she said, exasperated, lifting up her arms and letting them drop by her sides again.

He went to open his mouth to speak, probably to say no again, and she held her hand up to stop him. 'You know what? Don't worry. Let's just walk in silence. I'll save my energy to keep me warm.'

The temperature was dropping the higher they were climbing, and she was starting to feel the chill. Or she was just getting that from him. She wrapped her cloak tighter around her and stormed on ahead of him up the path. It was hard going and she was flagging—not that she'd ever admit it to him. Instead, she used her frustration at him to push herself on. He was maddening!

He didn't seem comfortable in her company. He seemed tense. Perhaps he was just used to being surrounded by men, fighting in the emperor's battles. But did he not have a life outside the Emperor's Guard? She couldn't understand how he wouldn't want one. And yet she found it hard to believe he didn't have experience of being with a woman...he was much too attractive not to have spent time in female company. He was right, she couldn't imagine him living a monastic life! And she was cross with herself for her line of thought—for why did she even care?

Suddenly, she felt her arm being pulled back and he spun her round to face him. 'Livia, look... I'm sorry.'

She tugged her arm out of his hold and he let her go. He raked his hand over his hair.

'I'm not used to…this. All these questions. I'm a man of action and very few words. I like to keep my head down, get the task done.'

The 'task' being her, of course!

'This is not my usual mission,' he continued. 'I'm usually sent to the front line to fight in the emperor's next cause.'

She folded her arms across her chest, not willing to let him off the hook, although she was surprised he had apologised.

Was it so wrong to be polite, to show some interest in him and about where he'd come from? As the royal princess, she had been raised to ask questions, in preparation for all the people she would meet from many different countries at her father's palace. She'd never met a Norse man before and she was genuinely intrigued. Perhaps more than she ought to be.

'I don't usually share things about my life, my past, with people.'

'Why not?'

'Perhaps I don't want them to know. Perhaps there's not too much to share.' He shrugged.

'I don't believe that. You come from Norway. You've travelled down rivers and across lakes and mountains to get to Constantinople. I wish I was able to do that. You've fought in battles, seen so many places—much more than me. You've lived a life of adventure. I've been starved of it. It seems rude not to share it.'

He studied her. 'You're interested to know about all that?'

'Yes.'

'Then ask me. I'm much happier talking about places than people, than myself.'

'Why?'

'I was raised to keep my thoughts and feelings guarded. The more people know about you, the more they can use it against you. It makes you vulnerable. Weak.'

'And dull!' she said. 'You have to have friends. Allies. People you can trust. Maybe you should try it. It's a miserable existence if you don't. Don't you trust me?' she goaded him.

'I don't know you!'

She thrust her chin up in the air and he relented, as if impatient, wanting to get moving. 'Sure, Princess,' he said, exasperated. 'I trust you.'

'Yet you expect me to trust you on this journey, you expect me to put my life in your hands, but you won't even share any details about yourself with me. So I tell you what, I will continue to walk up this mountain with you, if you tell me something about you. Something real. Something true,' she challenged him. 'And I promise, you can trust me not to tell anyone.'

He sighed. 'You know I could force you to move. I could carry you...'

She stood her ground, crossing her arms over her chest, although she was slightly unnerved at the thought of him putting her over his shoulder.

He sighed. 'All right,' he relented, as if he couldn't believe he was playing this little game. 'Something true... I didn't want to come on this mission,' he said, shrugging his one good shoulder.

She raised her eyebrow. 'Why not?'

'Because of all those things you've said…about all the places I've been, all the journeys I've made. I've had enough moving around to last a lifetime. I'd be pretty happy staying in one place for the rest of my days, but obviously whatever the emperor commands, wherever he sends us, we have to go. So perhaps we're not so different, you and I? Perhaps we're both being forced on journeys we can't get out of, unsure where they will lead.'

She nodded, satisfied.

'Is there a reward for coming to get me? For putting yourself in danger and doing this?'

'Coin, as I told you. And my own satisfaction of doing my duty.' She didn't need to know that he was hoping to increase his status because of this. That probably wouldn't go down too well. 'Now can we please get a move on before we both freeze—or starve—to death?' He reached out and curled his hand around her arm. 'Let's pick up the pace and get to the hospice.'

'Will they let us in?' Livia whispered.

'They're monks. They should be generous.' Destin grimaced. He hoped so anyway. He didn't like the sallowness of her skin, or the way her body was dithering. They'd been out on the mountain pass all day—far too long—and it had rained and rained, soaking them through to the bones. He needed to get her in front of a fire, fast. But he also hoped he was doing the right thing by bringing her here. He hoped these men wouldn't recognise the princess—he wasn't sure how good the relationship was between the Pope and the Roman king.

'But they're monks, I'm a woman, and you're a...a...' Her voice trailed off.

'A what?' he said, his eyes narrowing on her.

A kindly looking old man opened the door, saving her from answering.

'I'm afraid we've got caught in the storm. We were hoping we might be able to seek shelter here for the night?' Destin asked, offering a smile. 'I don't think we'll make it back down the mountain before nightfall.'

The men whispered between themselves from behind the door.

'Where are you heading?' the one asked.

'Rome.'

'You're a Christian?' the man said, raking his eyes over Livia, then him.

'Yes. I am. Actually, I am an acquaintance of the Pope,' Livia said.

The man's eyes opened wide, and Destin swung to look at her.

'We don't usually have women or warriors here, but, as the weather is so bad, it would be unchristian of us to turn you away.'

The door slowly opened to let them in and Destin sensed Livia almost wilt in relief at his side. The holy men must have taken one look at their frozen faces and taken pity on them. Or were they just intrigued by her connection to the Pope? So much for not sharing too much information. Now they would have questions... But Destin too was glad of the respite from the bitter wind and rain, and he was glad she would have a bed for the night. They had travelled without food and sleep and she must be exhausted.

'You'll have to leave your weapons outside.'

Destin hesitated.

Livia gave him a look.

'Very well,' he said reluctantly, leaving his sword leaning against the wall. But he made no move to lay down his hidden knife in his belt. Her eyes on him, he knew she was aware of it.

'Thank you so much,' Livia said, grateful to the men as she stepped inside.

'I'm Father Sebastian,' the white-haired man said. 'We have some pottage on the fire, which won't be long, and one last room available you can have. It's our smallest, I'm afraid. Basic but comfortable enough.'

'Thank you,' Livia said again. 'You're most kind.'

'Come, I'll show you the room.'

Destin followed behind Livia, his body already tense from the monk saying he had *one* room. He would have no reprieve from her, and yet what did he expect? If he was to watch over her and keep her safe, this was for the best.

'Here it is,' Father Sebastian said, pushing open a door.

The room was certainly basic—in fact, it was rather desolate. There was a bed, a few furs, a chair and a writing desk.

'Thank you,' Destin said.

'It's very good of you,' Livia added, her voice sounding strained.

'I'll leave you to make yourselves comfortable. Come

and have some pottage and warm yourselves by the fire when you're ready.'

When Father Sebastian shut the door, Livia turned on Destin, wide-eyed and panicked. 'We can't share this room! Why didn't you ask for another?'

He understood her reservations. Hadn't he just been having exactly the same thoughts? And for a woman of her standing to share a room with a warrior, alone, before she was wed, it would all but ruin her reputation. But they didn't have a choice.

'He said he only had one room. And how can I protect you if I'm halfway down the corridor? What if your uncle's men come here looking for you?'

She shivered at the thought, running her hands up and down her arms.

'Your safety means more to me than your reputation.' And not just because he'd been tasked to bring her back to Constantinople. He felt protective of her—more than he should. *Helvete!* He didn't want to feel this way.

'This hospice might be a target. After your uncle's men search the village and rip it apart, it's likely they will come this way looking for us. No, unfortunately, we're stuck together,' he said, just as disturbed at the thought as she was.

'What would my father say—and Emperor Alexios? It's improper! It's not right.'

He stared at her, feigning nonchalance. 'I'm sure they'd understand, given the circumstances.' Only he wasn't sure if he was trying to convince her, or himself. He didn't like the idea of spending the night in such close proximity to her either—it would be intolerable. Her floral scent was wrapping around him even now, and he wondered how the delicate fragrance hadn't washed off in the rain. If anything, it had grown stronger. 'But I don't see how they would even find out. I'm not going to tell them, are you?'

She shook her head.

'So who is going to know?'

'I'm not sure if that makes me feel better or worse!' she said miserably.

'Look, I'm not going to come near you, Livia. You have my word. You can take the bed and I'll have this chair here,' he said, rattling the back of it. It looked like a torture device. 'It's not like I'll be going to sleep anyway, I'll be guarding you all night. You're safe with me.'

She nodded, and yet he noticed she bit down on her lip, unsure.

'I suggest we give ourselves different names when speaking to the monks. We'll need to make up a story, get our facts straight, about why we're here and where we're heading. Father Sebastian obviously thinks we're married...' he said, gesturing to the one bed. 'Perhaps we can say I'm a soldier in the King's Guard and you're a nobleman's daughter...'

She nodded, but then looked around, as if distracted.

'It's rather basic. Not what you're used to, I know...' he said.

She shrugged. 'It's better than the stables last night.'

He grimaced. But she didn't know real hardship... He walked over to the small opening in the wall, big enough to let in air and light, and he could just see a light smattering of snow falling, covering the tall pine

trees and the glittering lake. After checking no one was
outside, he closed the wooden shutter. The scenery reminded him of those adventures with Áki—the glorious views of the mountains meeting the fjords, and
how they'd wanted for nothing but the clothes on their
back, the food they could find and the next shelter for
the night. He actually felt at home out here, like this. Or
would, if he didn't have an enemy pursuing them and a
maddening, beautiful woman at his side.

'I bet even the luxurious palace and warm weather of
Constantinople is seeming pretty tempting right now...'
he said, turning to look at her over his shoulder.

She cast him a glance and shook off her sodden
cloak, hanging it over the back of the chair. Her tunic
and stola were wet through, clinging to her breasts, and
he swallowed. He forced himself to look away.

He placed her satchel down on the bed. 'I think you'd
better change before dinner,' he said. 'I'll wait outside.'

She nodded, rubbing her arms which were bristling
with goose flesh. 'Thank you.'

He was glad to step out into the corridor, to put some
distance between them for a moment. He hadn't been
out of her proximity since they'd fled the castle. His
stomach growled in recognition of the fact he hadn't
eaten in that long either, and yet his rumbling belly
couldn't distract him from his thoughts of what was
going on behind the closed door. He'd been given a
glimpse of what those perfect swells looked like beneath
her tunic and when he pictured her peeling off her wet
garments, his lower body hardened in response. Good
grief, how was he going to endure a whole night in the

same room as her? Perhaps it would be better to sit out here, on guard, but then he'd worry someone might try to get in through the small window.

He started when the door opened. 'I'm ready,' she said. And then looked him up and down. 'What about you? You're wet too.'

He shook his head, eager to be among others so they didn't have to be alone for a moment longer. Maybe then he would stop thinking about her beautiful body and the long night ahead. He took her by the arm to lead her down the corridor. 'I'm fine. I'll warm up by the fire.'

He thought how ironic it was that he was relieved to be in the company of a group of monks. Usually, he'd walk straight back out again. They were worlds apart. If they knew he was a pagan, they'd probably turf him out of here, leaving him on the side of the mountain to freeze to death. But right now, he was glad to have them around.

The men were all sitting at a long wooden table and Father Sebastian, who had greeted them at the door, gestured for them to join them and take a seat. Livia slipped into the bench first and Destin followed her. He was excruciatingly aware of her nearness, his thigh pressing against hers, their arms brushing.

The monks served them a bowl each of pottage and the men put their hands together to say their prayers. Destin copied them, closing his eyes, aware Livia was watching him. He was glad when it was over and they all tucked in. Livia must have been as ravenous as him, as she ate heartily.

'What brings you out here and why are you going to Rome?' Father Sebastian asked.

'We are visiting family there, although we foolishly mislaid our horses in the settlement today. Do you know where we might be able to source some other animals, or a cart?'

'I'm afraid we can't help you there. We make all our pilgrimages on foot, and only have one mule to get to market between the lot of us. But there is a farm in the next valley along. They make regular trips into Italy and might allow you to ride with them.'

Destin nodded. 'Thank you.'

'What did you do to your arm?' Father Sebastian asked.

He flinched at the age-old scrutiny. He should be used to it, only there was something about Livia sitting next to him, hearing it, that made him uncomfortable. She looked up from her bowl and to his surprise, she interjected.

'Foolish accident,' she said, answering for him, placing her hand lightly on his good arm. 'My *husband* can be so clumsy. He tripped and fell down the stairs at our home in Saxony. Bashed his head at the same time and I'm not sure he's been quite right since. I keep telling him he must be more careful.'

His gaze swung to look at her, and he saw her mouth twitch at the corners. So she was beginning their story, was she?

'Yes, I really must,' he added, his own mouth curving up into a smile. For the first time in his life, he enjoyed the light relief rather than the serious answers or excuses he often made.

'What are your names?' the monk beside Father Sebastian asked.

'This is Cassius,' Livia said, her hand still on his arm.

He stared down at it, and then up at her. Her eyes were glittering with amusement. 'I was warned it means hollow, but I assure you, he's anything but.'

His eyes narrowed on her. Deciding on revenge, he sat back in his chair, moving his arm to place it around her shoulders. 'Isn't my wife, Serena, just the best?' he said. For added effect, he gave her upper arm a squeeze, and she froze. It pleased him. 'She is a wonderful singer in church. I'm sure she should like to perform for you after the meal.'

'Oh, I'm sure they don't want to hear that, dear,' she said through gritted teeth.

'How long have you been married?' the monk asked.

'It's a recent collaboration,' Destin said.

'Although sometimes it feels like we've been together for far too long…' Livia said, smiling a little too sweetly. She caught his gaze and something passed between them, making his breath stall, and he found he didn't want to look away.

'Marriage is hard,' the elderly man said. 'It's a commitment. It takes work on both sides. I know I couldn't do it, which is why I'm wedded to the church. Wine?' he asked, as he offered them the jug.

'Thank you,' Destin said, releasing Livia from his grasp, taking it from him and pouring her and then himself a cup. He took a large swig, slaking his thirst.

When the monks turned to speak to one another, Destin leaned in and whispered in Livia's ear. 'You're going to hell now,' he jested.

He couldn't believe it, but he was actually having a good time.

'So, tell us how you know the Pope?' Father Sebastian said, his attention coming back to them, and suddenly it seemed as if all the table had stopped talking and turned to look at Livia.

Destin gave her a warning look.

'My father is friends with him,' she said truthfully. 'I have been lucky enough to meet him on two occasions, when he visited the king's palace in Rome.'

The whole table practically leaned closer to hear her, their mouths gaping.

'What is he like? We are all very eager to meet him ourselves…' Father Sebastian said.

'He is a quiet and proud man. You feel as if you are in great company when you are with him.'

And as Destin listened to Livia speak, he turned to look at her. A pinkish glow had entered her cheeks, from the fresh mountain air, or the wine, and her golden-brown eyes looked like yellow diamonds in the candlelight. She really was beautiful. She seemed to have warmed up a little from the food and the roaring fire. And she was speaking clearly, engaging the priests who were hanging on her every word. She could certainly hold her own with a roomful of men—even if they had all taken a vow of celibacy. She was a good fit for the emperor; she would make a good wife and queen. And yet he felt a burning sensation in between his ribs at the thought, and he rubbed his chest where it ached. But he mustn't do that. She was not his to feel jealous about.

'Did you hear the king is dying?' Father Sebastian asked them, putting his spoon down in his empty bowl.

Livia tensed and Destin instantly wanted to reach out to her, to comfort her. She put down her cup and wiped her hand on her skirt.

'We had heard he had been injured,' Destin said, stepping in to answer for her, as she had done for him at the start of the meal. 'We weren't sure how serious it was. Has there been any further developments at all?'

'The word is he has a fever, from the wound getting infected. We have been told the Electoral College are preparing themselves for his death. They'll vote for a new successor.'

Destin placed his hand over hers under the table and for once, she didn't cast him off.

'And who are the people calling for?' Livia asked, raising her chin.

'It is not for us to speculate, dear,' Destin said. 'And it is pointless to. Perhaps it is time for us to go to bed.'

'I am interested to hear what the priests have to say on the matter,' she said.

'Some feel the crown should go to the king's brother,' Father Sebastian said.

Destin's grip tightened around Livia's fingers, trying to offer her reassurance.

'Others are calling for the Princess Livia. Rumours are rife, of course. It is an uncertain time for all.'

She nodded, and he gave her hand a final squeeze before reluctantly releasing her.

As the meal came to an end and the monks began to leave the table one by one, departing to read, or write or sleep, Destin excused himself to do a last check of the building, and to make sure all the doors were fastened shut, before coming back to fetch Livia.

He was shocked to find her helping the men wash the dishes in a bucket of soapy water.

'What are you doing?' he asked her, through gritted teeth.

'I'm helping!' she said exuberantly. 'My dear husband won't let me lift a finger at home, so I'm enjoying doing some chores for a change,' she said to the remaining monks around her.

'My dear wife has had too much wine. I believe it's time for bed,' he said.

She picked up the bucket to pour away the dirty water and he went to take it from her, and the water sloshed all over the side, down his tunic.

'*Helvete!*' he cursed quietly.

He eased the bucket from her hands and drained it, before picking up a candle and coaxing her away, leading her back down the corridor. 'If your father could see you washing dishes he'd be appalled!' he whispered.

'I think he'd be appalled by a lot more than that!' she said. 'I'm sorry I got you all wet after you'd finally dried off.'

She carried a tankard of spring water and took the candle from him in her other hand as he opened the door and held it open for her, letting her step through first. 'Thank you,' she said.

When she spotted his sword on the desk, she gasped. 'You're not allowed that in here!'

'I'll need it if anyone comes here looking for us,' he said, taking the candle back off her, closing the door behind him and leaning against it, watching her.

'Will they?' she asked, hesitating in the middle of the room.

'I hope not. Not tonight anyway. It's getting pretty late, and it's dark and lethal out there on the mountain pass. There was a light falling of snow earlier, it might have iced over.'

She sat down on the edge of the bed, looking up at him, her hands awkwardly stroking over the furs.

'You've had a busy day. We have another journey ahead on the morrow. You should get some sleep now, Livia. I'm going to have to take this tunic off and hang it to dry,' he said with a grimace. 'If it's going to offend you, I'd look away now.'

She duly looked away as he undressed, busying herself with pulling off her own boots.

With his one hand he lifted the sling from around his neck, loosening it, allowing him to shrug himself out of the wet garment and hang it over the back of the chair with her damp cloak.

'You know, if I'm going to hell, like you said, I think it must be confession time,' she said. 'I didn't like you much when I met you.' She looked up at him and her eyes widened, raking over his upper body, before quickly glancing away again, her cheeks turning a pretty pink colour.

'No?' He mocked. 'I would never have guessed.'

'But I'm starting to think you're not so bad. I had fun tonight. Who'd have thought that would be possible—with a Norse man and a group of monks.'

He nodded. He had felt the same. 'Good. But enough talking. Bed now,' he said gruffly.

'I think I blamed you for everything. For forcing me to leave Harzburg and travel to Constantinople. For pushing me towards a wedding day I don't want. It felt good to lay all the blame at your feet. I know it's not your fault that you're making me do this.'

'I am sorry anyone is forcing you to do anything. But perhaps it won't be as bad as you think,' he said. Only he was starting to think he didn't want her to marry Alexios either. He didn't like the thought of her with any man, which was madness. He had no right to feel this way.

He vigilantly checked the door and the window were both locked, and when he turned back round, she was lying down on the furs, making herself comfortable, rolling over onto her side. He moved to the chair, putting the candle down on the desk, before blowing it out, descending the room into darkness.

'I'm sorry they brought up your father.'

'At least we know he is still alive. For now.'

'Yes, I'm glad. Goodnight, Highness.'

'Livia,' she corrected him.

'Goodnight, Livia.'

Livia lay there wide awake in the pitch-black room, so aware of him. She could hear the sound of his steady breathing from his position on the chair at the end of the bed. She had been lying still for ages, trying not to move, but she was parched. She needed water, her mouth dry from the wine.

She couldn't get the sight of his magnificent body out of her mind. It had shocked her.

His tunic covered a multitude of scars and strange, swirling patterns of blue dye. She had never seen a man's naked torso before, and she hadn't been able to stop her eyes from roaming over his skin… It had only been a moment, but it had made a lasting impression. The scars and ink etched across his muscles were like some kind of tapestry, giving a glimpse of the battles he'd experienced, the brutal story of his life. She had wanted to ask about them, find out how he'd got the injuries and what the intricate symbols meant, but she had stopped herself. She knew it was inappropriate. But now she wondered how she would ever get the vision of him out of her thoughts.

She sat upright, trying to focus in the darkness. Where was the tankard of water the monk had given her?

She threw off the furs and tiptoed out of bed, but almost immediately tripped on her boot, stumbling, muttering a curse, and fell into something solid. Something warm. Something awake and very bad-tempered.

His muscles bunched. 'What are you doing?' Destin barked, his hand coming round her wrist to steady her.

'Sorry,' she gasped. 'I didn't mean to wake you.'

'You didn't.'

'I'm looking for the water.'

He righted her, before standing and finding the tankard with ease in the blackness, before pressing it into her hand. How did he do that?

She took a big swig, quenching her thirst.

'I probably had too much wine,' she said.

'Well, it was holy wine.'

His voice sounded deeper in the darkness. Velvety and smooth. And he was so close, she could feel his warm breath on her cheek.

She passed him back the jar and his fingers brushed against hers, making her tingle.

'Better?' he asked. She nodded, before realising he couldn't see her.

'Yes.'

'Good. Now go back to bed.'

'I can't sleep.'

'Try.'

She felt her way back to the bed and lay down, curling back up, closing her eyes. But it was no use. She flipped over again and sighed.

'I don't think I thanked you—for saving my life today,' she said.

'It's what I'm here for.'

'I still don't understand why you'd risk your life for me. You must want to please the emperor very much.'

'It's what he commissions me to do. What I'm best at.'

He was certainly the better man today against those soldiers.

She heard him shift in his seat.

'That chair can't be comfortable,' she said, propping herself up on her elbows, trying to make out his frame in the darkness. He must be exhausted. 'You could lay the furs on the floor instead?'

'I'm good here,' he bit out, his voice sounding strained.

She felt as if the air was vibrating with something, something palpable. She had felt it at the meal, too, when their eyes had met and their thighs had collided under the table. His blistering gaze had burned into hers, his mouth curling up into a wide smile, and she had been caught in his spell. She hadn't wanted to look away. She didn't know how she had thought he had cold eyes when she'd first met him, because now it was as if she saw fire burning within them. And when he'd put his arm around her, pretending she was his wife, she had felt her pulse rocket, her blood heat. Had he felt it too?

'Do you have a woman back in Constantinople?'

'What's that got to do with anything?' he asked, incredulous.

'I was just wondering…why don't you want to get married?' she asked. 'I don't understand it. You've achieved your goal of becoming a commander in the Varangian Guard. Why wouldn't you want a wife and a family?'

'*You* don't want to be married.'

'That's not true. I do want to marry one day. I'd just like to choose my husband for myself. So why don't you?'

'It would put a stop to me being a warrior, would it not?'

'I don't see why. Many soldiers have families… There must be more to it than that. What's the real reason? Did you not like being part of a family growing up? Did your parents not get along?'

'*Helvete*, Livia. All this prodding and probing. You never stop, do you?' he said, and she sensed him get off the chair and stand.

'I'm sorry. I just…want to know you, that's all.'

She heard him sigh in the darkness. 'If it's going to mean you'll stop asking me all these questions so I can go to sleep, I'll tell you. I don't have a family, Livia! I don't know much about my background, where I came from… I was raised by strangers…so enough of the personal questions, all right? If you must know, it's a miracle I survived past childhood. But somehow, I did. And I thought if I achieved enough, I might be deemed worthy.'

Of love? She wondered. Or was he talking about praise and accolades?

She was shocked at the revelation, and felt a sudden pang of sympathy for him—and a little guilty that she had forced him into admitting it. But she was glad he had. If he was an orphan, that explained a lot. She knew what impact the loss of her own mother had had on her at such an early age and she wondered what effect this had had on him. To not know who he was or where he'd come from.

'I'm sorry,' she said. 'I didn't mean to pry. But I don't understand. You don't want to marry because you didn't have a family growing up?'

She sensed him stop pacing. 'No. I won't marry because, well, why would I subject anyone to that?' he said bitterly.

'What?'

'In Constantinople, as in most cities or settlements, disfigurement is seen as a disgrace. I won't subject a wife to that. And I don't know what my impairment would mean for children. It would be too cruel to bring a child into this world knowing they could be like me. I won't leave that legacy behind.'

'But that's…that's irrational' she said, shaking her head. She couldn't believe he thought of it that way. If only he could see what she could see when she looked at him. He was the most attractive man she had ever met—and suddenly she wondered what it would be like to touch him, to run her fingers over the scars and ink on his skin. To kiss him… The thought shocked her.

'Take the emperor,' he said, pacing now, on a roll, his words more prolific than she'd ever heard from him. Perhaps the darkness was helping him to talk more freely. 'He's God's sovereign ruler, is he not? His wholeness, his looks, are meant to represent the perfection of heaven to people, yes? That's why deposed Emperor Constantine was blinded, and Emperor Basil mutilated by Alexios's father, so they can never take back the throne. Looks mean everything to you Christians.'

She wondered if her uncle meant to do the same to her, and she shivered.

'I guess you're right… I have been at the mercy of that too…plucked from the line-up of the twelve maidens deemed the most beautiful for the emperor's bride show—and chosen for my looks alone,' she said bitterly. 'I didn't want my marriage to be based on that. I am so much more than just a face, a body…

'I know that,' he said quietly.

And she felt a rush of pride and pleasure. Did he really think so?

'So are you.'

He stopped pacing.

She still couldn't believe he was saying he thought he was monstrous. Unlovable. He was far from it. Her heart went out to him and she wanted to show him that wasn't true. That there was so much about him to admire.

'I read that *your* God, Odin, had only one eye. That he gave the other up willingly, as a sacrifice, throwing it into the well to learn the knowledge it contained.'

He stilled. 'You study our gods?' he asked, surprised.

'We're not meant to, no, but I couldn't help it. I found the stories fascinating. So what about Tyr? Didn't he only have one hand, after the wolf, Fenrir, bit off his right one? But he is still the most powerful warrior of all the gods...like you, the most powerful of men. Perhaps you need to start comparing yourself to your own gods, rather than ours?'

Silence reigned for a few moments as her words sank in.

'I've never thought about it like that before,' he said.

'Maybe you should start now.'

She stood, taking a step towards where she thought he was in the middle of the room. She reached out her hand and her fingertips met the warm, smooth skin of his bare solid chest. Tentatively, she flattened both her palms against him. He inhaled deeply.

'What are you doing?' he rasped.

She roamed her hands up, over his chest. 'Can you feel this?' she whispered.

'Yes, but...'

She ran her fingers over his shoulders, curling over them. Leaving one hand where it was, the other stole higher, up his neck, to hold his jaw, her trembling thumb finding the corner of his mouth.

She raised herself up off the ground, on tiptoes, and she leaned in and placed a soft, sweet kiss on his lips.

He pulled back, urgently. 'Livia, what the—' In an instant he'd reached out and snatched her wrist up in his hand, hard, holding her away from him. 'What are you doing?' His tone seemed angry.

'I just—' She didn't know what she'd been thinking; she'd just wanted to touch him. To show him she cared... She wanted him to be the first man she kissed.

'Don't,' he warned her.

'But...'

'No!' he bit out. 'I won't discuss this again. Now go back to bed and stay there.'

Chapter Four

Destin couldn't believe Livia had kissed him.

It had been a brief, soft kiss, and perhaps she hadn't meant anything by it, but because of the feelings it had triggered inside him—a burning, overwhelming need—it had him coldly, brutally, pushing her away.

He didn't want her pity.

And he could not kiss the emperor's bride.

Courage, consult, fealty, he repeated to himself, over and again. He would not have his loyalty called into question.

He must not feel anything towards her. It would get in the way of his ability to protect her. It would jeopardise her safety. And his own life too.

He was in a foul mood, and it wasn't helped that he had had to spend the entire night sitting on that too-small, rock-hard chair, watching over her, her body tossing and turning, her beautiful chest gently rising and falling. And all he could think about was the feel of her hands on his skin, her soft lips brushing against his.

As soon as the sun had risen over the mountains and he'd felt it was safe enough for him to leave her, he'd exited the room and the hospice and checked the periphery of the building, looking for signs of any unwanted visitors. Thankfully, all was quiet.

He took in a few lungfuls of air and admired the dramatic scenery. It helped to calm him. And yet it wasn't anywhere near as beautiful as the scene back in that room... Livia's slender body stretched out on the furs, her silky black hair having come loose and spread across the pillow, her cheeks still rosy from the mountain air.

She had eventually fallen asleep last night, and he'd known it by the way her breathing had changed. But he'd listened to her having a dream, muttering and shaking her head against the furs, agitated, until he'd come off his chair, sat down next to her on the bed and stroked her hair, soothing her, until she'd fallen back into peaceful slumber.

How could he continue to take her on this journey to be the emperor's wife, when he wanted her for himself? How would he be able to hand her over, when with every step they took together he seemed to enjoy her company even more?

Heading back to the hospice, in search of some hot spring water and lemon, his heart lurched. There, in the light dusting of powder-white snow before the door, were three sets of footprints. His, and two others'. But his went in the direction away from the door, the others disappeared inside...

Crunching over the light patches of snow, he pressed

his ear against the door and he heard the sounds of Father Sebastian and two men talking. He went cold all over. Were Prince Lothair's men in the building? No! Livia was asleep inside.

He checked his surroundings again, a prickling sensation rippling over him, feeling as if he was being watched from the line of trees. If he was, he didn't want to give away where she was. And yet, he had to get to her...

As quickly and quietly as he could, he made his way around the hospice to the little window of their room. He was glad he'd opened the shutter to let some light in this morning, as his heart nearly overflowed with relief when he saw she was still lying there on the bed, fast asleep. He rapped on the wall. 'Livia,' he whispered.

She stirred, but she didn't get up.

He tapped again, this time a bit harder. 'Livia,' he said, louder.

She sat bolt upright, her tousled hair tumbling loose over her shoulders. She looked around under hooded eyelids and gasped when she saw his face at the window. She swung her legs off the bed and came round the room to the window.

'Livia, listen to me,' he said calmly. 'There are two men inside. I think they're your uncle's soldiers.'

Her eyes widened, her lips went taut.

'Get your things. We need to go now,' he said.

She nodded and raced to pull on her boots and cloak, stuffing the satchel with her wet things, before rushing back to him at the window.

'All right. How do I get out? How do I get to you? Do we break the shutters?' she asked.

'No, they'll hear,' he said, shaking his head. 'They'll come down the hall straight away the moment they hear the noise. I'm going to go round the front and create a distraction. Wrap those furs around your elbow. When you hear a commotion, break the shutters and crawl through. Understood?'

She nodded, and he went to leave.

'Destin,' she said, placing her through the small gap, her ashen face full of concern.

He placed his own hand on top of hers, gripping her fingers tight. 'I'll be right back. I promise.'

He had to force himself to go. He knew he shouldn't let her out of his sight, but he had no choice. It was the only way to get her out of there.

He rushed back through the slush, his heart pounding, towards the log store he'd seen at the front of the building. The monks had enough wood in there to last them through the winter. He hoped they'd forgive him for what he was about to do.

Crouching down, he removed two flint stones from his belt. Áki had told him they would always come in useful, and they had. Rubbing them together quickly, he created a spark, and gently lit up the pile of wood. He waited a few moments before the fire raged into life, and then, using his sword, he toppled a few of the logs, beginning an avalanche, causing an almighty crash, setting off chaos. And then he ran.

Appearing back at Livia's window, he was pleased to see she'd broken the wood, splintering it into shards. He wasn't pleased to see she was bleeding. *Helvete!*

He used the fur she passed him to knock out the rest

of the broken shutter and then helped her through the small gap in the thick walls, pulling her arms. It was a tight squeeze, and when she finally came through, she fell on top of him, his arm coming around her.

'Are you all right? You're bleeding,' he said, trying to ignore the sudden tension in his body, the way her warm, soft curves felt pressed against him. He was glad they were back together again, with no stone wall separating them.

She nodded. 'It's just a scratch.'

Not believing her, he deftly swiped up her sleeve to see how bad it was. He didn't like to see her injured, but assessing the gash, although there was blood, he didn't think it was too urgent. 'We'll patch you up later, but first, we need to get away from here. We have moments till they realise we're not in the room and they'll come looking.'

They ran around the back of the building, towards the stables, but inside, there was just one lone scrawny-looking mule, like the priest had said.

'He'll have to do. We'll have to ride together,' Destin said, ascending the animal first, before helping Livia up. And as she settled herself between his thighs, he swallowed down a wave of desire.

He could hear the monks shouting outside, no doubt panicking about the fire but hopefully dousing the flaming wood with water and snow to put it out—that's what he'd do. He knew that Lothair's men would be looking for them by now, and the moment they rode out of here, they'd be in danger, pursued again. He only hoped those men didn't have horses of their own.

He pressed his feet into the mule's sides and spurred it on into an immediate gallop, forcing Livia back into his chest—and his groin—and she gripped onto his arm to steady herself, trying to hold herself away from him. But it was no use, the speed was too great, and she finally gave in, her body slackening against him, clinging onto his chest and arm. They tore across the uneven ground, heading for the mountain pass, aware the monks and the men were all standing there, looking at them in disbelief. And then he saw the two men in uniform charge, racing towards the forest.

Reaching the pass, he was glad to see the morning sun was bursting through the clouds, already melting the snow. Good. It shouldn't hinder their progress, and he urged the mule to go faster. He glanced behind him, to check if the men were following. Not yet.

He took a last glance at the monks and the hospice, guilt prickling, after the men had taken them in last night and looked after them. They were shaking their heads in disappointment. They didn't deserve this. At least the flames had been put out before any real damage had been done.

'It's them, isn't it? My uncle's men?' Livia asked, turning her face to look up at him.

'Yes.'

'So they'll be after us now? Right behind us again?' He didn't like to see her golden eyes wide with fear.

'I'll try to lose them further up the pass, but it will mean us getting off the track, which I'm not too keen to do. It can be treacherous out here. But it will be all right, Livia. I promise,' he soothed.

He hadn't slept in days, and he felt tense, and irritable—not just because they couldn't seem to shake Livia's uncle's men, but because of the way she felt in his arms, nestled against him, her scent getting up his nose. The movement of the mule was unsteady, and she clung to him like mud, and he couldn't deny he didn't like the feel of her hands holding on to him, as if she needed him. It was as if someone was trying to test his resolve and his loyalty to the emperor by putting his greatest temptation in his way. But he needed to keep his head—he had to remain alert, he had an enemy hot on their tails.

When they reached a three-way junction in the path, surrounded by forest on all sides, he looked back to check no one was coming, before halting the animal. He jumped off into the undergrowth, careful not to leave any footprints on the path, before gripping Livia around her waist and lifting her from the animal. He carried her and she wrapped her arm around his shoulder, before he set her down in the shelter of the trees.

He quickly urged the scrawny mule up the path to the right and the animal trotted on unwittingly, happy he had lost his heavy load.

Destin took Livia's hand and tugged her further into the forest. 'Hopefully they'll see the mule's tracks and think we carried on along the path,' he said.

'But what now?' she said.

'We wait. I want to see how many of them there are. See which way they go. And that mule wouldn't have made it much further anyway, not carrying the both of us.'

'What if they don't come and we're stuck here?'

'They'll come.'

And sure enough, within moments, he saw the two soldiers charging down the track on horses. He weighed his options. He could attempt to take them out, but he didn't know if any others were behind them. And he didn't want to put Livia in any more danger. No, he thought their best bet was to keep hidden, for now, and see what route they took. Perhaps they could work out what Lothair was planning.

'Here they come,' he whispered. 'Stay low.'

As they reached the crossroads, the soldiers began conferring about which route to take.

'What are they saying?' Livia asked.

Destin placed his finger over her mouth to silence her. 'Quiet,' he hushed. 'I'm trying to hear.'

She looked up at him, her golden eyes blazing in anger, his finger across her plump lips, and he struggled to concentrate. He sensed her breathing change, as if she was aware of him too, and he moved his hand away from her mouth.

'They're not behind us,' the one soldier said. 'Our best bet is to meet up with Lothair and the rest of the men at the border. Trap them in between us. They'll never get through into Italy.' And finally, they carried on up the right-hand path, the way Destin had sent the animal.

'They're gone, for now,' he said, letting out a sigh of relief. 'And it sounds as if Lothair has overtaken us and will be at the border when we get through the mountains.'

'That's not good.'

He grimaced. 'Let's take a look at that arm of yours while we decide what to do.'

'It's nothing.'

'I'll be the judge of that.'

He gently cast her cloak over her shoulder and pushed up the sleeve of her tunic, holding it in place above her elbow. She winced as the material moved over the wound.

'Sorry,' he said.

She had a gash to her forearm, but it wasn't too deep and the bleeding had stopped. He rummaged in the satchel for her damp tunic from last night and tore a strip off it with his teeth, before wrapping the material round her arm.

'Will you hold it in place while I wrap it?' he asked.

She nodded.

'You've been very brave,' he said, as he wound the material around her skin, before tucking the end in. 'Better?' he asked.

She nodded.

He bent down and plucked a small, star-shaped white flower from the ground and pressed it into her hand. It was a little furry, but it was beautiful. Intricate. 'Your reward,' he smiled.

'Pretty. What is it?' she asked.

'I've been looking for one of these since we left the settlement and started on the mountain path. It's an edelweiss. They're rare. It looks delicate, but it's extremely hardy. It can withstand most storms. Its name means noble, pure—and it's a symbol of resilience… It reminds me of you.'

She smiled up at him. 'I think that's the nicest thing you've ever said to me. Thank you.'

He felt the air change between them, and he pulled away a little and sat down, his back against a fallen tree.

'Are we going to talk about it?' she said, biting her lip, wary.

'What?' he bristled.

'Last night.'

He gave her a stern look. 'There's nothing to talk about.' He'd already said far too much. He shouldn't have been so vocal. Perhaps he'd had too much wine. But he knew that wasn't true. He was always careful never to drink too much, especially when he was on guard. It had everything to do with her, and he knew it. She made him want to share things he'd never told anyone. And she'd astounded him—knowing about his gods, likening him to them... He'd never thought of his impairment in that way before—that perhaps by having a weakness, it made him stronger in other ways? She had totally reframed it in his mind, bolstering his confidence. If ever there was a reason to embrace his uniqueness, she had found it. She had certainly given him something to think about in the long, dark hours...

'I kissed you,' she said, matter-of-factly.

He groaned inwardly, remembering the feel of her soft lips pressing against his. His body had gone rigid in shock and desire. He still couldn't believe it. It was only a brief, sweet kiss yet his reaction had been fierce. But why had she done it? To thank him for looking after her? Or was it out of pity? He couldn't believe he had been careless in revealing his thoughts about his impairment. Did she feel sorry for him? Had that been what had prompted her to press her lips against his?

'You were tired. It's been a worrying couple of days. Let's just forget about it.'

'Oh, that will be easy, won't it?' she said sardonically. 'Especially as I go around kissing lots of men. I'm certain not to remember it—especially the humiliating part where you pushed me away.'

'Livia!' he warned. 'We need to stay focused. All these questions, all this talking—it compromises my ability to protect you and keep you safe. I don't think you understand how much danger you're in—the seriousness of the situation.'

'I don't think you do either.'

'What's that supposed to mean?'

'I like you,' she said simply.

The silence stretched. Had she really just said that?

And she laughed then, a shrill sound echoing out across the quiet landscape. As if she knew what she'd said was absurd.

His brow darkened. 'You're mocking me,' he said, his voice ice-cold.

And all her light-heartedness fled. 'No,' she said, shaking her head. 'No, I'm not. That's the laughable part. You're aloof and intrusive, formidable and hateful at times, but I still *like* you. And I know I shouldn't. I know it's madness, because the only reason you're here is because I've been promised to someone else, and you're taking me to marry him.'

'You're right. It's absurd,' he said, rising to stand, trying to put some distance between them.

'You don't like me?' she said, curling upwards, standing to join him, placing her hands on her hips.

And he wondered how she could be so straightforward in her questions and answers.

'What would be the point in that when you're engaged to be married to someone else? When you're a princess and I am a member of the emperor's Royal Guard.'

'You didn't answer the question.'

'I think you're confusing my protection with my feelings. Livia, you must know—there can be nothing between us... I'm not the way out of this marriage alliance of yours.'

She reeled. 'I know that,' she said, her beautiful forehead furrowing. 'All right...have it your way. Let's forget it. It was nothing,' she said, her voice sounding cool, her body moving away from him, and he knew that he'd hurt her.

He felt a bitterness burn his throat, a pain in his chest, as if he was turning down something truly special. Because the moment her lips had met his he'd felt fire. A spark he had never felt before. A connection, and he'd wanted to pull her closer, open her mouth with his and kiss her fully. It was all he'd thought about all night long. But his fealty to the emperor would never allow it.

Recklessly, he gripped her wrist and tugged her back. 'I don't think a kiss like that, between you and me, could ever be described as nothing, Livia,' he said. But then he released her and dragged his hand over his cheek. 'But no good can come of it. And no one can know.'

She nodded. 'Like you said last night, I'm not going to tell anyone, are you?' she said.

'No. Not unless I want to lose my position—and my head,' he said wryly. 'Come on, let's go this way,' he said, leading them up the left-hand path. 'It might be slightly longer, but hopefully we won't encounter any more of Lothair's men for a while.'

'What's the plan? How are we going to get past the border if they're blocking it?' Livia asked.

'Let's keep within the tree-line but follow the path. The priest said there's a farmstead up this way. Perhaps they can help us,' Destin said.

Livia nodded, and trudged through the trees behind him, along the root-strewn forest floor, their conversation from moments before running through her head. She knew he'd disapprove of what she was saying. That he'd try to dissuade her from her thoughts—that his duty would always win out. And wasn't that one of the reasons she was starting to like him—that he took his fealty so seriously? That he was loyal. Wasn't it why in the space of two nights, she had started to feel safe with him?

And he was right, of course. What had she been thinking? She was the future queen of Constantinople, if not Rome—there was no way anything could happen between them. So why did she feel so disheartened? She needed to pull herself together. She needed to stop thinking as if her marriage to the emperor wasn't going to happen. It was what her father and Alexios wanted. And she was powerless to stop it. She had to start getting her head round the fact that soon she would be Alexios's wife. And the only way she could do that was to start imagining herself in Constantinople. To find out more about the emperor. And to put as much distance as possible between her and Destin. From now on, she should keep her thoughts—and her lips—to herself.

They walked all morning, the warm sun beating down on them, the hum of the insects in the hedgerows filling the gaps of silence. And finally, they came over the cusp of a hill and saw the sprawling farm buildings down below. Destin made them stop for a while to watch who came and went, to check there were none of Lothair's men around, but it looked as if it was just the farmer and his wife and their help.

Her thoughts returned to Destin's men back at the castle—and her people. It was torture not knowing what had happened to them, not knowing if they were safe. And her father…last night the monks had said he was still alive. She craved more information.

To add to her frustration, Destin made her wait half the way down the track towards the farm as he went and spoke to the man and woman at the door. She could hear their voices, and see them gesturing, but she couldn't make out what they were saying. When he finally made his way back up the track towards her, she tried not to look at him, and the way he walked, his rugged, riveting maleness, and his smouldering stare, but instead focused on the warm sun on her face and the scent of alpine flowers. She fingered the flower he had given her, which she'd tucked into her stola. Did he really think she was resilient? And she wondered, if she went with him to Constantinople to meet Alexios, would she see him every day? At least she would know someone. At least she wouldn't feel alone. Would Destin still guard and protect her, as well as the emperor?

'Finally, we're in luck. They've said they'll take us to the border this afternoon.'

'That is good of them,' she said, breathing a sigh of relief. 'Did they say whether they'd seen my uncle's men?'

'She said four men passed by yesterday evening and asked about a man and a woman, then carried on their way.'

He shuffled his feet. 'I may have told them who you were…'

Her head shot up. 'What? I thought we were travelling in disguise. I thought we were keeping our identities secret?'

'It was the only way I could get them to take us today. I could tell they were loyal supporters of your father, from their shields and swords lined up in the house. The farmer even served in his army for a while.'

She nodded. 'Did you tell them about my uncle?'

'Yes, they know what they're getting themselves into and are prepared to go anyway. They don't want to see Lothair on the throne. It seems you have supporters, Livia.'

She nodded thoughtfully.

'They have a small building round the back by the lake. They said we can wait in there, out of sight, while they load and ready the horse and cart. Let's go and take a look now.'

Dustin led them round the buildings, past the pens

of pigs and chickens running loose, and they came to a little barn.

'This must be it,' Destin said, pushing open the door. 'The farmer's wife says she makes him sleep out here when he's had too much ale.'

Livia smiled at the thought.

It was cosy inside, with a small bed, a hearth and a smoke hole.

Destin threw the satchel onto the ground and she felt awkward. The afternoon stretched out before them. 'Did they say how long they'd be?'

'No. I doubt it'll be too long.'

'At least we don't have to stay till morning,' she said. The thought of spending another night with him wasn't too appealing.

He gave her a look, arching one perfect eyebrow.

'What? Am I supposed to feel happy about sharing another room with you again?'

'I wouldn't exactly be thrilled with the idea either,' he said with a grimace. 'But I'm afraid you're still stuck with me for now.'

'So what are we going to do all afternoon?'

'We could take a walk?'

'Oh, no, please, no more walking…' she said, flopping down onto the bed.

'There's a lake…we could paddle? I don't know about you, but my feet are killing me.'

She shook her head. 'I think my body has been frozen enough these past couple of days. What about a game?'

He looked at her, as if she couldn't be serious. 'A game?'

'Yes, have you never heard of a game before?'

'Sure, I just didn't think grown men and women played them.'

'Perhaps that's why you're so serious all the time,' she smiled.

He gave her a look. 'What game did you have in mind?'

'What games did you play growing up? Maybe you could teach me one from Norway.'

'Not many. *Hnefatafl. Kubb.*'

He looked around and his eyes settled on the chopped pile of wood. 'We could try *kubb*,' he said. And she watched, amused, as he got to work setting up the chopped pieces of wood at the end of the barn. When he came back to her, he handed her a small stick and she took it from his fingers. Would she ever get used to the spark between them when they touched?

'Right, you throw this and see how many pieces of wood you can knock down. The ones you do, you get to keep. The winner is the one with the most wooden pieces at the end,' he said, amusement dancing in his eyes. 'I warn you, I play hard—and I'm good.' He winked.

She laughed. 'I might be a natural.'

He gestured with his arm for her to take a turn and prove herself so she stepped forward to have the first go.

She planted her feet apart, weighing up the pieces of wood, taking it seriously. And she swung her arm back, aiming her piece of wood at the others. Finally, she released it, letting it fly, and it knocked down three out of the nine pieces. 'Yes!' she said, making a fist with her hand and cheering.

He laughed at her delight, and she thought how different he looked to the man who had stormed up her hallway in Harzburg to demand that she come with him to Constantinople. She had seen so many different sides to his character these past two days, and she admired them all.

She stepped back, allowing him to take his turn, and he blew on his piece of wood and winked at her, as if it would bring him good luck. Her heart swelled. He was utterly gorgeous. She still couldn't believe he didn't realise it.

He drew back his hand and then launched the wood forward, knocking down four of the pieces.

'Not bad,' she said, raising her eyebrows. 'But you haven't won yet.'

'It's going to be close.'

She took up her position again, and blew on her own piece of wood, flashing him a grin, and then she assessed her target and let go of it. To her amazement, she knocked down the last two pieces, winning the game.

'I won!' she gasped in delight, throwing her hands up in the air to celebrate, turning round to face him, and he caught her waist lightly in his hand.

'You did! Well done! I can't believe you beat me. You really do have natural talent!' he laughed.

It was only a game, but his words of praise pleased her. 'Or it's just beginner's luck.'

'You do realise we have to play again now, so I have the chance to win back my reputation at being the best at this.'

She smiled. Despite the danger they were in, despite

being out on the mountains not knowing where their next meal or bed was going to be, she was enjoying herself—again. And she knew it had everything to do with the man at her side.

They were just finishing their third round, and he had indeed beaten her, two—one, when there was a knock at the door.

She saw the change in him instantly. His smile left him and his hand was on his sword, ready. He moved to open the door a fraction, and he released some of the tension in his body when he saw it was just the farmer's wife, come to offer them a small feast—some cold meats and bread, grapes and ale, and he thanked her, gratefully.

The woman peered through the slit in the door, and Livia came to say hello.

'Your Highness,' the woman bowed, slightly in awe of meeting her, and Livia felt Destin's eyes on her.

'It's lovely to meet you. And thank you for allowing us to rest here a while and travel with you. We will remember your kindness.'

'Oh, it's nothing, Your Highness. The least I can do. It is such an honour to meet you.'

'What is your name?' Livia asked.

'Marta, Your Majesty. And my husband's name is Charles. We will let you know as soon as the cart is ready. It will be a bit of a bumpy ride, but we'll do our best to make it as comfortable as possible for you.'

'Thank you.'

When she was gone, Destin propped the door open to let the sunlight in, and they sat on the floor and had a picnic, both famished from their day's walk.

'You don't cope well with being recognised—or adored, do you?' he stated.

'I'm just a person like everyone else,' she said. 'It was one of the reasons I preferred to live in Saxony. Away from all the drama of being watched and expected to behave a certain way all the time. Will you tell me a little about what Alexios is like? How does he cope with the attention?'

He looked up at her, surprised. He finished his mouthful and put down the rest of his bread.

'What do you want to know?'

She shrugged. 'What does he look like these days?'

His eyes narrowed on her. 'I thought looks weren't important.'

'I should like to know if he still looks the same as I remember, so I don't have a shock. Will I even remember him? Will I melt at his feet when I see him?' Her lips curved up, as if to tell him she was jesting, but she felt her smile crumple at the sides.

A muscle flickered in his cheek. 'He is still fair. He has a slender frame and delicate facial features. I would say he is a handsome man. The women seem to think so anyway. He is popular. And a lot vainer than you. He definitely likes the attention. He cares a great deal about his clothes and his appearance.'

'Delicate?' she queried.

'Let's just say he's not covered in scars, like me.'

Shame, she thought. 'Are they all battle wounds?'

'From fighting, as a child and an adult, yes.'

She nodded. 'What of Alexios's character? What are his interests?'

'He hosts many feasts and enjoys elaborate entertainment, like the chariot races in the hippodrome, much like your Coliseum. I'm sure you will enjoy those events. There are also parades, and staged animal fighting and hunting.'

'Do the animals get hurt?' she asked, wrinkling her nose.

'Sometimes.'

'I don't think I shall enjoy those.'

'No, neither do I. I always say I have training on those days...' He smiled.

'It's funny. I've spent my whole life preparing for how I should be as a princess. But I've never been taught how I should behave as a wife. How will I be treated?'

'Well, I hope. With respect,' he said, his voice sounding strained. He took a large swig of his ale, and then didn't stop until he'd drained his tankard.

'Does he want children?'

'I imagine it would be expected,' he said, clipped.

'What if I don't?'

He put down his cup. 'You don't want to be a mother?' he asked, his eyes wide.

She shrugged. 'I saw what my mother went through. What happened to her. I am unsure.'

'You were there with her when she died?'

'Yes. My father made the choice to save the baby, his second son, over her. Then they both died. I was angry with him for a long time over that.'

She'd had a bad dream about it again just last night, unable to get the images out of her mind. It had weighed heavy on her today.

He shook his head at the thought, and reached out to touch her hand. 'She also had two healthy children, Livia. Remember that.'

She nodded.

'All men want a legacy…' His brow furrowed at the thought. 'That's probably why your father behaved how he did. It is a king's duty to produce an heir, to carry on their bloodline. It's why the emperor will want children.'

'You don't.'

He pushed his hand through his hair. 'I don't see what that has to do with anything. We weren't talking about me. Are you done with your questions?' he asked brusquely. 'If so, I think I'll go and see how the farmer and his wife are getting on with readying the cart.'

'But you haven't finished your food.'

'For some reason, I'm suddenly not hungry,' he said, getting to his feet. 'I'm going to get some air.' He stormed out of the barn and slammed the door behind him.

'Did I say something wrong?'

Destin was angrily skimming stones into the emerald-green waters of the lake, and he spun round, startled by Livia's approach. He was disturbed he'd lost his temper back there. He'd been surprised by her questions concerning the emperor, first wanting to know what he looked like, then asking about his character. Where had this newfound interest in the man come from?

'No,' he bit out.

'You seem angry.'

'I'm not.'

He knew he shouldn't be. Livia was preparing herself to be married, which he'd told her she should do. He should be pleased, only he wasn't. The thought of the two of them together was bad enough, let alone thinking of the things they'd have to do to make a child... Thoughts of Alexios taking her to bed had not been pleasant. He didn't like it. And yet it had no right to bother him, not one bit.

He shook his head, as if to shake away the terrible images in his mind. He wanted her for himself, he admitted. How had he allowed this to happen? How had he allowed himself to begin to like her? He prided himself on staying on task, never veering from his duty, never allowing his emotions to get in the way. But he'd never expected her to be so alluring. He was fighting to remember his vow of conduct and his oath of loyalty to the emperor.

He threw another stone across the surface of the water.

'I thought you didn't care. I thought you wanted me and the emperor to be wed,' she said.

'I do.'

'Fine.' He saw her blanch and he hated himself. He usually prided himself on being honest.

'What are you doing? Is this a new game I can beat you at?' she said, obviously trying to lighten the mood. And she went to take the stone out of his hand. He gripped her wrist, pulling her up against his chest, hard.

She gasped.

'Look, I'm glad you're readying yourself for what's to come. But it doesn't mean I enjoy talking about it, answering your questions about him or thinking about you with him. I do care, more than I should.'

She was so close, staring up at him, and he could see the tiny little flecks of gold in her widened eyes. He saw her swallow, and he released her. She stumbled backwards.

Knowing he'd said too much, that he'd revealed too much of his feelings, he bent down and picked up another stone, rolling it round in his hand. He needed to get this back onto safer ground. 'Want me to show you how to play?' he asked.

'Yes,' she said, her voice sounding shaky. And he could have cursed himself. He had no right to say what he had said. He was giving her mixed messages, being unfair. And this helped neither of them.

'You need a flat, smooth rock that fits in your hand. Put your finger beneath it like this, and flick your wrist forward, throwing it across the water. You have to try to get it to bounce across the water as many times as you can. More than your opponent.'

He threw his stone, showing her his technique, and it skipped over the water. 'Now you try.'

She held the stone like he'd told her to and she let it go. It bounced once, before sinking beneath the shimmering surface.

He bent over to pick up another two stones, selecting the best ones, but when he stood and passed her one, she rounded on him.

'I don't really care about the game right now, Destin.'

He sighed and turned to face her, stroking his hand round the back of his neck. He'd brought this on himself.

'I know that nothing is allowed to happen between us. I know we have our lives marked out for us, determined by others. That we both have duties we have to fulfil. But don't we get anything that *we* want?'

'No.'

'I don't think that's right,' she said, bravely stepping towards him. 'I don't want to settle for that.'

'What do you want?'

'Right now? I want you to be the first man to kiss me.'

The breath left him. He was not expecting such honesty. He flipped the stone round in his hand. 'And how exactly will that help either of us?' It would surely destroy him.

'It probably won't. But perhaps I just want this one perfect moment. Here, in the mountains, with you. Is that too much to ask when I am prepared to give up the rest of my life based on what others expect of me? You... you're free to go off and live your life however you want to. Can you not give this one thing to me?'

'Livia...'

'No one is around. Like you said last night, who is even going to know?'

He had no right to touch her... 'I'd know.'

'And you couldn't live with yourself?'

Could he?

He cast the stone angrily into the water, giving up on the game, and sat down on the pebbly shore. She slumped down next to him. He stared out across the crystal-clear lake, hemmed in by the mountains, watching the birds swoop down low over the glittering surface.

'How can you live with yourself if you let this moment pass by…'

The air surrounding them felt as if it was crackling with the tension between them.

Destin felt her hand on his arm and he turned to look at her. She was so beautiful. She was right. How could he not do what she was asking? A huge battle was playing out between his duty and desire.

'Just one kiss?'

She nodded.

He knew he'd made his decision. He couldn't resist her any longer. And slowly, he bent his head and leaned towards her. Her eyes fluttered shut as she waited for him to reach her, and he gently covered her soft lips with his. He had intended to give her the kind of kiss she had given him last night, to keep it chaste, to stop as soon as their lips met, but as she turned her body into him, pressing herself closer, her chest brushing against his, he lingered, not wanting to be parted from her. His lips gently moved against hers, coaxing hers open, and he carefully slid his tongue inside her warm, forbidden mouth.

He half expected her to pull back in shock, but instead her hands reached out to touch his chest, to hold his jaw close, holding him in place as she met his tongue, caressing it with her own.

He was lost. His hand came up to cup her cheek, her skin smoother than Byzantine silk, running his fingers into her glossy hair, drawing her closer, deepening the kiss, and he felt her whole body tremble. His gave a responsive shiver as something he'd never felt before rippled through him, and he finally pulled back, disturbed.

Her eyes flickered open and she looked up at him, smiling. 'Thank you,' she said.

He stared down at her, not sure he could string two words together. He wasn't sure what had just happened. His whole world had been rocked. That wasn't a chaste kiss between friends, that was a kiss between...

'I'll find great comfort in that in the following weeks.'

Comfort? he thought, incredulous. That was not the word he would use to describe it.

He wondered how she could look so content. So satisfied, when he felt anything but. Was that enough for her? It *had* been the perfect kiss, but now he knew once would never be enough. No, now he was ruined, because one kiss had just made him want a whole lot more.

Chapter Five

The sound of a voice calling broke through the moment, helping Livia to recover her sanity. She looked behind her to see Marta, the farmer's wife, bustling towards them.

'Your Highness. Commander,' she said, giving an awkward little bow again as she drew near. 'The weather looks promising for the afternoon. My husband is almost ready to leave, if you both are?'

'That is good news,' Destin said, quickly rising up to his feet to greet the lady. Was he worried the woman had seen something between them? 'Thank you so much for taking good care of us.'

Had he not felt anything when they'd kissed? For her, it had been everything she had hoped it would be. The quivers in her stomach when she'd bravely told him what she wanted, and the breathless anticipation when his dark eyes had stared down at her, and she'd realised he was actually going to do it. Her heart had raced when he'd leaned in closer, almost taking flight. And she'd felt a jolt through her body, a heady rush when his firm lips had met hers, and the pleasure and surprise of his mouth moving, taking control, increasing the delicious pressure as his tongue tenderly swept inside. She was glad they'd been sitting down as she'd felt a shiver from her head to her toes. It had made her feel light-headed and euphoric.

He had tasted of the cool ale and grapes, his skin warm, his beard soft to her touch, and she'd wanted to get closer, pressing herself against his solid chest. And his hand in her hair, drawing her in, sending tingles down her spine, had felt intimate, like he'd wanted that too. Yet he had been careful, taking it slow, and she couldn't imagine it ever feeling better.

When he'd pulled away, his breathing ragged against her cheek, she'd wanted to follow. But she'd forced herself to look up at him and smile. He had given her what she'd asked for. At least, whatever happened from now on, she would have that one perfect moment to remember, etched in her memory.

He seemed relieved to be going, more eager than ever to be on their way, but Livia was now reluctant. After that kiss, the prospect of staying here and spending the evening with him, sharing a room, seemed far too tempting. It was beautiful here, with mountains as far as the eye could see, the glistening lakes and fields a sight to behold. She thought she could stay here for ever. Somewhere people barely knew her, where she felt free, with him. But her thoughts were running away with her and she mustn't do that. One exquisite kiss had to be enough. She could not ask Destin for more. She knew he lived by his code of honour and it wouldn't be right. Not when every step on this journey was taking her closer towards her future with the emperor. It was time to go.

She got up to her feet and they walked back over to the outhouse in silence. They gathered their things, and tidied up the wood, the bread and tankards. She hesitated as she gave the barn a final glance before going to open the door, but he put his hand on it, preventing her from leaving.

'Are you all right?' he asked gruffly.

'Yes.' She nodded. For some reason she felt a huge lump grow in her throat.

'You've gone quiet. It's not like you.'

No, she wasn't all right! She didn't want to carry on their journey, she had never wanted to make a start on it in the first place. When she hadn't wanted to marry before, she had just thought she would be happier alone. But that was before she'd met him. Before she'd started to like him. Before he'd kissed her like that… Surely it was a sign of their growing affection for each other? It was on her part, anyway. Now, her fate seemed so much worse. She didn't want to take one step further and yet she knew that she must. So she nodded.

'From now on, we won't be alone. We'll have company. We'll need to be careful what we say, and how we act…'

'I know that,' she said quietly.

'There can be no more…'

'I know!' she snapped. It was obviously a lot easier for him to put aside than it was for her. And suddenly she wished she hadn't closed her eyes when he'd kissed her. If she'd kept them open, she could have watched the emotions crossing his face, to see if it had affected him as much as it had her.

He nodded.

'You seem very keen to get going,' she accused.

He frowned. 'It is good of them to offer to take us. The journey will be much easier by cart, and we won't stand out so much travelling in a group. We should get to Rome much quicker than I expected…'

'Good. I can't wait,' she said sardonically.

'Livia,' he warned, his voice stern, a muscle flickering in his cheek. 'I thought you were desperate to get back to see your father.'

'I am!' She was. She wanted to see him, to hold his hand and tell him that she loved him. She still couldn't believe he was as poorly as everyone was saying. She needed to see it for herself. And she also now desperately wanted to ask her father if he still thought she should marry Alexios. But she couldn't tell Destin that. Because that's why he was here, wasn't it? He had been sent to fetch her. He had a duty to fulfil, to bring her back to Constantinople. But if her father said she didn't have to marry Alexios, where would that leave them? Would Destin be pleased?

'But am I supposed to be happy about carrying on, about nearing our destination? After what just happened between us out there?'

He gave her a pained look and ran his hand over his beard. 'This is why I said it was a bad idea.'

'Do you regret it?' she asked, tipping her chin up.

'To be honest, I am regretting ever convincing you to come with me on this damned journey,' he said wryly.

And she smiled at that, releasing her shoulders, letting out a little of her tension. Perhaps he was suffering just a little bit?

He released his hold on the door then and they slipped out, into the bright afternoon sunshine.

The farmer and his wife had their horses and cart ready to go, and were looking up at them expectantly, from the front seat. Marta seemed very proud they were about to embark on this important journey with their precious cargo.

Destin helped Livia up into the back of the cart, filled with bundles of hay and covered with wool to keep it dry, and they set off immediately to make the most of the daylight.

It was a bumpy ride as they traversed past cattle grazing in fields and a mountain stream kept them company as they descended the valley. They saw more farmers out in their fields planting crops and logging trees. The rolling mountains, the meadows full of flowers and the vast, glistening lakes all made Livia feel small, almost making her problems pale into insignificance. There was no snow at all on the slopes lower down, and everything seemed greener, more vivid and vibrant, like it was bursting into life.

At some point, Livia must have dozed off, because when she woke, her head was nestled into Destin's shoulder, his arm wrapped around her, and there were different-looking mountains in front of them.

'Sorry,' she said, sitting up, dragging her hands over her face and patting down her hair.

'It's all right. No one can see back here. You must have been tired. You slept right through the night. We stopped and let the horses rest for a while. You didn't even stir, you were in such a deep sleep.'

'Was I?' she asked, mortified.

'Snored a bit too,' he said, and then he grinned, letting her know he was provoking her in a gentle way.

She elbowed him, but smiled at his gentle teasing.

'Don't worry, you didn't miss anything. Apart from Marta's singing.' He gave her a wide-eyed look of fear and mouthed, *It's terrible*, and she giggled.

'Did you not sleep?'

'No. I'll rest when we stop off in Rome and I know you're safe.'

'You must be tired,' she said. They'd been travelling for days and she didn't think he'd dropped his guard once. Studying him, she realised he had dark circles around his eyes, which were much softer now than when she'd first met him, and his beard had grown, but he was still rakishly handsome. She wanted to trace her fingers over the scars on his face and ask how he'd got each one.

He leaned across to touch her and her breath hitched. 'You have straw in your hair,' he said, removing the strand and letting it flutter to the ground.

'I think you were having a bad dream,' he said. 'Does that happen a lot?'

She shrugged. 'I have nightmares sometimes. Often about my mother. About my father not giving her a choice about the baby. I can still picture what happened to them both.'

He frowned. 'It must have been traumatic for you, Livia. I'm sorry. Your father shouldn't have allowed you to be there.'

'I wanted to be. I wanted to be by her side, to help. To meet my brother...' She looked around, trying to shake the thoughts from her mind. 'Where are we anyway?'

'We're coming down the last valley now, into Italy. I was going to wake you shortly. We need to be alert as we approach the border.'

She pulled her cloak tighter around her.

'Cold?' he asked.

'Just disorientated from having slept too long,' she said.

She should have felt pleased that they were nearing their destination, and yet, she wondered what would be waiting for them when they arrived in Rome... She hoped her father was still with them. Perhaps the healer had been able to treat his wound and he'd be on the mend. Oh, that would be just the best outcome. To find him sitting up in bed, healthy. Smiling.

It took a while longer to get down the winding valley, stopping every so often to take a break. Marta enjoyed handing them food and ale, making a fuss of them, to keep them going. But when the cart began to slow for the third time that morning, the farmer called out to them urgently and Livia knew from his tone it couldn't mean anything good.

'Commander, there's trouble ahead,' he shouted over his shoulder.

Destin held the rail and twisted his head to try to see what was in front of them, without being seen himself, and he cursed, making Livia's hairs on the back of her neck stand on end.

'What? What is it?'

'Soldiers,' he said. 'They're blocking the road. They look like Lothair's men.'

Her eyes went wide. 'What do we do? They can't stop us now. Not after we've come so far. Should we jump off? Shall we try to hide?'

Destin shook his head. 'No. This is the only way through. Get down. In here,' he said, quickly making a space for her in the middle of the cart between the bundles of hay. 'Lie down.'

'Carry on,' he called to the farmer. 'Don't give the princess's whereabouts away, no matter what.'

Livia did as she was told, lying down on her back, and she was surprised when Destin came down next to her on his side, pulling the hay all around and over them, before tugging the cover back into place as best he could over the top. She was holding her breath, and she wasn't sure if it was because she was frightened because they were nearing Lothair's men, or because Destin's powerful body was tucked in tightly next to hers, curling around her.

Lying next to each other, as the cart continued along the winding, bumpy track, their bodies were thrown together, and she couldn't believe, given the circumstances, that she still felt awareness ripple through her.

When the cart began to slow, and she heard the sound of male voices talking, barking questions at the farmer and his wife, she held her breath. The smell of the sickly-sweet hay was overwhelming. Destin's hand came round her waist to reassure her. 'Just stay quiet. Stay still. It will be all right.'

She was so glad he was here. She would never have got through this journey with anyone else. Thank goodness the emperor and her father had sent him.

They heard voices and footsteps drawing nearer, and the sides of the cart being shaken, as if the soldiers were inspecting it. She couldn't bear it. She turned into Destin, burying her face into his chest, seeking his protection, and he pulled her close. Her own hands splayed across his chest and curled around his waist, clinging onto him tight.

'Close your eyes, it'll be over in a moment,' he whispered.

She thought perhaps there were far worse places to die than in his arms. She sought comfort in the outdoorsy pine forest and leathery scent of him, the feel of his strong arm holding her, his long fingers stroking her lower back.

Suddenly the woollen cover was pulled back, allowing light to filter through the hay, and she bit back a gasp, but he had hidden them pretty well. When they heard the sound of swords being drawn she felt him tense, and then so fast she didn't have time to think, he rolled her onto her back and covered her body with his, his weight crushing her beneath him, his arm covering her head. It was as if he was trying to touch every part of her and heat swept through her.

'What are you…?' she whispered.

And then she realised why, when swords began slashing through the hay.

Her body went rigid, and she squeezed her eyes shut, trying to stay as still as possible.

'Stop that! You're ruining my hay!' the farmer said, suddenly outraged. 'There's no need!'

And finally, after what felt like for ever, the slashing noises stopped.

The cover was loosely thrown back over the straw, descending them into half-darkness once more, and moments later, the cart jolted, beginning to move again.

Livia allowed herself to release the breath she'd been holding. It had been the most terrifying few moments of her life.

'Are they gone?'

She felt him nod against her hair. 'I think so. Are you hurt?'

'No,' she said, shaking her head.

He raised his head to look down at her, inspecting her. 'You're sure?'

'Yes, I'm fine.' She nodded. She thought she must be in shock. She couldn't believe they'd done that. She felt sick to her stomach.

'Thank goodness,' he said, pressing a kiss to her forehead.

'What about you?' she asked. 'Are you all right?'

'It's just a scratch or two.'

She gasped, trying to move from under his weight. 'Let me see.' And when she shifted beneath him, her thighs pressed against his, her belly nudging into his groin, and he cursed.

'Livia, just…keep still for a moment, till we've passed through,' he said. 'They might still be watching us. I'm sure the farmer will stop when it's safe to do so.'

And then she felt the hard ridges of him digging into her and heat flooded her body. She went still. Had she caused that reaction? He was heavy, his huge body pressing down on top of her, but she didn't mind. It felt…nice.

When he pulled away, rolling off her back onto his side, she strangely felt disappointed. She wanted to pull him back, to wiggle against him some more to see what would happen…when she felt moisture on her arm. She looked down and lurched. It was covered in blood.

'You're bleeding,' she said, distraught.

He grimaced. 'They caught me a few times with the tips of their blades.'

'No!' she gasped, horrified, shaking her head. 'How bad is it?'

'I'll live.'

She felt panicked, wanting to get a better look at his wounds, and it felt like an age until the cart stopped again. They heard the farmer come hurrying around the side of the wagon. He threw off the woollen cover. 'Commander? Princess?'

Destin pushed the straw out of the way and sat up, curling himself out of their little den, and when he stood, they all stared at the blood dripping down his good arm, and his leg. Blood was seeping through his tunic at the side of his waist. Just a scratch? It looked a lot worse than that. 'But you…you didn't even flinch,' Livia said, shaking her head, paling.

Still, he held his hand out to help her up, and then apologised to the farmer for the blood on the hay. Clambering down onto the rocky track, he lifted Livia down by her waist, and then inspected the damage to his skin. He had a deep gash in his upper arm, a wound just above his hip, and a cut across his lower leg.

'I thought you were past recovery. I thought I was going to have to take your dead bodies to the emperor,' Marta said, ashen-faced. And then she burst into tears.

'What brutes!' the farmer said, pulling his wife into a hug. 'I wanted to beg them to stop, but then I thought you were certain to be killed. I can't believe Prince Lothair would order something like that,' he said, getting angry. 'He doesn't deserve to rule.'

The farmer led his wife away to sit down on a grassy bank, comforting her, while Livia turned to Destin, concerned. 'How did you not cry out? Or even react?' she asked him, trying to get a closer look at his injuries to see how she could help him.

'I'm surprised you didn't hear me silently curse a few choice words into your ear,' he said, with a grimace.

But she knew he hadn't said anything, or even moved. It was astounding. His tolerance for pain must be great. It had her wondering why…what had he suffered to make him so tough? To make him not flinch when someone inflicted suffering on him? To just take it like that.

With trembling fingers, Livia rummaged in the satchel and pulled out her torn tunic from the day before and passed it to him. He ripped off three strips with his teeth, before passing them back to her.

'Would you mind?' he said.

And she knew he must be hurt, because he was asking for help.

'Sit there,' she said, instructing him to perch on a nearby rock, and he just did as she said.

She tackled the leg first, wrapping the material around his blood-soaked breeches. 'You'll need to change this later. We don't want it getting infected.'

He nodded, grim-faced.

Then she moved onto his arm, first mopping up the blood trickling down his muscles, before tying the material tight around him. 'I hope this helps,' she said. 'I'm all fingers and thumbs.'

His hand closed over hers, steadying her. 'It's all right, Livia. It's over now.'

She swiped a tear away from her eyes. 'I can't bear to think about what might have happened. I hate that you're hurt. And I can't believe you didn't say anything.'

'Better me being hurt than you. And to be honest, you distracted me from the pain.'

He stroked his finger over the top of her hand, holding her tight in his grip. 'I'll be fine. Don't worry about me.'

She swallowed, nodding, before attempting the next wound. He gingerly lifted up his tunic and she gasped when she saw the deep gash to his torso, just under his ribs. 'This is bad!' she cried.

'I've honestly had worse. Just do what you can.'

'It will need a stitch, but I don't have anything on me,' she wailed, letting her tears fall now.

He nodded. 'Just patch it up and I'll have it seen to when we get to Rome.'

She sank down to her knees before him, and looked up at him, as she wrapped the material around his waist. She was reminded of touching his bare chest the other night, and him pushing her away. He was always trying to do the right thing, she realised, but by others, not himself.

'I can't believe you did that for me. You saved my life,' she said, shaking her head. 'Again.'

His hand came up to brush her cheek, stroking a tear away.

'That *is* what I'm here for,' he said.

After the ordeal at the border, none of them could stomach any food, and they decided to press on, eager to get to Rome now. Even Livia. Marta came to sit with them in the back, worried about Destin's wounds almost as much as she was, her bubbly demeanour having turned serious, perhaps realising just how precarious the situation was.

It took the whole of the afternoon to reach the city. Destin actually slept for a while, demanding to be woken up if anyone came near, and Livia was concerned he was hurting more than he was letting on. He wouldn't have succumbed to rest otherwise. She kept pressing her hand against his forehead, worried he was getting a fever, but he kept casting her off, reassuring her he was fine. She wanted to take care of him, she realised. How had she allowed herself to get so attached to him?

As they drew nearer to the city walls, they all gave a collective sigh, pleased to see the King's Guard was manning the ramparts, not her uncle's men. Rome was still under the king's control.

As they approached the gateway and the cart slowed, Destin jumped down and walked ahead to speak to the soldiers. As they spoke, she watched how they at first eyed his arm and wounds, but as the conversation went on, they straightened up and answered him with respect, realising who he was and what they had overcome to get here. She almost crumpled in relief when the gates began to open, like giant arms welcoming her home.

Destin hopped back onto the cart and the farmer urged the horses forward, to take them into the city. Livia even felt the flicker of excitement as the iconic dome of Saint Mark's Basilica rose up before them, dominating the skyline. They had made it.

She was surprisingly glad to see the place. She had been away for so long, and had thought she hadn't missed it, but now that she was here, taking in the familiar landmarks, she felt proud of the colossal amphitheatre and familiar grand columns of the Pantheon. But she felt as if she had changed so much since the last time she was here. She'd changed so much these last few days, and she knew it had a lot to do with the man at her side.

She turned to look at him and he smiled, his eyes shining. 'We made it,' he said, sharing her satisfaction. 'Halfway, anyway.'

It was a moment of great significance. Despite their rocky start, he had kept his end of the bargain and brought her here, unharmed, and she was grateful. But now she would have to keep hers. She would be expected to go on with him to Constantinople, and she wondered what the next stage of their journey would bring.

'Thank you for getting me here,' she said. She didn't know what state her father would be in when she arrived at the palace, but she felt like after these past few days, whatever happened, somehow, she would be strong enough to cope with it.

'You're welcome,' he said.

She wondered, if the farmer and his wife hadn't been around, whether he would have taken her hand, like she wanted to take his, in solidarity and support.

Word spread quickly that the princess had returned, and people began to step out of their houses to line the streets, cheering as they rode past. She waved and smiled, delighted. It had to count for something that they were pleased she was here, didn't it?

Marta puffed out her voluptuous chest in pride that she was riding with them—that her husband had been the one to bring them here, and Livia suddenly felt like laughing. It had been quite the journey.

'They're all staring,' she whispered to Destin.

'And not at me for once! I've found my ruse. Give them something far more interesting to look at. I'll need to stay by your side from now on,' he said, jesting.

She rolled her eyes at him and laughed lightly, but she felt a pang in her chest. If only he could…

When the cart entered the palace gates and stopped in front of the impressive frontage of her father's palace, the king's servants filed out onto the steps to greet her, and Destin finally took her hand to help her out of the cart.

But now they were here, she found she didn't want to get out. Placing her feet down on solid ground, her knees trembling, she was reluctant to let him go. Would they ever be alone again?

'Your Highness, welcome home,' a man said, stepping forward to greet her, and Destin quickly released her from his grasp. She recognised him from when she was younger. It was Matthias, chief amongst the king's councillors.

'Thank you. It is good to see you Matthias. I should like to see my father at once,' she said.

'Certainly, Your Highness,' he said, giving a little bow. 'If you would like to follow me?'

She tentatively started to walk with the man up the steps, and then looked back at Destin, aware he wasn't coming with her.

'Will I…see you later?' she asked.

'I'll be around, keeping guard,' he said. 'I'll be here if you need me, Your Highness.'

Chapter Six

Destin spent the afternoon learning the lay of the land and the security of the palace. He spoke to the Royal Guard in the city, asking about any sighting of Lothair's men, suggesting doubling the soldiers on the gates, making sure their weapons were all sharp and they had the right armour. He couldn't be sure what Lothair was planning, and he wanted them to be prepared for every eventuality. When he had spoken to each man on every post, making sure they understood their instructions and were being vigilant, on alert, he was confident Livia was now safe. He didn't think Lothair would dare attack her here. Lothair wouldn't risk losing his claim to the imperial seat if anything were to happen to her within the city walls.

But he was disturbed that no one had seen or heard anything from his own contingent of men—were they still in Harzburg? He hoped they had got out, along with the women and children. He wouldn't be able to settle until he knew they were all right. He didn't think Livia would ever forgive him if they weren't.

Trying to keep himself busy, to distract himself from thinking about Livia and how she was getting on with her father, he found a place for the farmer and his wife to stay for the night—it was the least he could do to thank them for all their help.

Then he'd seen a healer who had stitched up his wounds. When he'd felt the tips of those swords slice into him, he'd thought that was it, that his life was over. And with a strange sense of calm, he'd accepted it. He'd been willing to die in Livia's place. He couldn't think of anyone more worthy, not even the emperor. When he'd felt the cart move on, and he'd realised he was bleeding, but still alive, he'd felt euphoric. That he was still with her, that they had made it. He had wanted to kiss her again, to hold her tight and never let go. He'd wanted to tell her what she meant to him. And he'd become so aware of their bodies being so close, of her every curve pressed against him, of her every movement, he had felt his groin respond. *Skit!* Had she felt it? If he hadn't just saved her life, he didn't know what she'd think of him, and he'd forced himself to roll off her.

Heading back to the palace for the evening's feast, he was desperate to see her again, and it had only been a few hours since he'd let her out of his sight. He missed seeing her smile. He missed the camaraderie between them. He even missed her incessant questions. But when he arrived in the great hall, the news of the king's passing reached him.

Despite knowing that this was going to happen, he wished it wasn't true. He had found himself needing to sit down as he'd tried to process it. He'd asked Matthias questions, to better understand what had happened, but mainly, he just wanted to know if Livia was all right.

The feast in the hall had been a sombre affair, the bells in the Basilica ringing out over the city. They continued throughout the evening, and when the hour began to grow late, Destin began to worry. He hadn't seen Livia all afternoon, and he needed to know how she was coping. But no one had seen or heard from her since she'd left the king's quarters. When he could bear it no longer, he went to the kitchens and piled a plate full of meat and vegetables, asked the servants to show him where her rooms were, and headed up to see her. He knew it didn't look good, but it was an unsettling time. The palace was in disarray, with everyone in a state of shock and mourning, waiting to be told what would happen next. Perhaps the rules of conduct could be put aside for one night.

A guard was manning the door, and he bowed in respect as Destin came towards him.

'Have you seen or heard anything from the princess?'

'Not since she locked herself in here after the king's passing, Commander.'

Destin nodded. At least he knew she was inside. 'Very good, soldier. You can take your leave. I will stand guard for a while now.'

He was relieved the man didn't argue it, but instead nodded and marched away, down the corridor, trusting him implicitly. It seemed word had spread fast that he was the man who had helped the princess escape the siege in Saxony and how he had protected her on the journey here. He had the feeling the farmer and his wife were to thank for that.

He pressed his ear against her door and could hear Livia softly sobbing, and he couldn't stand for her to be suffering all alone. He wanted to ease her pain. Against his better judgement, telling him to leave the food there and walk away, he placed the plate down and rapped lightly on the door.

He heard her footsteps approach the wood, and she tentatively opened the door, her face pale and streaked with tears. 'I asked not to be— Oh. It's you,' she said, when she saw him.

'I came to offer my condolences. I'm so sorry to hear about your father...'

She stared up at him, her golden eyes huge and sad, and he dropped the pleasantries. 'Are you all right?' he asked her, concerned.

'No. No, I don't think I am,' she said, her lips trembling, her voice cracking. She crumpled before him and he pulled her into his chest, lifting her off the ground and carrying her back inside the room, kicking the door shut behind him.

He walked her over to the bed and sat her down on the edge of it, holding her for a while, stroking her hair as she cried.

'Everything's going to be all right,' he soothed. 'Your father's at peace now.'

He studied the surroundings over her shoulder, as he always did when he was somewhere new, taking it all in, assessing it for danger. But he thought it was the most beautiful room he'd ever been in. There was a small window, letting in a cool evening breeze, and soft drapes hung loosely around her bed, floating about. All her belongings were scattered around, just as messy as the room she'd had back in Harzburg, but it felt more opulent somehow. There were trinkets and books all over her desk, and wisps of smoke filled the room, from little sticks that were burning, giving off a scent of lavender and incense.

Eventually, when she'd cried all her tears, Livia pulled away slightly and looked up at him from red, puffy eyes.

'Sorry,' she sniffed. 'I guess this isn't how I'm meant to be behaving. Was everyone expecting my presence down in the hall, at the evening's feast?'

'No,' he said, inclining his head. 'He's your father, you're allowed to grieve, Livia.' He pushed her damp hair out of her face and tucked it behind her ears.

'I'm just not ready to face anyone. Or to address the court. Not yet.'

'People will understand. Are you hungry? I brought you some food.'

She shook her head. 'I don't think I could eat anything... Thank you for getting me here in time to see him, Destin. He was grateful to you.'

He nodded. 'I'm sure he would have got great comfort from having you with him at the end.'

'I think he was waiting for me, holding on till I got here...'

'But you got to speak to him? To say everything you needed to say?'

'Yes.' She nodded.

He wanted to ask what they'd spoken about, whether

her father had given her any advice about her future, but he also didn't want to pry.

He didn't like to see her like this, her shoulders bowed.

'I can't believe all my family, the people who knew me best, have gone. My mother, my brothers, now my father…'

'I know how you feel. I know the feeling of abandonment all too well. It does get easier as the winters pass.' Only his parents had chosen to leave him, hers hadn't. 'But *I'm* right here,' he said, taking her hand and squeezing her fingers in his. 'There are a lot of people who care about you, Livia, take comfort from that.'

'For how long?' she whispered. 'How long will you be here?'

'As long as you need me. I promise you, even when we get to Constantinople, I'll be there, watching over you. You'll be sick of the sight of me,' he said, trying to make light of it. He would make sure she was safe, even if it killed him seeing her with Alexios every day.

'Doubtful,' she said, gripping his fingers back. 'Will you stay with me now and talk to me for a while? I don't want to be alone…'

He looked towards the door. 'I sent the guard away…'

'Good. Then no one is going to disturb me. They think you're guarding my door. Please?'

He nodded stiffly, leaning back against the wall, resting against the piled-up furs, bringing his legs up onto the bed, and she curled up into his shoulder, carefully resting her hand on his chest.

'What will happen now?'

'That depends… Do you want to be queen?' he asked.

And she raised her head to look at him. 'No one has ever asked me that before. Isn't it just expected that I do? It wasn't ever something I had to think about growing up, as Otto was always next in line. When that changed, it was there, at the back of my mind that this could one day happen. But the thoughts of my impending marriage overshadowed it somehow. I guess I didn't ever think anyone would allow a woman to take the throne.'

He shrugged. 'If you don't want the position, then you can abdicate and your uncle will probably be successful in his claim.' She settled back down, resting her cheek on his chest. 'But if you do…while you are the rightful heir to the throne, Livia, I believe there will be an election. You and Lothair will both be asked to petition the Electoral College, usually in Frankfurt, on why you should be the next ruler, and then they will decide.'

'Will I have to see my uncle?'

'Yes, but remember the whole court will be there. I'll be there. You'll be safe… He can't hurt you now.'

She ran her hand over his waist, over where he'd been stabbed, and he felt his muscles tense. 'Or you… I owe it to my father to try. I don't know how they can even consider Lothair being ruler, after the things he's done.'

'He is a man with a legitimate claim… The rest is only hearsay. Our word against his. There is no proof, unless we send people to Harzburg to check the damage.'

'If he is successful, what happens to me then? Will Alexios still want to marry me?'

His heart clenched. 'Your engagement is set in stone.

The emperor agreed to marry you when your brother was next in line to the throne, I doubt your uncle being king would change anything… There may be some terms to negotiate.'

'And if I am crowned queen?'

'Then you and Alexios will be rulers of not one but two great empires…'

'But you don't think that will happen?' she said.

'I never said that. I think the more allies you have, the more people who support your claim, the more chance you have of being successful. Those who knew your father may be rooting for you. They may dislike his brother. Especially if word has reached them of what he's done this past week.'

'Families are so complicated.' She sighed. 'Sometimes I wish I'd been born into a normal one, like Charles and Marta, and I'd been brought up on a farm and had a simple life.'

He nodded.

'How is it you came to be raised by strangers? Will you tell me about it?' she asked, changing the subject, looking up at him.

His lips twisted. 'I don't like to talk about it.'

'Please? It comforts me to hear your voice, to learn of your past. I want to know more about you, Destin. And it will distract me from thinking about my father.'

He sighed. 'I'm afraid there's not much comfort in this tale, Livia. Where I come from, in Norway, settlements removed the sick if they didn't think they'd be able to contribute to the village, or if it was thought they'd bring shame upon the family. I believe, because

I was born how I was, my parents thought they had to abandon me to keep the others in their settlement strong. Growing up, I would have been expected to work and to fight and they no doubt took one look at me and deemed I wouldn't be able to…so they put me out to die.'

She gasped, pulling away from him a little to look into his eyes. 'Just because of your arm? How could they do that?' she said, outraged.

He shrugged. 'It's how things are back there. I told you, it's a warrior culture.'

'But it's so…so cold. So wrong.'

And he smiled at how she was so defensive of him. 'I don't blame them. I don't feel any ill will towards them. Or try not to anyway. They probably thought they were being merciful.'

She shook her head, before lying back down on his chest, her hand curling over his stomach, and he wrapped his arm tighter around her. 'How can you be so understanding, so forgiving?'

'Because I believe they thought they were doing it to be kind. And the couple who found me in the woods, Áki and Gerdur, became my family. It was all I knew. They were good people. They told me I struggled to crawl, but I don't remember that.' He shrugged. 'And it took me longer than most to learn how to do things. So I don't look back and think my parents were evil. I like to think of it as though they were trying to save me from living a life of shame.'

'And has it been, a life of shame?'

'For many years, yes,' he admitted. 'You've seen what it's like. Every day I have to explain myself…

why I am like I am… You saw how that monk looked at me at dinner that night. How your people looked at me in your hall… You must have heard the whispers. And the soldiers today. People are curious, they always have questions. They want to know why I'm different.'

'But they can see it doesn't hold you back.'

'No, it doesn't. *I* know that. I hope I have more than proved my worth to myself and the emperor and my men.'

'And to me.'

He smiled into her hair, breathing in the familiar floral scent of her. 'But it isn't a life I would want to subject others to. It's a constant battle to prove myself.'

'Not having you in their life must have been a great loss to your parents, Destin. And the fault for your abandonment lies with them, not you and how you are. If only they could see you now… Are you not tempted to seek them out, to show them the type of man you have become?'

He shook his head. 'Norway is a big place. I wouldn't know where to start. Besides, I'm not sure how I'd feel if I found my family now.' He shifted beneath her. 'Anyway, I came in here to see how you were, not to talk about me…'

'I like talking about you,' she said, turning herself round in his arms to lie on her front, her hand splayed out on his chest, and his fingers curled around her upper arm. She lifted her head to look up at him. His dark eyes were focused on her and he wondered how they had got here. How they had grown so close in just a week, so that he felt comfortable sharing his deeper thoughts. He welcomed her questions now, and didn't hold back from answering. But her touch? He really should be going…

'Did you get your wounds seen to?' Livia asked.

'Yes. All good,' he said.

She narrowed her eyes on him. 'Did they need stitching?'

'Only the one.'

'Show me?'

'Don't trust me?' he asked, grinning, and when she gave him a look he sighed, and tugged up his tunic, revealing the wound to the side of his stomach. It looked a lot better than it did before.

She nodded, satisfied. 'Who did it for you?'

A healer at the hospice in the centre of the city.'

'A woman?'

He raised his eyebrows, amused. 'I didn't really have a choice in who did it.'

Her lips twisted. She didn't like the thought of another woman touching his body, soothing his wounds, making him feel better.

'I still can't believe you did that,' she whispered. 'That you were prepared to sacrifice yourself for me.'

Livia's fingers strayed to the bruising around his wound, tracing it lightly with her fingers. She flattened her hand against his skin, sliding it up beneath his tunic, over his bare chest. She wanted to touch where she could feel his heart pounding.

'Livia,' he said sternly.

But she didn't want to heed his warning. Her hand moved up, under his other arm, strapped across him, and settled over the solid warmth of his chest muscle, and she felt his nipple harden beneath her palm. Unable to help herself, she reached up and placed a soft kiss on his mouth.

He tensed and pulled back, his hand tightening around her arm.

'Livia. We said we weren't going to do this again. You said just the once…'

'I know. I've changed my mind,' she whispered.

'I should leave you,' he said, attempting to sit up.

'Don't go…' she said, increasing the pressure on his chest. She clung to him, needing to keep him close. 'If my father's death has taught me anything, it's that life's too short. You should make the most of it. Be with the people you care about, before it's too late… And I care about you.'

'Livia, you know that we can't.' His voice sounded strange. Strangled.

'Why can't we? We're not hurting anyone. I'm not married yet… Alexios and I don't even know each other. Are you saying the emperor has never been with a woman? Never kissed anyone before? I'm not going to judge *him* for it.'

'That's different and you know it,' Destin said, trying to remove her hand from under his tunic, but she wasn't budging, resisting him.

'Why is it?'

'It just is!' he said, sitting up and gently pushing her away, finally working her hand free. 'If he knew about this, he would have me killed, and you…well, I don't know what he'd do to you,' he said, shaking his head.

'I thought you said he was kind,' she retorted, her lips pouting as she tucked her legs beneath her.

'He's also ruthless. He has to be. And every man has their limits. This is a matter of honour…'

'You've already kissed me once. What does it matter if you do it again?'

He dragged his hand over his face as if tortured by the reminder, or the temptation she was putting before him. 'What do you want from me?' he said, shaking his head. 'What do you see in me?' he whispered.

'Everything…'

She sat up on her knees, reached out and curled her hand around his neck, drawing his head towards her. Her stomach fluttered, her heart hammered, and she knew, as her mouth covered his, he was past resisting. His lips were firm as they met hers, and she opened her mouth, inviting him inside, wanting him to caress her tongue with his again, as he'd done the other day. When he did, her hands slid wildly into his hair, drawing him closer, needing to breathe him in. This was what she wanted. To be in his arms again, his mouth on hers, soothing her, to feel close to him and forget all else.

She pressed herself against him, pushing him backwards on the bed, so they were lying chest to chest, her knee curled over his thigh, and their mouths clung together, testing, exploring, letting the kiss go on and on. She could feel the hectic thud of his heart beating and it reassured her, that she wasn't alone in how she was feeling.

Her hand crept beneath his tunic again, and her fingers splayed out over his skin, up to his right shoulder.

'Can you feel that?' she whispered, wondering where the sensations stopped for him.

He covered her hand, moving it down to the middle of his chest. 'Now I can.'

His other arm was in the way and she nodded to the sling. 'Can I take that off?'

'Livia,' he said, almost hesitant, uncertain.

But she ignored the warning in his tone and reached for the strap around his neck, lifting it up over his head, before pulling the splint away. He eyed her warily, but she continued. She carefully moved his arm to his side, so there was no barrier between them.

'Are these all battle wounds?' she asked, holding her palm against his cheek, smoothing her thumb over the silvery scars. He was so close, she could see the tiny brown flecks in his dark eyes, and she wondered how she could have ever thought they were brittle and hard. There was warmth and passion behind them.

'All from fighting, as a child and a man.'

'They fascinate me. You fascinate me.'

He covered her hand with his and kissed her again, his beard softly grazing her skin.

She moved her hand back to his chest, running her hands beneath the material again. 'And these. All injuries from fighting too?'

'Yes,' he said, his dark gaze on her, watching her face as she traced her fingertips over the ridges and lines of his skin.

'Did they hurt?'

'Some. Although not having any feeling in some parts of your body can be an advantage if you're injured there.'

She bent her head to press her lips against the skin at the base of his throat, and lower, wherever she could see his burnished skin, savouring the spicy taste and fresh pine scent of him. Flattening her lower body against his, she became aware of other parts of him that were definitely working. She gasped in surprise, pleased to have caused the same reaction as she'd felt in the cart, feeling a reciprocal excitement between her legs, and he tried to push her away but she resisted, kissing him on the mouth again.

'Livia,' he said, tearing his lips away. 'We must stop. I'm in danger of losing control with you and I mustn't. I won't let you compromise your position. You can't put your reputation, your marriage and throne in jeopardy... Not for me.'

But didn't he realise his words only made her like him even more?

'We're just kissing,' she whispered, placing little kisses up his throat, coming back to his mouth again, and he groaned. And yet she was aware of her body reacting with force, liquid heat pooling between her legs. She was feeling the increasing need, the desire for him to touch her right there, and she recklessly pressed her belly against him, cradling the hard ridge of him, and he tightened his grip on her waist.

'What are you trying to do to me?' he groaned.

She gave a little wiggle as her answer.

He growled and rolled her gently onto her back, lying on his weaker side, and his hot mouth left her lips to trail down to her chin and along her jaw, and she lifted her head, wanting, willing him to move his mouth lower.

When he didn't, she gripped his hand and brought it up to place it over one swollen breast, flattening his palm against her.

She thought he was about to resist once more, to continue to fight his feelings and her needs, and she prepared herself to have to hold him in place, but then his thumb grazed over her nipple, teasing it into a hard peak beneath the material of her tunic, and the movement felt so good, she whimpered. She wanted to get closer. She wanted him to peel off her clothes and press his mouth to where his thumb was gently stroking her.

Her fingers stole between their bodies and beneath the bottom of his tunic, roaming up over his muscled torso, bunching up the material, and he reached down to help her, lifting it over his good arm and his head, before pulling it off his other side. He looked at her, wary, as if he expected her to recoil, but she stared at him in awe. His left side was less muscled, yet he was still magnificent. She pressed her mouth to his bare chest, over his ink.

'What is all this?' she whispered, tracing the dark, swirling lines with her fingers.

'In Norway, we dye our skin with symbols. They all mean certain things to me.'

'Will you tell me about them?' she asked, her eyes raking over them.

He pointed to some of the sharp, angular shapes. One was an arrow, pointing upwards. 'It means Tyr.'

'The god we were talking about the other day?'

'Yes.'

'And the other?' It looked like a tall fork. 'It means man. Áki did them for me.'

'I'll tell you more about him sometime. He was a father to me in every sense of the word. He saved me.'

His statement settled, bringing home just how close he had come to not surviving as a child. To not being here with her now. That was unthinkable.

She wondered at the impact that knowledge, that his parents had left him out in the cold, helpless, to die, would have had on him growing up. That the very people who were meant to love him, unconditionally, hadn't wanted him because they'd thought he was less able, when it couldn't be further from the truth.

She had the flash of a thought that her father had treated her mother that way. That he had put her out to die, during childbirth, choosing to save the child over her. But it had been an impossible choice...yet one that had haunted her nonetheless.

No wonder Destin thought he was unlovable. No wonder he'd had to fight for praise and recognition.

'Perhaps Áki and I think along the same lines...' she said. 'That you and Tyr have a lot in common.'

He kissed her again, harder, more passionately than before, and she began to fumble with her brooches on her kirtle, her fingers trembling with nerves and need. 'Will you help me take this off?' she whispered. And suddenly he pulled back, disturbed. He stilled, placing his hand over her trembling fingers.

'Livia, we need to stop now,' he said seriously.

No! She didn't want to stop. She wasn't ready for

this to be over. She wanted more… She wanted him to make her his, if only for the night.

'Many a person has seen me naked in battle or bathing…but you…your body should only be seen by your husband. And that's not me,' he said, his voice hardening, as if he'd decided for the both of them enough was enough. 'It wouldn't be right. It's *not* my right…'

'But I want to do this. With you,' she said.

He shut his eyes momentarily, as if he was in pain. 'I won't like myself very much if we go any further. And neither will you.'

She sighed heavily, feeling hopeless for their situation. She wanted him, she cared for him, and yet she couldn't have him. 'I don't like you very much for stopping me.'

He raised an eyebrow, making her smile.

'Look, you've been through a lot today. Your feelings must be in turmoil. I won't take advantage of you when you're at your most vulnerable. I think you need to get some sleep now. You must be exhausted, after our journey, after everything that's happened.'

'What if I don't feel this way about the emperor?' she blurted.

Any hint of a smile disappeared from his face. 'I'm sure you will grow to care about him.'

'And if I don't? What if I never feel like this again? What if he touches me and I feel nothing?'

'He should be gentle with you, take care of your feelings,' he said, though his voice sounded tight, as if he was forcing the words through his lips. He shook his head, as if to shake away the thoughts. He went to move away from her and she hated the distance between them.

'Please. Don't go. Will you stay with me? Just hold me until I fall asleep?' She felt safe, stronger, whole, when he was with her.

For a moment, he looked conflicted, and then he relented. 'Yes, if that's what you want.'

'Promise you won't leave me?'

'I promise, Livia.'

Destin lay there awake, Livia curled into the side of his body, her head resting on his bare chest. She had slept half the night, muttering things in her sleep, and he'd stroked her hair, soothing her. He knew he should get up and leave before the sun rose, and yet he couldn't bring himself to move. He didn't want to be parted from her. Not yet.

He shouldn't be here, and yet, she had chosen him over anyone else to comfort her in her time of need. So how could he not? It made him feel wanted, special, for the first time in his life. Surely it was worth the risk?

A breeze drifted through the window and she shivered. Stirring, she pressed herself closer to him, curling her hand into his chest, and he held his breath. He reached over to grip the edge of the blanket and pull it up her body, to keep her warm, and she sleepily took it from him, tugging it, helping him to cover them both. And then she surprised him by bringing it up over their heads, descending them into darkness and stretching up, her body coming down on top of him, and she planted a kiss firmly on his mouth.

'Now you can deny ever seeing me,' she whispered.
He was hard in an instant. 'Livia, what the—'
'Shh,' she hushed him.

He had never wanted anyone or anything so much in
his life. And by the way her hands were moving over
his jaw, over his chest and down, neither had she. She
was persistent, he'd give her that! And the moment her
fingers curved over the straining, hard ridge of him,
touching him through the material of his breeches, he
was gone. There was no going back.

He hauled her closer to him, his lips on hers, his hand
on her back, roaming down over her buttocks, pressing
his thigh between her legs, and she whimpered.

He began rucking up her dress, wanting to touch her
in return, and his fingers gathered up the skirts of her
stola, trembling as they trailed up the back of her bare
legs, over her smooth thighs, until they curved over one
round buttock and gently squeezed.

He was aware of his heart thudding erratically as she
flicked her tongue against his in a hot, open-mouthed
kiss and he lost all restraint. His fingers slipped lower.
When the tips reached her slick, silky flesh, she gasped,
and he stilled. 'Do you want me to stop?' he rasped.

'No,' she said, her forehead resting against his, their
frantic breath mingling. 'Don't stop.' And as if to prove
it, she moved against the curve of his hand, impatient,
encouraging him on.

He rolled her over onto her side, his hand coming
round the front of her for better access, and he pushed
her bunched up skirts out of the way, his large hand
smoothing over her stomach. He swallowed, nervous,

now he'd decided to do this. Moving lower, he stared down into her eyes as his fingers stole through her delicate curls, making her body shudder. Her hand curled around his neck, drawing him closer, and she restlessly parted her mouth—and her thighs—as his fingers stole lower, to where he knew she wanted him to touch her, and when he did, softly seeking her most sensitive parts, she moaned. She was soaking wet, and she writhed beneath him, her cheeks flushing. He touched her slowly, gently. 'Is that all right, like this?' he asked, ready to take any instruction she gave him, seeking her approval.

'Yes,' she choked, her breathing quickening. He grazed his knuckles along her crease, opening her up, before flattening his fingers back against her, learning the feel of her body. He found her tiny nub and circled it with the tip of his finger, and she groaned again as if in disbelief, pulling his head down to kiss her again and again.

Lips clinging, tongues swirling, forehead to forehead, he moved his finger lower, pressing it gently inside her tight, silky entrance, before drawing it out with a fresh rush of moisture and swirling it back over her little bud. Her muscles began to tense and he knew she was close, and he was desperate to give her the release she so obviously craved. He pushed his finger back inside her once more and she cried out into his mouth, clasping his hand between her thighs as her body shuddered through her climax, and he kissed her, holding her close until she settled.

Chapter Seven

When the warning horn sounded out over the city the next morning, Livia's heart lurched.

The date had been set for her father's funeral in a week, and for both her and her uncle to petition the Electoral College in just two days, giving Livia what the council deemed enough time for her to deal with her grief and Prince Lothair enough time to travel to Rome. Anger flared at the thought. She couldn't believe they were allowing Lothair that concession, given all he and his men had done. She was furious with him, and she was determined she would not let him get away with it.

Upon hearing the warning horn, her skin prickled. Had Lothair arrived already, come to try to take her father's throne? She stepped out of the bath and her maids wrapped her in a huge silk sheet, but she wasn't interested in getting dressed. She wanted to see what was happening outside. She peered through the small window, trying to see out over the grand courtyard down below, to work out what was happening.

She could see the Royal Guard manning the walls,

but scanning their positions, she saw they were opening the gates, letting in a convoy of marching men. And
she reeled. They weren't wearing the Royal uniform
of Rome, or the phoenix of her uncle's banner, but the
burgundy cloak and dragon emblem of the Varangian
Guard. And then she saw who was leading them. It
wasn't her uncle who had arrived, but Emperor Alexios
and a contingent of his army.

No! Had he really come all the way from Constantinople to claim her? And would he use force?

This could not be happening. Not now.

She believed Alexios's presence here would make
the nobles anxious, unsure of what the Byzantine emperor's arrival meant for their own empire. They would
not like the thought of a foreigner ruling over them, and
she didn't want his arrival to ruin her chances of suc-
ceeding the throne. Because she had decided now, after
speaking with her father, and listening to Destin's words
last night, that she was going to petition to be queen.
And her engagement to the emperor might be the very
thing putting her crown at risk.

When she had gone to see her father, he had looked
so small and frail, lying there in his grand bed. A
shadow of his former self. He'd reached out for her
and she'd run to him, taking his hand and kneeling beside him. He had spoken slowly, as if he was in a great
deal of pain, and he had apologised for putting his wars
and greed for glory and more lands before her. He'd
said sorry for being a different man since Otto had
died, thinking only of warfare and vengeance for his
son's death. He had told her he'd regretted some of the

decisions he had made, including how he'd dealt with her mother's death. And she had squeezed his hand and stroked his brow and told him she forgave him.

She had seen how weak and pale he was, and she had felt guilty bringing up her impending marriage to Alexios, but she'd needed to know her father's thoughts on it.

'It is a good match,' he had said. 'He will protect you. You could achieve what I never could…you could reign over two great empires.'

She had nodded, a lump growing in her throat. 'So you wish for me to be queen?' she asked.

'I wish for you to be happy,' he had said. 'I cannot tell you what to do. A great ruler will decide their own destiny. But I know, whatever path you take, will be the right one.'

It made her realise, if she'd been in any doubt before, just how much she did want to secure the crown for her father's legacy, not just for him, but her mother too, so she hadn't died in vain. Also, for herself. Deep down, she thought she could do this, with the right people supporting her. She hadn't realised just how much it meant to her until now. But now she knew she had to become her father's daughter. The princess her people expected her to be. And the queen she wanted to be. To make them all proud.

And yet, staring down into the courtyard, watching her intended husband approach the palace, she knew there was no way she could turn Alexios away. Destin was right, she needed all the allies and supporters she could gather at the moment.

But why had he come today, of all days, when she had spent the night in the arms of another man?

As her maids dressed her in a beautiful dark mourning tunic and stola, she saw a familiar figure move towards the gates and welcome the visitors. Destin.

Her breath stalled. She hadn't seen him since he had slipped from her arms and her bed while she had been sleeping. He had promised her he wouldn't leave her and yet she had awoken alone.

Still, the memory of the things he had done to her, the way he had touched her so intimately, remained. She had never known it could feel so good. The excitement he had caused as his fingers had stroked up her naked thighs, touching her between her legs, and inside her body, had been like nothing she'd ever felt before. And the overwhelming pleasure he had given her... She flushed at the memory of her muffled screams as her climax had crashed through her, and he had kissed her, quieting her quivering body. It had all been so unexpected. Incredible.

After she had got her breath back, she had felt the hard ridge of him still throbbing against her thigh, and her hand had roamed down, knowing it was her turn to touch him, wanting to pleasure him in return. But as her trembling fingers had curved over him, he had stilled her hand.

As controlled as ever, he had stopped them from going any further. He had pushed her away, denying himself his own release, and she wondered how he could be so restrained. Did he not feel this infuriating longing that she felt for him? She had wanted to show him, through her touch, how much he was beginning to mean to her.

And yet, if anyone found out… She dragged a hand over her face. She wasn't sure how she would be able to face him, and now the emperor, today, when thoughts of Destin's fingers touching her body were at the forefront of her mind. When all she wanted was for him to do it again. And yet she knew that she must go and greet them. There was nowhere to run, not this time. There was nowhere to hide.

She wondered how Destin would feel about his ruler's sudden and unexpected arrival, after what had happened between them last night. But, to her surprise, she watched as the emperor descended his horse, removed his helmet and embraced his commander, smiling.

The scene took her breath away. They were *friends*? Destin had never said they were close. She knew Alexios must trust him, to give him the position of commander in his army and such a task. But *friends*? That would explain a lot. Destin didn't just respect his ruler, he cared for him. No wonder he was conflicted. No wonder he kept pushing her away… She forced herself to step back from the window, troubled.

And yet, the sight of them embracing also gave her a little bit of hope. If Destin liked Alexios, if he thought he was a good man, perhaps she would too. Perhaps the emperor would listen to what she now knew, without a shadow of a doubt, she had to say to him.

As soon as she entered the great hall, her father's councillors gathered round her, offering their condolences and asking about arrangements for the funeral, wanting answers to endless questions. She tried to deal with each one in turn, calmly. Finally, when all the tasks had been delegated, she tried to gather her courage and announced that she was ready to receive her visitor.

Gripping the sides of her father's elaborate wooden throne tight, her knuckles turning white, she took a deep breath and steeled herself for what was to come.

The ornate doors suddenly swung open and two figures and a small convoy of men came in, walking up the hall towards her. Her eyes scanned her guests, assessing them. She recognised the emperor at once. He was, as Destin had said, a handsome, well-groomed man. Not much older than herself, he had blond hair that fell across his bright blue eyes, which were slightly too small for his face, and she could now see what Destin had meant. His nose and lips were indeed delicate. He was attractive, but he didn't compare to the man who towered over him at his side.

In that moment, she knew she could never be attracted to the emperor. She knew she could never have a future with him. She had thought so before, but now she was absolutely certain. He didn't have any impact on her, not like Destin had when she'd first met him. He was the only man who had ever and would ever stir her heart. He made her knees go weak, he made her feel feverish, her breathing quicken. He made her want to open up to him and share her thoughts and listen in return. To know everything about him. He made her appreciate the world and everything in it, from a tiny alpine flower to a grand palace she had previously been disillusioned with. He made her feel complete. No. No man could ever compare to the Norse warrior striding up the hall towards her.

Their gazes clashed and she felt the familiar thud in her chest, the jolt of recognition, and she could only think of last night and the things they had done. She fought against the attraction, tearing her eyes away, forcing herself to glance back at the emperor, afraid of what he and her councillors might see behind her eyes, what she might unwittingly disclose if she continued to look at his commander. She tried to keep her face impassive, trained on Alexios, and she kept telling herself they couldn't see the trembling of her legs beneath her skirts as she rose to greet them. They had no way of knowing what she was feeling inside.

They stopped just before her and bowed. Emperor Alexios offered her a broad smile, Destin did not.

'Princess Livia, it is good to see you again after all these years,' Alexios said confidently.

'You're very welcome here, Your Highness. We were not expecting you, but it is a pleasant surprise nonetheless.'

'I was getting rather restless waiting for news back at home. I was starting to worry about the many days the journey was taking and thought I should heed my commander's advice and meet you halfway, see what the delay was,' he said.

Had Destin advised the emperor to come in the first place? How different everything might have been if that had happened. But she imagined the end result would still have been the same. She would still have had the same reaction to Destin when she'd finally met him.

'I trust you had a safe journey from Saxony?'

'The scenery was beautiful. There were some fraught moments along the way—I'm sure your commander will relay all the details to you.' She tried not to look at Destin.

'I sent one of my best men, knowing he would take good care of you. I trust he has?'

'Yes, well enough.' She felt the flush rise in her cheeks as she recalled Destin taking good care of her last night, causing her to throw her head back in pleasure.

'Please allow me to extend my condolences for the passing of your father, Your Highness. I was sorry to hear the news. I always liked him when he visited Constantinople.'

She nodded solemnly. 'Thank you. I believe the feeling was mutual.' She still couldn't believe her father had gone. It almost didn't seem real, as if he might walk through the door at any moment. She felt the lump of emotion grow in her throat and tried to swallow it down.

Her father had thought he was making a good match for her with the emperor, but how could he know her heart at four and ten years of age? She hadn't known it herself till recently. And the thought gave her the confidence she needed to say her next words.

'Emperor Alexios,' she said. 'I appreciate you have come all this way and I am flattered. Really, I am. But I have something to say and you're not going to like it.'

He stared down at her, his brow furrowing.

'I fear you have made a wasted trip in coming here. I have been trying to tell your commander this for days.

But I'm afraid I cannot return with you to Constantinople, at present.'

Two pairs of eyes widened in shock and bore into hers.

'Your Highness—' Alexios said, moving forward towards her. Her council seemed to draw closer to hear her next words.

'Please understand. My circumstances these past few days have changed beyond belief. My empire is in a state of unrest. As am I. Right now, I'm needed here until the succession is decided. I mean to fight for my throne, for my people and my empire. I cannot think about marriage at the moment, not until I know my empire is safe.'

Alexios reeled, his face turning a funny shade of purple, as if she had humiliated him in front of all the people in the hall. That had not been her intent.

Destin quickly stepped in, seemingly perturbed. 'Emperor Alexios, I'm sure Princess Livia is just in a state of shock about all that has happened these past few days. We had a far more dangerous journey than I led you to believe just now, and we arrived here to learn her father had just hours to live. Now, her crown is at risk. Perhaps the princess just needs a day or two...'

Alexios nodded. 'Of course. I can accept that,' he said slowly. 'What is an extra day or two when you have already made me wait four winters?' But his mouth formed a thin line and she knew he was displeased.

'You seemed in no rush yourself to hurry it along, until now,' she countered.

In fact, it had always surprised her that when she had fled from Constantinople, he'd sent no messengers, no words of encouragement or support across the ocean, to try to win her affections. She had barely heard from him these past four years. They were strangers.

'Princess Livia,' Destin interjected. 'As I have stated from the start, I believe you will have more power and protection here if you align with the emperor. Whether you are or aren't successful in ascending the throne, you will need allies...'

Her gaze moved from Alexios to Destin and her eyes narrowed on him. She felt wounded—and angry. He should be on her side. Surely, he didn't want or expect her to still go ahead with the marriage after everything that had been said between them this past week, and after she'd slept in his arms last night? After the way she'd let him put his hand on and inside her body so intimately. Had it meant nothing to him? How could he still be pushing her towards a future with another man? Did he not know she cared for him? Did he not feel the same?

The emperor clapped his hand on Destin's shoulder. 'Even though you haven't quite made it to Constantinople, I think you are worth every coin I will be paying you—and that reward I promised you, Commander,' he said.

Livia froze. 'Reward?'

'For fetching you for me. I promised to make him a very rich man.'

She nodded. She knew that.

'And my right-hand man, in fact.'

She went cold all over. But of course there would be a reward. Destin was a mercenary. She had known he was being paid for his mission, not doing it out of the goodness of his heart, for he had told her so when they'd first met. No doubt it was why he had been so insistent at first that she came with him. But she had begun to hope his feelings on the matter had changed, and that he had begun to protect her because he cared about her, not just because he was obliged and wanted the coin.

Now she was uncertain. He was set to gain so much more from her union with the emperor than she had first believed. Did he still want a grander title? Over her?

Suddenly, she was livid and she'd had enough of him pushing her towards the emperor. She clenched her fists tight and lifted her chin.

'Perhaps you're right, *Commander*,' she said, her voice like acid. 'Perhaps I just need more time to think things through. To forget about my ordeal—no, *everything* that's happened this past week!'

His body barely flinched, but she saw the flash in his eyes and knew her words had hit home. Good.

She turned back to the emperor, a steely resolve settling in her stomach. 'Emperor Alexios, I cannot return with you to Constantinople right now, but you are welcome to extend your trip. Perhaps it would be wise for us to take some of your commander's *insistent* advice and become better acquainted while you are here. I have much work to do for the petition on the morrow, but if you're not too tired from your trip, perhaps you might allow me to show you around the palace gardens before this evening's feast?'

She got a small slither of satisfaction from seeing the muscle working in Destin's cheek.

'I would like that, Your Highness,' Alexios said. 'And I look forward to us getting to know each other better.'

Walking around the grounds of the palace, a few paces behind Livia and Alexios, Destin couldn't relax. He was on high alert, as he now had not one but two people to protect. He felt as if he had crossed over into *niflheim*, the dark, suffering world of the Norse dead.

This was the second time in so many weeks he'd been to the Roman king's home, but on this occasion, he'd made sure he was aware of all the entrances and exits, and the defensive strengths and weaknesses. The stone building itself, in the heart of the city, was impressive, with a grand hall and opulent rooms, which wrapped around a large, central courtyard. The gardens were vast and home to many sculptures and fountains. But right now, the magnificent setting wasn't doing anything to ease the tightness in his chest. The torment he was feeling.

He followed behind Livia and Alexios at a distance, as they walked through the manicured gardens, stopping every so often as Livia pointed out a statue, a perfectly cultivated plant, or an unusual bird in the trees, and he realised he wasn't worried about a threat from an enemy right now, he was concerned about their proximity. He was aware of Alexios's every move. His hand touching Livia's arm, his ruler's disarming smile. He felt a burning sensation in his chest and stomach, and with every step they took he regretted his suggestion that she align with the emperor even more.

He hadn't wanted to come on this outing, and yet he

hadn't been able to stay away either, needing to see it unfold. It was like some kind of self-inflicted torture.

He had sensed the anger behind Livia's words when she had asked Alexios to go for this walk, and he wondered if she was trying to punish him. There was no doubt he deserved it, after pleasuring her last night and then asking the emperor to give her time to come round to the idea of their marriage this morning. But he was only acting out of concern for her safety. He really did want what was best for her. And *he* wasn't it. Plus, revealing to the emperor what had happened between them wasn't going to help either of them.

As his quarry stopped to crouch down and look at another perfect flower in bloom, Destin tried to look away, to not seem interested at all.

'A lily, if I'm not mistaken,' Alexios said.

'Correct! It is the Italian flower of Rome,' Livia smiled.

'Which represents purity and exquisite beauty, Your Highness,' Alexios said. 'As do you.'

Destin cringed. He had compared her to a wild plant, an edelweiss, when they had travelled together through the Alps, whereas the emperor was likening her to this stunning, elegant flower.

'Thank you, that is so kind,' she said, and Destin's patience waned. How could he compete? And the thought caught him by surprise. Did he want to? Was he trying to get himself killed?

He frustratedly pushed his hand through his hair, thinking how immaculate, how different this place was to the rugged castle Livia had been living in in Harzburg. She had grown in confidence this past week, and dressed in an elegant black silk tunic and stola, her long dark hair woven up in a sophisticated style, she looked stunning. Rome suited her well, he thought. Perhaps she had finally grown into it and was ready for life at court.

He was pleased she was going to petition the college tomorrow. He was proud of her. At least this way, whatever happened, she would have no regrets.

In contrast, he felt like a shadow of a man. He had lost a little of his desire for power and glory somewhere in the mountains, and he was bone-achingly weary. He had lain awake half the night, wondering what he was doing. Livia had been nestled into his naked chest, sleeping, and his arm had been wrapped tightly around her, holding her close, and he had never wanted to leave. He should never have gone to her room and comforted her. He had ended up doing a lot more.

He had known he should get up, put his tunic back on and stand guard all night from the other side of that door, and yet he hadn't been able to bring himself to move. He hadn't wanted to be parted from her. With her leg curled over his, her breath fluttering across his shoulder, he hadn't wanted to be anywhere else. And he had been pleased that for the rest of the night, she hadn't had a nightmare.

He should never have kissed her, or touched her, but when she'd told him she wanted him, curving her hand over his rigid shaft, nothing could have prevented him from doing so. He'd been like a man possessed, and he hadn't been able to stop until he'd worked her into a frenzy, until he'd pressed his fingers deep inside her and she'd cried out her intense climax. Had it been her first one?

Only when she had gone to reciprocate and touch him in return had he stopped her and said no. To take his own pleasure would have felt like a complete loss of his honour. He already felt overwhelmed with guilt.

When he'd seen the emperor's convoy approach the palace gates this morning, his heart had stalled. He couldn't believe Alexios had come here, and he'd known whatever this thing was between him and Livia had to be over. It had to be the end of it. But as he watched their interaction now, he wondered how he would be able to put his feelings aside.

'What if I never feel like this again?' she had asked him.

What if *he* never felt this way again?

And yet, now she was walking next to the emperor, sharing her thoughts with him, as if Destin wasn't following them, as if he didn't exist, as if she couldn't still taste him on her lips, like he could her. She was smiling up at Alexios, and when his ruler leaned in and said something, she threw her head back and laughed. Destin clenched his fist.

How would he be able to continue in his role if she returned with them to Constantinople? He would have to pretend to be happy for them both. But seeing them together every day, and every night, might just break him. And how could he continue to guard and protect the emperor, when his gaze was drawn to her, when she stole his focus? The emperor would no longer be his priority. His judgement would be off.

When Alexios placed his hand on her back to lead them towards the hall for the evening feast, Destin wasn't sure how much more of this he could stomach.

It put him off his food, not wanting to eat the meat in his bowl, the pork feeling dry in his mouth. He struggled to swallow it down. He was envious of Alexios sitting next to Livia as he had at the hospice the other evening, and his leader was keeping her deep in conversation. He was aware of a few of the nobles trying to engage him in talk, but he didn't want to speak to them, he was too busy trying to listen to what Livia was saying, so he sullenly gave them one-word answers until they gave up.

Alexios was being polite, asking her questions about her childhood and her interests, no doubt having had the same rigorous training on how to conduct yourself as a royal as she had, and she held her own, answering fully and eloquently. They were perfect for each other, he realised. The emperor could give her everything she needed. And who was he to stand in their way?

All of a sudden he felt a huge sense of dissatisfaction with his life. Perhaps he did want more.

He put down his spoon and pushed his bowl away, suddenly not hungry. Surely no one would notice if he disappeared for a while? He got up out of his seat, a crease carved into his forehead, and stormed out of the hall.

This was his comeuppance for allowing himself to get close to her, he thought. Usually, he was the master of restraint, but he'd let down his guard with her. He'd overstepped the mark, and now he was being punished for it. He had been sent to fetch her in return for being the emperor's chief commander. He'd wanted the recognition and the title. He'd thought it would make him happy. But it was the emperor who was going to get the real prize. Alexios was going to get Livia.

'Where have you been?' the emperor said, finding Destin in the palace courtyard after the feast.

'I needed some air. I thought I'd stand guard out here instead.'

'Princess Livia has retired to bed, but the night is young, Commander...' Alexios said, slapping him on the back. 'Let us make the most of it.' He began to lead them across the square towards the gates.

'What did you make of her?' Destin asked, unable to help himself.

Alexios shrugged. 'What's not to like? If I'm going to marry anyone, it may as well be her.' He stopped and rounded on him. 'I noticed you couldn't keep your eyes off her...'

He faltered. For a moment, Destin felt as if his emotions were being exposed—had he been found out?

'I've been protecting her for the past few days. You sent me here to do just that. I *have* to watch her,' he answered coolly. 'As I do you.'

The emperor's piercing gaze held him in place. 'Did something happen between the two of you?'

Destin raked a hand through his dishevelled hair, his brow furrowing.

And then the emperor threw his head back and

laughed. 'I'm just jesting, Commander. Of course it
didn't. This is *you* we're talking about.'

Destin bit the inside of his mouth. Hard. He was unsure what that meant, but he told himself he shouldn't
care—that he should just be relieved the emperor hadn't
seen his true feelings. That he wanted her for himself.
But if such a truth was revealed it would mean losing everything else. His honour. His position. All he'd
achieved.

'Come on, let's get out of here. I've been on my best
behaviour all day. I need to relax.'

'Where are we going?' Destin asked, following his
ruler out through the opening gates.

'Back to where I'm staying. It's just outside the city
walls. I'm meeting someone there at dusk.'

'Who?'

They turned down the street, past an alehouse where
lively revellers were spilling out onto the road.

'I can't protect you if I don't know where we're going
or who we're meeting,' Destin said. 'Do you not wish
to take the horses?'

'No. I could do with the walk.'

Destin was unsettled. He didn't want to stray too far
from the palace. Too far from Livia. Not tonight. She
had an important day ahead of her tomorrow, and this
was the furthest he'd been away from her all week. He
knew she wasn't his responsibility any more, not now
she had the King's Guard to protect her, but he still
didn't trust her safety to anyone else, and he felt the
distance between them in every step they took.

When they came to a grand private villa, surrounded

by a huge estate of land, he felt his skin prickle in apprehension. 'Where are we? What is this place?'

'My father used to stay here when he came to Rome,' Alexios said. 'He was good friends with the late Roman king when I was a boy.'

'So did you know Princess Livia when she was a child?' He wondered what she'd been like as a young girl. She seemed to have had a happy childhood, at least until her mother passed away.

Alexios shook his head. 'Not that I remember.'

As they approached, a big burly man opened the door and ushered them both inside. They stepped into the vestibulum and Destin went rigid in shock when he saw Prince Lothair standing at the far end of the room, surrounded by his men. Destin's hand immediately reached for his sword.

'Don't,' Alexios said. 'I arranged this meeting.'

'What? Why?' Destin said, incredulous.

'You're late,' Lothair bit out.

And Alexios nodded and went to step forward to greet the man. 'I know, we got held up. Thank you for coming. For waiting.'

Destin didn't like this. He put his body in front of his ruler, blocking Alexios's path. He wanted to get back to the palace, to warn Livia her uncle was here in Rome and make sure she was safe. 'Why?' he asked again, his need for answers, to understand, greater than his care for obedience.

'Because I need to make sure this all works out for me, one way or another,' Alexios said through gritted teeth.

'Is there a problem?' Lothair asked, his men all poised to protect him if there was.

'No, not at all,' Alexios said, trying to sidestep Destin and move forward, to shake Lothair's hand.

But Destin wouldn't allow it. If Livia could see this… He got in his ruler's way again. 'Explain it to me,' he hissed.

Alexios sighed. 'Would you give us just a moment?' he said to Lothair, and beckoned Destin to the side of the room. 'Look, if Princess Livia becomes queen, then fine, when we marry, I will get to rule over two empires,' he said, under his breath. 'But if she doesn't become queen, it would be foolish of me not to align myself with the new king, for us to be allies. And I will need to make sure the terms of the marriage that I agreed to with the princess's father still stand. That Lothair will still give me all that I'm due.'

Destin reeled. 'And what was that, other than a dowry?'

'Land. Gold.' Alexios shrugged.

He felt a flash of anger. 'You don't need any more land or gold.'

'I may not *need* it, but I do *want* southern Italy,' he smirked. 'I'm going to propose to Lothair I take Livia off his hands in return for the lands the late king conquered there. Her father's no longer around to bargain with and I need to make this worth my while.'

Destin looked at the emperor, shocked. For the first time, he couldn't understand where he was coming from. They had always been aligned in the past on their thoughts and reasons for doing things. But not on this occasion. He couldn't understand why Alexios would need anything other than Livia. Surely, she was enough? Did he not realise how lucky he was? Disappointment in his leader washed over him.

'I don't feel right about this,' Destin said, his hand curling into a fist.

'You don't need to. It's between me and the prince. You forget yourself, Commander. You're just here for your sword,' Alexios said, slapping him on the upper arm as if to say the conversation was over, and leaving him at the side of the room as he went to welcome his guests. He led them into the atrium.

Reluctantly, Destin followed.

The emperor gestured for Prince Lothair to sit down, while Alexios stood, with Destin behind him, watching on.

Lothair was a heavy-set man with greying hair and dark eyes. Destin had known it was him in an instant— he had met him just a few weeks before, at the King's bedside—but he also recognised the emblem of the phoenix on his tunic. The same as the men had who had attacked the castle in Harzburg. He looked a lot like his brother, the late king, only there was something about his face, the slant of his eyes, that wasn't as trustworthy.

He pursed his lips. It took all of Destin's restraint not to grab the man by the neck and demand answers as to what had happened to his soldiers and the people in Saxony. He knew it couldn't be good, especially as they had heard no word from them since. He wanted the brute to drop his claim to the throne and leave Livia be.

Instead, he had to stand there, watching on, as the men set to discussing her, making plans for her future, negotiating land and gold, as if those things were the real prize, not her. He felt sick to the core that they should talk about her as if her feelings didn't matter. That the emperor would align with her enemy. It was traitorous.

If he wanted to destroy any feelings Livia might have for her future husband, Destin thought he could go back to the palace and tell her what was going on. Vent to her and reveal Alexios's unworthiness. But he had to remind himself who he served and why he was here…

After they were done, agreeing to their terms for Alexios to still marry Lothair's niece when he became king, in return for her relinquishing her father's lands and properties here, but giving Alexios southern Italy, he watched them shake on it, pleased with themselves. And Destin felt dirty. How would Livia feel if she knew they were discussing her losing her father's home and Lothair claiming it for himself?

He hadn't wanted to be privy to the discussion because he didn't want to have to lie to her.

When they rose to their feet, Alexios came over to Destin. 'There's a room made up for you, Commander. You've earned it. Stick around, the night is just about to get interesting…' Alexios grinned at him. 'As a sweetener for our deal, the prince has kindly organised for us all to have some *entertainment* for the rest of the evening.'

And as if planned to arrive at exactly that moment, Destin heard a group of women drift through the vestibulum, laughing, and got a waft of their cheap scent as they approached the men.

Destin felt the bile rise in his throat. 'What about your bride? The woman you've spent the afternoon with. Are you even interested in this marriage?'

'I'm interested in what it can bring me.' Alexios shrugged. 'But just because I'm getting married, it doesn't mean the finer things in life have to stop, does it? I doubt the princess will be able to keep me content for a night, let alone a lifetime. And I'm the emperor, I can have as many women as I want.' Alexios shook his head. 'You really need to live a little, Commander. When we get back to Constantinople, I'm going to make sure of it. You take everything much too seriously. But tonight, I'm not in the mood to argue. And I don't need a guard dog, so if you don't want to partake in the entertainment, don't wait up for me.'

Chapter Eight

Destin had been pacing up and down the courtyard for the past hour and it was driving Livia mad. What was the matter with him?

The hour was late and she could hear the sounds of distant revellers across the city, but her father's home was quiet and peaceful. That was, apart from the sound of crunching footsteps marching up and down, and a man cursing beneath his breath.

Earlier, she had been so furious with him for suggesting that she align with the emperor that she had wanted to make him suffer. She had gone out of her way to make him burn with jealously, but she had only made herself miserable in the process. Every time Alexios put his hand on her arm or leaned in close, she felt reviled. She didn't want to spend time with him, or get to know him; it left her feeling hollow. She didn't want to encourage him. Not when the man she truly cared about was in the same room.

She'd been pleasantly surprised that she and Alexios had a lot in common. She thought they could become friends, but his touch had left her cold. And she'd found herself excruciatingly aware of Destin's presence, as he'd followed them around the gardens. During the feast, her gaze kept wandering across the hall to the Northman who was sitting at the far end of the table, brooding, shutting everyone out.

She'd felt bereft. She'd wanted to go to him, to talk to him and be near him, and yet she'd known she couldn't. It would not look good to the emperor, or her people. And she wondered if this was what it would be like, if she married Alexios, always wanting something else, someone else she couldn't have. It would be unbearable.

When Destin had left the hall, it was as if the light of a candle had gone out, descending the room into darkness. And she'd got a glimpse of what her life would be like with him not in it.

She was relieved when she'd finally excused herself from the emperor's company, telling him she needed to go and work on her speech for the Electoral College tomorrow, and he rose out of his chair and bade her goodnight. From the window in her apartment, she'd seen Alexios and Destin leave the palace, wondering where they were going, wishing Destin back, not wanting him to stray too far, and she'd been restless ever since. She'd done a lot of aimless wandering around her room, wrapping her arms around her waist.

But a short while ago, he had returned, alone. And now he seemed to be the one ill at ease, striding out across the courtyard before doing an about-turn and marching back again, biting out angry words beneath his breath.

She couldn't bear it any longer. Making a decision, she grabbed her gold silk robe, wrapped it tightly around her and left her room. The guard on duty stood to attention. 'Your Highness.' He nodded.

'I won't be long. Stay here,' she said, padding along the corridor in her bare feet.

She crept down the stairs and walked through the dark and quiet hall. Everyone seemed to have retired to bed. She made her way out to the cloisters, keeping within the shadows, in case anyone should be about.

'What are you doing?' she whispered, approaching Destin.

He looked up to the arched walkway, shocked to see her there.

'Can't sleep,' he said gruffly.

'Neither can I with you stomping up and down like this!' He certainly seemed like a man with a lot on his mind. 'Shouldn't you be guarding the emperor or something…?'

'He's not here,' he said, his brow darkening.

Was that what was bothering him?

He ran his hand around his neck. She noticed he always did that when he was agitated, or nervous. She was beginning to learn all his little habits.

'Did you know the emperor has a villa just outside the city?'

She nodded. 'Yes, I did know that. His father used to spend time there, when I was younger. Are you not staying there with him?'

'No,' he said, frowning. 'Not tonight anyway. My

things are here... I could see your candle on. I was waiting for you to go to sleep.'

'Oh.'

'I thought you'd be exhausted after your busy day.' She detected a hard edge to his voice.

'It was pretty tiring,' she admitted, the cool evening breeze, or his cold tone, making her shiver, and she rubbed her hands up and down her arms.

He took a step towards her, his movements stiff. 'You *looked* to be enjoying yourself.'

Her gaze narrowed on him, unsure of his mood. He seemed tired; there was a tightness around his eyes she hadn't noticed before.

'Did I? I would have thought you might be able to tell between my real enjoyment and when I'm faking it by now,' she said, tipping her chin up defiantly.

His gaze raked over her. 'I'm sure it helps that he's attractive,' he said, ignoring her pointed comment.

'You think so?'

'Don't you?'

'What does it matter to you? I'm sure you'd tell me I should still marry him whether I thought he was attractive or not. You wouldn't want to miss out on that reward. All those titles and riches.'

He pushed his hand through his hair. 'It's not about that.'

'No?'

'No. Whatever you might think, he proffered those rewards before I met you, Livia. And who wouldn't accept such an offer? But believe it or not, I don't care about that any more. My advice is based on what's best for you.'

'And that's the emperor, is it?'

He swallowed, glancing away. 'I thought it was.'

'What does that mean?'

'Nothing.'

'I don't see why you want me to marry him,' she said, shaking her head. 'Especially after the way you touched me last night.'

He groaned at the mere mention of it, drawing his hand over his beard, a pained expression crossing his face, as if he was both horrified by what he'd done and also tortured by the reminder. He glanced around, as if to check if anyone was about.

'If you're unsuccessful tomorrow, you may not want—or be allowed—to stay here. It might not be safe to do so, as your uncle will see you as a constant threat. This marriage could protect you. I am thinking of your safety.'

Was he really still trying to look after her? Was he still putting her own needs before his? She let out a long, slow breath. She'd spent most of the day feeling livid with him and she didn't want to be angry any more.

'And I'm thinking about my future.' She wanted him in it.

'It's the same thing,' he said.

'No, it's not. Not really.'

'Are you saying you didn't like him?' he said, boring down on her.

'I'm saying he's not you,' she said honestly. Bravely. She closed the space between them, placing her hand on his chest. She hoped her touch would reach him, even if her words didn't. She really wanted him to listen, to hear her. 'He doesn't make me feel the way you do.'

Destin stilled.

He stared at her for a long moment, and he was so close she could breathe him in. She thought she felt the tension of the day ebb a little from his body too, and he leaned in closer. He shook his head and closed his eyes briefly. 'This is madness…'

'I can't help it… I've been waiting for you to get back. What were you doing, back at his villa?'

He shrugged. 'Not much.'

Her eyes widened. 'You're a terrible liar.'

He gave her a look and she held up her hands. 'All right, don't tell me. I'm probably better off not knowing…' She took his hand in hers, entwining her fingers with his. 'I don't want to talk about him anyway. I missed you today. Did you miss me?'

'Livia…'

Yet she was determined now. She needed to convince him that the emperor wasn't what she needed. But he was. She started to walk down the outdoor corridor, tugging him behind her. 'Can I show you something?' she said.

His brow creased.

At the end of the cloisters she opened a door which led into a grand corridor, with rows and rows of paintings on the walls. She knew he hadn't been in here before, because straight away he looked around the room, scanning it for any danger. They walked past huge portraits of kings and queens, princes and princesses from the past, all seeming to be peering down at them, before she stopped in front of a more recent one of a very elegant young woman.

'This was my mother,' she said, looking up at the picture in awe. 'She was very beautiful, don't you think?'

He studied it carefully, tilting his handsome head to one side. 'Yes. Very beautiful,' he said, and then he turned to look at her. 'I can see the likeness.'

Livia smiled. 'She was a wonderful queen. The people loved her. She was kind yet strong. Fair. Whatever happens tomorrow, I hope that I am like her. I don't want to let my parents down.'

'You couldn't, Livia. Whatever the outcome, they would have been proud of you.'

She nodded, grateful for his kind words. 'My father was lucky to have her at his side. And I know I've been lucky to have you by my side this week. And I need you here, on the morrow too.'

He nodded. 'I'll be here.'

She had lost her mother at such a young age, they'd never discussed marriage or love. She wondered what her mother's thoughts were on it. She wondered what her mother would have thought of Destin.

'Do you know what you're going to say? Are you prepared?' he asked.

'I think so. But I was hoping…well, do you think I could read it to you?'

'Of course,' he whispered.

'Will you meet me in my room in a moment?'

'Livia…'

She knew he was going to protest. Was he still trying to keep her at arm's length, thinking it was what was best for her?

'It's important to me. Please?'

'All right,' he said unsteadily.

Destin's heart was pounding as he approached Livia's corridor, but he was surprised to see she had managed to discharge the soldier standing guard. He would be sure to find out which soldier it was and have a word. These men should know they must watch her at all times, in spite of her commands, to protect her against men like himself...

He took a deep breath. If Alexios and his men caught him here, it would mean certain death. Still, he knew he was the last thing on the emperor's mind tonight. And so was she. The thought gave him the impetus he needed to raise his hand to the door and knock, gently.

It opened instantly, and Livia ushered him in, still in her gold silk robe, her feet bare. She looked so beautiful, her long dark hair trailing down her back, the silk wrapped tightly around her curves.

'How did you get rid of the guard?' he asked, stepping over the threshold, and she shut the door behind him.

'I said I thought I'd heard something downstairs and asked if he could go and check it out.'

He nodded. 'You know he'll be back.'

'It looks like you're stuck here then. Either that or you'll have to go out the window,' she jested, and he rolled his eyes.

'So what can I help with?' he asked, running his

hand round the back of his neck again, suddenly feeling awkward. The fact he'd come to her room for a second time seemed to have even more significance. 'Do you want to go over your speech?'

'Would you mind?' she asked. 'I would value your opinion on it. I'm more than a little nervous.'

'Go ahead. I'd love to hear it.'

'So I'm going to walk in, like this, perfectly poised,' she said, practising her slow, steady walk down the aisle in front of the College, emphasising it, bending her knees for effect. 'I'm going to hold my head up high, stand tall and say, "I want to be your queen because…"'

He gripped her fingers, prising them off her skirts. 'Don't fidget,' he instructed. 'Stand tall. Chin up. And speak clearly. And slowly.' She caught his fingers with hers, not letting him go. He sighed. 'Just be yourself, Livia. How could they *not* want you?'

The air was thrumming with something heavy between them.

She moved closer towards him and came up on tiptoes, pressing her lips to his and this time, he didn't argue it. He had known this was inevitable when he came up here. That if she still wanted him, he didn't have the strength to resist her. Not after the suffering of today.

And he was angry with Alexios for this evening, scheming behind her back with her uncle. Livia deserved so much better. He knew he should tell her about it—that he'd been privy to their conversation. And yet, what good would come of it? It would unsettle her, disturb her, and she needed to have a clear head, to focus on the morrow.

He wondered if this would be the last night they could be alone together. If by some miracle she was voted queen, everything would change in an instant. And if she wasn't, she would have to accept Alexios's hand and leave for Constantinople immediately, as her uncle would have all the power. Knowing that, he wanted to kiss her one last time.

He covered her lips with his, pulling her up against him, crushing her breasts against his chest, his hand firmly around her waist as he took control. His lips moved against hers, slowly, his tongue tenderly gliding inside her mouth, making it last, making them both shiver.

When she tried to pull away to look up at him, to speak, he held her fast, as if he never wanted to let her go, and she smiled.

'Do *you* want me, Destin?' she asked.

His heart pounded, his body trembled.

Her golden-brown eyes were focused on him as she stepped back, still holding on to his fingers, and she sat down on the edge of the bed. With her other hand, she parted her robe, running her fingers along the opening, revealing the curve of her creamy swells.

He felt his eyes widen, his heart stutter.

'Because I want you,' she said, gently pulling him towards her.

'I shouldn't be doing this,' he whispered, his voice strained.

'You're the only person I want doing this,' she countered, tugging him harder, and he followed her down, his mouth coming back over hers, drawing her body up the bed as he came over her, and she clung on to his shoulders, holding on to him as he pressed her into the furs.

He was rock-hard, and he knew she could feel the ridge of him, nudging into her belly. He should probably lift himself away, but he wanted her to know how she made him feel. He didn't want to deny it any longer. He couldn't hold it back any more. She wriggled against him, wrapping her legs around the back of his, holding him in place, as if she wanted to cause more of a reaction, and he groaned.

His lips left hers to roam down, under her jaw, along the column of her throat and further, between her gaping robe, nipping and kissing as he went. His hand closed over the knot of the tie around her waist, and for just a moment he paused, staring down at her, before he slowly unfastened it, smoothing the silk fully apart on either side of her body. His eyes devoured her. So much for everything he'd said last night about not looking at her…he couldn't not. He'd lost all restraint. He lifted his head to take in the view of her beautiful pert breasts with their taut, rosy tips, her smooth, flat stomach and the tight curls of hair at the apex of her flawless thighs. She was so beautiful it made him ache, and she writhed, restless, gripping his head, pulling his lips down to her breast. He cupped her swollen flesh in his hand and his hot mouth covered one dark peak and she whimpered.

Her fingers trembled as she reached for the bottom of his tunic, drawing it up between them. He sat up on his knees, unhooking his sling, and then tried to lift off his top and she sat up to help him, before discarding it on the floor.

Her smile slipped as she stared at him, and his breath stalled. He wondered what she was thinking.

'You're the most incredible man I've ever seen,' she said, running her hands over his chest.

He pushed her robe off her shoulders, allowing it to slip down her arms, pooling around her wrists, and when she wrapped her arms around his neck, kissing him again, she left it behind on the bed, leaving her completely naked in his arms. His hand smoothed down her back as he came over her, laying her down again, and he began to leave another trail of kisses all across her chest.

She gasped when his tongue trailed even lower, down over her stomach, covering her hips in kisses, and then he dropped to his knees on the floor, pulling her to the edge of the bed, settling himself between her thighs. He knew he couldn't be inside her, making her his, but he could taste her. No one would ever know. He could give her something she would never forget.

'I want to kiss you everywhere,' he said. 'Is that all right?'

She whimpered, now knowing what he intended to do, and she looked him in the eyes, her cheeks feverish, and nodded, before lying back, bravely offering herself up to him, throwing her arms above her head in surrender. Her heated gaze locked with his just before his mouth covered her delicate curls and her glistening flesh, and he had a flash of a thought that if he was hanged for this, it would be worth it. That he would die a happy man.

The tip of his inquisitive tongue glided along her crease, before circling her tiny nub, intimately. And she thrashed beneath him, as if she could scarcely believe what was happening, and neither could he. He just knew he wanted to be this intimate with her. When he pushed her legs further apart, she responded, lifting her bottom up off the bed, as if she wanted more, meeting his mouth, lips to lips, and his tongue became more insistent, more demanding of her pleasure. As he slid a finger inside her, deeply, it was her undoing, and she came apart, crying out in wonder, shattering against his tongue, her thighs shuddering around him, and he dragged himself up to lie back next to her and hold her close.

When her breathing returned to normal, Livia turned into him, pressing a kiss to his lips. She could smell her own subtle scent on him and her face heated at what had just happened. She had never known about such things, or that it could feel so good. But the time for feeling embarrassed was long past. Especially after she'd told him she wanted him.

There was no way he could deny there was something between them now... Not after what he'd just done.

Knowing he had pleasured her twice now, Livia knew she needed to touch him in return, and she was desperate to finally see him lose control and take his own pleasure. Still, she was nervous as her trembling hand roamed down to curve over the hard, straining ridge of him.

'Livia…'

'Destin, so help me God, if you don't let me touch you after what you just did to me, I'm going to scream,' she said.

And he looked shocked at the force of her words. Or shocked that she wanted to touch him so badly. She wasn't sure. But either way, he eased his grip on her hand. And the moment her fingers dipped beneath the waistband of his breeches and she took hold of him, she knew he was lost. That there was no turning back. He hauled her to him so tight she could barely breathe, but she liked knowing she was having such a profound effect on him, as he had had on her. Hell, she was still recovering.

His stomach was taut, his muscles bunched, and as she ran her hand up and down him, he shuddered in disbelief.

Struggling with the restrictive material, she pulled herself away momentarily as she worked them down, pushing them to his knees, and then her hands came back to cradle him again, and he groaned. She couldn't help but look at him and he was incredible. His body was so powerful, even the part she was holding in her grasp. His skin was silky, hot and hard, and she marvelled at it.

'Am I doing this right?' she whispered, learning the feel of him.

'Yes,' he said, his voice strained, his forehead against hers. 'Very right.'

He moved his hand around her back, to curve over her bottom, pressing her closer, and as she stroked him harder, he kissed her fully and possessively on the mouth, scraping his tongue over hers.

'Livia,' he warned, against her lips, but it encouraged her on, wanting him to lose all restraint, and she moved her hand faster. He groaned, and his body tensed as his climax took over and she felt the rush of warmth against her hand.

She released him from her grip and held him close, elated after this first experience, feeling close to him, and hoping she had given him as much pleasure as he had given her.

Pressed against him, she could feel his heart beating erratically. He lay still for a long while, his arm still curved around her, his eyes closed, and eventually his breathing settled.

'Are you sleeping?' she asked him, her gaze studying every inch of his face. She knew each silvery scar intimately now, and loved his long dark lashes, which were resting on his cheeks. Her hand held his bearded jaw, which he'd trimmed since they'd got to Rome, but he hadn't removed it entirely. He was perfect, she thought.

'No.'

'Are you all right?'

His beautiful ebony eyes opened a little, focusing on her. 'Just about. You?'

'Yes,' she smiled. She couldn't believe she was lying here like this, with no clothes on, with him. The formidable man who had stormed into her castle in Saxony. She had thought he was such a brute, but in just a week, he had become her whole world. The person she wanted to seek advice from and share her thoughts with. She liked the feel of his hand curved around her body, his fingers stroking her skin. This was all so new to her and she wondered if he had ever been close to anyone before. She wanted to know everything about him and curiosity got the better of her.

'Have you done this a lot?' she whispered.

'Not compared to some.'

She propped herself up on her elbow, staring down at him. 'You mean the emperor?'

His brow furrowed.

'I don't mind. I'm not angry, or hurt. I don't even care…it's you I want to know about. How many women have you been with, like this?' she asked.

He rolled his eyes, as if he found her question distasteful. 'You and your incessant probing,' he said, disapprovingly, pulling away from her a little to roll onto his back and tugging the blanket up and over them.

'It's called being interested.' She pouted, and he sighed, deeply.

'In truth? Not many.'

'Really?' She ran her hand over his chest, her fingers tracing the blue lines of dye. 'Why not?'

'Because I didn't feel comfortable, you know, what with looking, being, how I am.'

She shook her head, still amazed he didn't see himself like she did—the strongest, most attractive man she'd ever met. Her fingers stalled. 'And you do, with me?'

'Yes,' he said, rolling back towards her and trailing his knuckles down her cheek.

She held his jaw again, pulling him in for a kiss.

When they broke away, she wriggled her eyebrows.
'So…how many is not many? Five?' she prompted,
smiling. 'Ten?'

'Livia!' he groaned.

'What? You know about my lack of experience…'

'Which seems to be gaining by the night,' he said
with a grimace. He flung the blanket off himself and
stood, naked, reaching for his breeches, beginning to
pull them up. She gawked at him. He looked magnificent naked.

'Is it so wrong I should want to know what experi-
ences you have had? Why can't you just tell me?'

He flew his arm up, exasperated. 'Because there's
nothing to tell. There has been none, all right?'

She looked up at him, shocked, her mouth hanging
open. *'None?'*

He shook his head. 'No.' He fastened the tie at his
waist and came back to sit beside her on the bed. 'There
have been women. Things happened. But never *that*.
There's never been any real intimacy. How could there
be? They didn't know me. My history. I couldn't bear
to see the looks on their faces when they knew I hadn't
just been wounded, but that there was something wrong
with me.'

Her heart went out to him. 'You feared their rejection.' Even though she couldn't imagine any woman
turning him down. Ever.

'Not like I fear yours.'

She shook her head. 'You're the one who keeps trying to resist me, turning *me* down, not the other way round,' she smiled wryly.

'And how am I doing with that?' he said, raising his eyebrows.

She grinned.

She couldn't believe he hadn't been with a woman. She would never have guessed it, not after the pleasure he'd given her just moments ago, his tongue doing those incredible things. The way he'd touched her so masterfully…

It all made her like him so much more. 'So…do you want to…do that…with me?'

He groaned, tucking her hair behind her ears. 'Livia, you know I do. I want to be inside you, making love to you, more than anything. But we can't.'

'Why not?'

'You know why not!' he said.

'Please say this isn't still because of the emperor,' she said, her eyes darkening. 'I doubt he is thinking about me at this very moment.'

'You *are* supposed to be marrying him,' he countered. 'Not that I can stomach the thought of it any more,' he said, placing his head in his hand. And then he looked back up at her. 'But what does it say about me, and the oaths I have made, if we do this? It wouldn't be right.'

'Yet the things you just did to me, the way you touched me and kissed me, was?' It certainly felt right.

He ran his hand across his brow. 'No, it wasn't,' he said, his voice quiet. 'I'm sorry.'

'I don't want you to be sorry,' she said, her anger flaring. 'I want you to do it again. I want more…'

'You know I can't take your virtue, Livia. Think about the consequences…' His hand came over hers, gripping her fingers in his. 'Someone has to be sensible here! You know how important your purity is. Can you imagine the outrage it would cause if word got out that the Roman princess had bedded a pagan? It would destroy your reputation. I'd be killed.'

She knew he was right, but she didn't want to hear it. She still wanted to do this with him.

'And even if we tried to keep it secret, you know I can't have—that I don't *want*—children, Livia. And neither do you. Not after what happened to your mother…'

He was right again. She knew actions had consequences…

'So stop it.' He leaned in and rested his forehead against hers. 'Give a man some peace and stop torturing me. You've got an important day tomorrow, so let's just lie here and let me hold you for one last night. Let's both try to get some sleep, all right?'

Sleep. It didn't sound that appealing, not when she had him lying next to her, in her arms. Her eyes narrowed on him. 'Are you going to stay this time?' She really didn't want him to leave.

'I will stay with you as long as I am able, Livia.'

Chapter Nine

Destin hadn't seen Livia or the emperor all morning. When he'd woken in her bed, she hadn't been there, and he was growing increasingly alarmed. When had she left him? Where had she gone? And how had he managed to let down his guard and fall into such a deep sleep? He'd let her slip from his grasp, out of his sight, and he hated not knowing where she was or if she was safe.

He'd thrown off the blankets and pulled on his tunic and belt quickly, fastening his sword in place. He'd opened the door slightly to check if the guard was standing there, but he wasn't. Good. He hoped he'd followed Livia wherever she'd gone. That was something, at least. If the man was protecting her, he might go easy on him for his lack of vigilance the previous night.

His thoughts drifted back to what had happened between them during the night. The way she'd touched him, so tenderly, but adamantly, demanding he let her, wanting to give him pleasure. He'd never known a woman like her. And then to ask him for more, to want to go further…he didn't know how he'd had the strength to say no. But he'd already taken things much too far. He wasn't sure how he was going to look Alexios in the eye today.

Courage. Conduct. Fealty.

He'd smashed the last two to smithereens the moment his mouth had covered her moist heat. Probably even before that. He had been set one simple task. He'd been honour bound to fetch her from Saxony and bring her back to Constantinople to be wed. Instead, he had spread her legs and kissed her, tasted her, violating his own moral code.

If anyone were to learn of it, she would certainly never be made queen today. And her marriage to the emperor would be off. Destin would lose his position in the Varangian Guard—everything he'd worked for—and maybe even his head. So why couldn't he bring himself to regret it?

He searched for her everywhere. In the hall, the cloisters and the gallery she'd shown him last night. He glanced up at the portraits of her mother and father. There was a smaller one of them together, with a boy, presumably Otto, by their side, and a baby in the queen's arms. Livia. The couple looked to be in love and Destin felt a pang, an ache in his chest. Did he want what they had? Love and a family? It was the first time he'd ever thought this way, and it was disturbing. Because it could never happen. Not with her. He had fallen for a woman who could never be his. And he needed to stop wishing for something that could never be.

He turned away, frustrated, wondering where else

she could have gone. He checked the stables and the gardens, but she was nowhere to be found. He was starting to feel slightly panicked.

When he went to speak to the guards on the gate, they informed him she'd left early this morning by cart, taking Matthias, her chief councillor, with her, but hadn't told them where she was going. He ran his hand round the back of his neck. Why hadn't she woken him and asked him to go with her? He didn't like it. But again, he had to remind himself the emperor was his responsibility, not her. Did she feel like she couldn't ask him for his protection?

He tried to quell his worries as he headed back to his room in the palace barracks. He pushed open his door, agitated, and threw his sword onto the bed. He stood there, his hand on his hip, breathing deeply.

'Where have you been?'

Destin spun round, startled by the emperor sitting in the corner of the dark room.

He tried to calm the wave of guilt tumbling through him. But he wasn't sure Alexios was in any state to notice his misconduct. He looked to be suffering from his own. His skin was sallow, as if he'd barely had any sleep, his hair dishevelled, and his breath reeked of ale. He could smell it from the other side of the room.

'Did you have a good night?' Destin asked.

'What I remember of it,' Alexios said, shifting guiltily. 'Was I missed here?'

'I don't think so.' Destin stared down at him, unsure of his mood.

'I thought we had a deal, Commander.' His voice was

deadly. 'You were oath-bound to fetch Princess Livia
unharmed—and untouched—to receive your reward.
I offered you the role of *chief* commander, to be my
right-hand man…' He pushed himself out of the chair.
'So I'm going to ask you again, where have you been?'

'Around.'

'You know you can't lie to me. We've been friends
for a while. I know you better than most. Tell me. How
is the princess? Did you ease her worries about today?'

Destin swallowed. What did he know?

Alexios stepped towards him. 'You couldn't keep
your eyes off her when we took a tour of the gardens
yesterday—or at the feast last night. You couldn't bear
to be parted from her while we were at our meeting.
You wanted to get back to her, rather than stay with me.'

Destin ran his hand over his beard, sweating now.

'I didn't like it,' the emperor said. 'I've never seen
you like this before. You like her.'

If he was going to lose his head, so be it. But he didn't
want to put Livia's position in jeopardy. 'What's not
to like?' he said, repeating the emperor's words from
yesterday.

Alexios braced his hands on his hips. 'Did you bed
her?'

'No.'

'She came to see me this morning. At the villa.'

Destin went very still. So that's where she'd gone.
She'd left the palace without telling him—and gone to
visit Alexios? Why?

'She started spouting some nonsense about her people not wanting a foreign ruler and that she didn't need one either.'

Destin's heart momentarily stopped.

'She said that her empire doesn't want to be taken over by Byzantium. She must really think she stands a chance today...' Alexios continued, his voice barely containing his anger.

'I reminded her that her father made an arrangement. That we have been promised to each other for four winters, if not before. Our fathers probably arranged our marriage at birth! And do you know what she said?' Alexios took another step towards him. 'She said, "Now my father has passed on, his words are no longer valid."'

Destin's eyes widened. He hadn't been expecting that. And going by the look on the emperor's face, neither had he.

Destin couldn't believe it. Livia had listened to his advice about marrying the emperor to keep her safe—but ignored it and done her own thing anyway. She was her own woman.

Had she done this for him? Because of what had happened between them last night. Surely she must know they still couldn't be together—that her councillors, her people, wouldn't allow it?

'Can you believe she doesn't intend to honour his agreement?' the emperor asked. 'After I've waited so long for her? After I've come here for her?'

'You haven't exactly been waiting...' Destin countered. 'You only decided you'd better wed her when you heard of her father being ill. Only then did this marriage become important to you. You even slept with another woman, or many others, last night.'

The emperor's eyes narrowed on him. Destin knew he wasn't used to being judged and he'd overstepped the mark. He would surely be punished for standing up to him.

Instead, the emperor grimaced. 'I think that's what I like about you, Commander. You always say it like it is. You're not worried about hurting my feelings. I get total honesty from you. And I thought loyalty, until now...'

A muscle worked in Destin's cheek.

'I am loyal to you. I have given you ten winters of my life.'

'Loyal...until you decided to claim my bride for yourself.'

'I haven't claimed her. I swear it.'

'So you're happy if I do?' the emperor asked.

Destin's stomach churned at the thought, and he reeled.

'No, I didn't think so,' Alexios said, seeing his reaction.

'I have told her over and again I think she should marry you.'

'So you're not the reason she came to see me this morning?' Alexios asked, his eyes narrowing on him.

Destin couldn't be sure. 'I don't know what she was thinking, she didn't say anything to me. She knows her own mind.'

Alexios nodded. And then he turned and began to pace. 'It was most humiliating. Especially in front of her chief councillor. I don't think I've ever been turned down before. I was angry. I told her that wouldn't do. That if she wouldn't marry me, she probably wouldn't be queen either.' He stopped pacing and looked up at Destin. 'And now, it seems, she won't be…'

'What do you mean?' Destin asked, his brow furrowing.

'Well, Lothair was still there…'

Destin went cold all over and he stepped towards his leader, suddenly uncaring of being insubordinate. Right now, he only cared about her safety. 'What happened? What did you do?'

'It all seemed like a good idea at the time. But now the wine has worn off…'

Destin didn't like the sound of this. The cold grip of fear clutched his heart. He gripped the emperor roughly by the tunic. 'Where is she? Where is Livia?'

'On first names now, are we?'

Destin pulled him closer. 'What have you done?' Anger clawed through him.

'They saw their chance and took her. Said they would hold on to her long enough so she couldn't get to the Electoral College and petition today. That way, Lothair would be certain to be crowned king, and I could have southern Italy, and all would be well.'

Destin cursed, roughly letting him go. He reached for his sword.

'Did they say what they were planning? What they were going to do with her? Where they were taking her?'

'They're still at the villa.'

Destin swung to look at him, his eyes wide. 'Do

you realise you could be implicated? That this could cause a war?'

The emperor slumped back down into his seat. 'I know. I thought they were just going to keep her hostage long enough for Lothair to appear at the College and be crowned. But then things started to take a turn for the worse...they got...brutal...and I began to feel uneasy. I started to realise I'd done the wrong thing.'

'You think?' Destin spat. He felt his blood drain from his face and he tightened his leather vest, readying himself to fight.

'I came here looking for you. I was hoping you'd know what to do. And when you weren't here...when I saw your bed hadn't been slept in... I put two and two together. Look, I'm not proud of myself,' he said, getting up again, starting to pace across the room. 'You know I didn't care much for the marriage anyway. I don't think any of us expect her to be made queen, so I've never thought I would rule over these lands. But I do care about southern Italy... Too long her father has campaigned in those regions, and I want them under my rule. I figured if Lothair became king and I got those, all would be good. But I don't want anyone getting hurt. And I can tell you don't either. So what do we do now?'

'We?' Destin asked.

'You're still *my* commander, aren't you? You say you still pledge your fealty to me?'

'Yes.' Although now he felt unsure. He wasn't sure Alexios deserved his loyalty.

'Then if you help me to rectify this, effectively, I will forgive you for your disobedience. I can see why your head would be turned. She is very beautiful. But you must know nothing can happen between the two of you. You can't marry her.'

Destin swallowed. 'I know.'

'When I leave, you will return with me to Constantinople and we'll both forget any of this ever happened. Are we in agreement about that?'

Destin gave a single nod. They'd already spent too long talking. He wanted to get going. 'Take me to her. Now.'

The streets of Rome were overloaded, buzzing with people getting ready for the election. It was the first time it would take place here, instead of Frankfurt, and there was excitement in the air about the great electors having arrived in the city. But all Destin felt was a looming sense of dread. He just wanted to get to the villa, to get to Livia, to know she was all right.

He felt so worked up, he was pushing brusquely through the people, trying to make way for him and Alexios. They'd brought a small contingent of men with them, although he knew Alexios didn't want him to use force. But he wasn't sure how he was going to retrieve Livia without things turning out badly. And right now, he didn't care about the consequences. She was his priority.

When they reached the city gates, they broke out into a run, and raced through the grounds of the villa. The same burly man who'd been on the door last night let them in, and they commanded their men to wait outside, to be on alert.

'Where's Lothair?' Alexios asked.

'Last I saw him, he was in the triclinium.'

Destin needed no further instruction. He barged his way through the building, gripping the hilt of his drawn weapon. If action had to be taken, he would do whatever he needed to do to keep her safe.

They headed through to an impressive room at the back of the property, and as they drew near, they could hear the men talking. But Destin was only focused on Livia. When they burst through the door, he saw she was sitting in a chair, her hands bound, tears streaking her face. His hand clenched and unclenched. He felt his nostrils flare.

Matthias was sitting on a chair next to her, also bound, a bloody gash to his face.

Her eyes widened in shock and relief when she saw them, her gaze focused on Destin. And she struggled with newfound fervour with the ties around her wrist.

'Let them go,' Destin said, moving slowly and deliberately towards her, limbering up his good shoulder, ready to fight anyone who got between him and Livia.

Yet looking at the state of her hair, her swollen, split lip and an angry red mark across her cheek it seemed Lothair had already put his hands on her. He knew Livia would have struggled and put up a fight. That was her. She was stronger than she looked. Had Matthias tried to protect her and they'd maimed him too? A fierce rage blazed in his stomach that any man would hurt her.

There was an unnatural silence as Lothair took in the scene, realising the emperor was no longer on his side, before he and his men drew their weapons, halting his advance.

'No. Not until the election has taken place. Then she's all yours,' he said to Alexios. 'You can force her to go to Constantinople with you. Everyone's happy.'

'Let her go, or I'll kill you,' Destin said.

'Emperor Alexios, what is the meaning of this?' Lothair sneered. 'I thought we were allies… Why don't you ask your one-armed heathen dog here to put his muzzle back on.'

'Prince Lothair, don't you want to know you won fairly today?' Alexios said, still trying to be amiable. 'I was thinking we should let the princess go.'

'No. Not yet. I'm disappointed you have come here trying to break off our agreement. It doesn't bode well for our alliance going forward now does it?'

'I just don't think I can let you do this,' Alexios continued. 'It's not right. I will support your claim to be king, I want us to be allies, but I don't want to put the princess's life at risk. Think about it. She's your niece! This is your brother's chief councillor. You don't want their blood on your hands.'

But to Destin's horror, Lothair moved his sword and placed it against her neck. 'She remains here till the election is all over today. Come one step closer and I'll make her bleed.'

'You're a traitor to your brother and your empire,' Destin raged.

The blade bit into her skin, drawing blood, and Alexios and Destin halted. Her frightened eyes met his.

'Drop your weapons,' Lothair ordered. Then he turned to his men. 'Seize them too.'

'You won't get away with this, Lothair. I have soldiers surrounding this villa,' Alexios said.

'By the time they realise what's happening, I shall be king. I shall command a great army. You will be the one who will need to be concerned, Emperor Alexios.'

The soldiers surrounded them and Destin struggled, as the whole room descended into chaos. They punched him in the stomach, four against one, and he bent double. Seeing Lothair's sword edge further into the column of Livia's throat, he reluctantly gave in, dropping his sword, and the men pounced on him and the emperor.

'You really shouldn't have chosen a one-armed man as your bodyguard, Alexios,' Lothair said, tutting loudly, mocking him, and they all laughed. The humiliation was great, but it only helped to fuel Destin's fury.

Lothair came forward, and Destin was relieved to see the blade move away from Livia's skin. His arrogance getting the better of him, Lothair yanked Destin's good arm, before twisting it behind his back. 'Perhaps we should remove the other, see where that leaves him,' he sneered.

But with a strength born from years of hardship, insult and pain, in one swift movement Destin rotated his body, moving in a circular motion around Lothair, colliding violently with him, winding him, grabbing his arm in return. He skilfully dropped down, launching Lothair into the air, over his shoulder, bringing him onto the ground on his back with a crack, shocking everyone. Destin placed his foot on Lothair's chest, pin-ning him down, and removed the sword from the man's hand, turning it on his captive. 'Everyone drop their weapons,' he barked.

And in a state of impressed shock, it took a moment for the soldiers to catch up, to realise they no longer had the upper hand. Seeing their ruler trapped, a blade to his throat, they did as they were told, releasing Alexios from their grasp in the process.

The emperor got to his feet.

'Take their swords,' Destin said, and Alexios went round the room, gathering up the weapons. 'Now untie them,' Destin barked. He couldn't believe he was shouting orders at his leader, and that Alexios was following them. Yet right now he didn't care. He would do whatever was necessary to get them all out of here, and it was as if Alexios knew it. The emperor stepped over to Livia and began unfastening her bonds, releasing her, and Destin allowed himself to take a breath, then Alexios moved on to Matthias.

Lothair squirmed beneath him, letting out a string of expletives.

'Shh, that's not the way a would-be king should speak, is it?' Destin said. 'You're lucky I haven't silenced you for good.'

When he saw Alexios and Matthias were helping Livia up, he noticed she was stumbling, limping. What had they done to her? He wouldn't be able to settle until he'd got her far away from this place. He wanted to pull her into his chest, to safety, but he didn't dare touch her, not in front of all these men.

'We're leaving now,' Destin said to Lothair. 'The emperor's men will escort you off the property once we're gone. After all, you have an election to be at. And I doubt Alexios will want to see you here when he returns.'

He watched his three comrades back away, towards the door.

'You'd better hope I don't become king!' Lothair roared, still pinned down beneath Destin's boot.

'I was already hoping that. Don't worry. You, there,' Destin said, turning to one of the prince's men. 'Tie your leader to that chair. See how he likes it.' He released his foot from the man's chest and watched as Lothair's own men imprisoned him, before he made them do the same to each other, leaving one lone man standing.

When he felt the others would be at a safe distance away from here, out of the villa, he swiftly removed himself from the room and used a small knife from his belt to seal the handles of the door shut. He raced through the atrium towards the exit, where he found Alexios commanding the soldiers to hold the men inside back, while they got the princess to safety.

A guard hurriedly brought them some horses, and Destin went to help Livia up. But Alexios stopped her ascent, tugging her arm.

'I'm sorry I got you into this mess, Your Highness. And Matthias,' Alexios said, turning to look at the councillor.

Livia nodded, her body still trembling, her face ashen. 'At least you helped us get out of it. Thank you,' she said, graciously accepting his apology.

And then she swayed and Destin expertly caught her, scooping her into his arm. 'Are you all right?' he asked.

'I am now,' she whispered, looking up at him.

And he never wanted to let her go. Or let her out of his sight again.

But he couldn't forget where they were and who they were with. He released her momentarily while he climbed onto the horse, before pulling her up, into his lap. He held her close, sending a silent prayer up to the gods, thanking them for keeping her safe.

'Are you coming?' he said, turning to Alexios.

The emperor shook his head, looking grave. 'You two get her back. I'll make sure the soldiers see Lothair and his men off the property. I'll meet you at the palace to go to the election later. And I will hope,' he said, turning to Livia, 'that the council make the right choice.'

Destin wrapped his cloak around Livia, pulling the hood up over her face so she wouldn't be recognised on their way back through the busy streets, and she nestled in close to him, glad to be back in his arms. Just the scent of him, of fresh pine and leather, helped to soothe her, as well as his strong, comforting embrace. She wished she had never left his side this morning, then none of this would have happened.

Fortunately, the guards manning the city walls recognised him and Matthias instantly, letting them in, and she released a huge breath when the gates shut behind them. For now, her enemy was shut out.

As they reached the palace and galloped across the courtyard to the steps, there was a commotion as her servants came rushing out to greet them, making a fuss of her and the councillor. But she didn't want to get down from her position on the horse. She didn't want to leave Destin's hold.

But he was taking control, dishing out orders. 'Ready the princess a bath,' he said to one. 'And she'll need some food,' he said to another. 'There's lots to do before the election this afternoon.'

And then he helped her descend the horse, taking her hand in his, lowering her down to the ground, and she hesitated, feeling at a bit of a loss, wondering what happened now. When Matthias approached them, thanking him for saving their lives, Destin let her go.

'Your loyalty won't go unrewarded,' her councillor said.

'I need no reward,' Destin replied. 'I'm just glad you're both safe. That is all I require.'

Livia began to wearily climb up the steps and into the hall, and she was pleased when he followed her.

It felt so good to be home. She would never be so foolish to go anywhere again without letting her guards know what she was planning. She had learned her lesson.

Once inside, she made her way to the hall and sank down onto one of the benches. She was grateful when the maids brought her some pottage, bread and ale, and she downed the tankard of liquid in one go. She was so thirsty.

'You're hurt,' Destin said, nodding to her face, when the maid had walked a fair distance away.

'He hit me,' she said, wiping the back of her hand over her lip, checking to see if she was still bleeding.

'Yet he hurt my pride more than anything else. I think I twisted my ankle trying to get away from them. But that's all. It could have been a lot worse.'

'That's all?' he grimaced. And then he looked around, checking no one was within hearing distance, before letting his barely contained anger spill over. He leaned forward, pressing his hand into the table. 'What were you thinking, Livia?' he hissed. 'Leaving my side. Going there by yourself. Not telling me. Not *waking* me.'

She shrugged miserably. 'I wanted to talk to the emperor before the election today.'

Livia had contemplated waking Destin, but he had looked so handsome, so peaceful, she hadn't wanted to disturb him. And she'd hoped she could speak to Alexios and be back before Destin rose, by which point she could tell him the marriage alliance had been cancelled—and it would have been too late for him to stop her. 'I never thought for a moment my uncle would be there.'

A pained expression crossed his face. He had known of Lothair's whereabouts. He should have told her. It might have prevented this.

'When I saw him, I was so shocked. And afraid.'

'I'm not surprised.'

She had been frightened, but she'd stood up to her uncle anyway. And so had Matthias. But when he'd hit her and commanded his men to tie her up, she had begun to panic. She had thought she might miss the election. That her people would think she had run, like she had from her father and the emperor in Constantinople once before. But she would not run away from her responsibilities this time.

And she had begun to worry what Destin would think when he woke and she wasn't there.

'Thank you. For coming to get me,' she said, reaching out and putting her hand over his on the table. 'You were incredible…what you did back there. You certainly proved them all wrong about you.' Once again, she had been in awe of his strength. She had never seen a man fight or move the way he did. He had stunned her, as well as all the men in that room. 'Did you know that Lothair and Alexios were collaborating?' she asked. He knew her by now. She wouldn't stop asking him questions until she learned the truth.

'Not until last night.'

'Why didn't you tell me?' she said, snatching her fingers back, as if he'd burned her. She stared at him with accusation.

'I wanted to,' he said, pushing a hand through his hair. 'I was torn. I didn't want it to worry you. I thought it was just talk about land. Coin. It's what men in power do. I never realised Alexios would go so far as to put you in jeopardy, Livia. If I had…'

She nodded, the tension in her shoulders abating. She believed him. 'So that explains why you were pacing the courtyard like a mad man when I came down to see you.' He had been tortured, unsure whether to tell her about the emperor's disloyalty. 'What will happen now?' she asked, tearing off a little of the bread and popping it in her mouth, but it felt dry on her tongue as she chewed it. She offered him some and he shook his head.

'You can still go to the College this afternoon,' Destin said, his tone softening. 'You could tell them what Lothair did. But if you've changed your mind... You know you don't have to do this. People will understand.'

She finally swallowed the mouthful and glanced up at him, surprised. 'The need is greater than ever for me to do this. My uncle has proved what kind of man he is, over and again. I cannot let him rule here. Not without putting up a fight. I have to at least try...'

She pushed her bowl away and gingerly rose to her feet.

'I'm going to take that bath,' she said. 'Would you... see me up the stairs?'

His eyebrows pulled together, but he nodded, running his fingers around the back of his neck.

She was so aware of him as they climbed the stairs together in silence. Her throat felt restricted and her words dried up. She took in his rigid posture and the muscle working in his cheek. Was he feeling it too? He dominated the stairwell, her space and her thoughts.

Turning into the corridor, she was both pleased and relieved to see there was no soldier guarding her door right now that she needed to dispose of, and as she stepped inside her room, she thanked the maids for running her bath and said they could leave her. She wanted to be alone with him, desperately.

Destin's eyes raked over her as he lingered by the door, waiting for the women to disappear out of view, before his hand reached out to take her chin between his fingers, tipping her face up towards him, as if checking that no lasting damage had been done. And his touch sent tingles through her body.

What must she look like? It wasn't a great look for her appearance at the council later on today. And it wasn't the ideal way to seduce him…but she knew she was going to try anyway.

His thumb smoothed over her swollen lip. 'You're getting quite the bruise on your cheek,' he said.

'It's throbbing. Will you kiss it better?' she whispered, leaning in.

His eyes narrowed on her. 'You're determined to ruin me, aren't you?' he said, shaking his head. And then he frowned. 'I can't believe I was with you, lying beside you, and I still didn't keep you safe. It was my one task and I failed.'

'You didn't. You saved me. It was my fault. I should never have left you,' she said. 'I don't want to leave you again.'

He removed his hand from her skin and braced it on the door-frame above her head. 'Or I you. So I'll wait here while you take your bath. I will guard the door. You're safe now, Livia. I promise I won't go anywhere.'

That wasn't what she wanted and he knew it. She stepped towards him, placing her hand on his chest. 'I'd be safer if you stayed by my side. If you came in.'

'Not a good idea,' he rasped.

She moved closer. 'Did Alexios tell you I spoke to him?'

'Yes,' he said.

'Then you know I told him I couldn't marry him. Because I can't. I won't. It wouldn't be right. Not after what happened between you and me last night.'

'Livia…'

She knew he was about to chastise her again, that he was going to give her another reason why they couldn't do this. And suddenly she felt overwhelmingly frustrated. She'd nearly lost her life. And being in such danger had only heightened her feelings. She knew what was important to her now. She had determined that if she survived the ordeal, she would show him what he meant to her. And then he'd rescued her. Of course he had. And she wanted him now more than ever. She wanted him to admit he wanted her too. To stop fighting it.

Leaving the door open, she removed her hand from his body and turned away from him, heading over to the filled, steaming bath, sunken into the floor. She unfastened her brooches, willing her fingers to stop shaking, praying for the confidence to do this. She let her stola sink to the ground, pooling at her feet, before pulling off her tunic, so she was standing naked before him, her back to him.

She glanced over her shoulder, satisfied to see the shocked, starved look in his dark eyes, which were raking over her body, trailing her every movement. 'It's still warm. Do you want to join me?'

She didn't know why she was being so brazen, but she felt she needed to be with him. He kept holding her at arm's length, as if he was playing a game of tug of war between his head and his heart. He needed a little persuasion.

As she walked down the steps, slowly, and sank beneath the surface, she heard the wood click shut, and for a moment she wondered if he had left. But when she looked up she saw he was still there, resting his back against the door, watching her, his body rigid. It seemed as if it was taking him every ounce of restraint not to come to her, to touch her, his breathing laboured. She would just have to be patient. She lay back in the water, her dark hair spreading out around her, and let her eyes momentarily flutter shut, enjoying the sensations of the heat lapping at her body. When he still didn't come to her, she eventually sat up and cupped the water in her hands, using it to wash the blood off her stinging, swollen face, and ran her soaped-up hands over her body, washing herself. By the time she was clean, she realised he still hadn't moved.

She sighed.

'Destin, can you pass me my robe?' she asked, gesturing with her head to her gold silk gown, which lay over the side of her chair.

He came off the door and swiped it up, bringing it towards her, and she stood, rising out of the bath, droplets of water cascading down her body. She turned to him, taking the silk from his fingers. But she made no move to put it on. Instead, she stepped closer to him and pressed her damp body against him, wrapping her arms around his neck. He bit out a curse of frustration and defeat, and in one swift movement he caught her waist in his arm and his mouth came down on hers, finally claiming her. He was gentle, careful of her bruised and swollen lips, and she was lost.

And by the way his mouth moved down to cover her neck, the tops of her breasts, his hand curling over her bottom and hauling her towards him, frantic with need, he was too.

He pressed his groin into her body and she could feel how hard he was. How much he wanted her, and it spurred her on. Her heart hammering in her chest, she unfastened his leather vest and ruthlessly tugged it off, before reaching for his tunic, desperately wanting that gone too, needing to feel his skin on hers again, her fingers barely able to grasp the material they were shaking so much. He removed his splint and his tunic, letting his left arm fall to his side, and then his hand was back on her, roaming down over her bottom.

He paused for just a moment, pulling away, looking at her, breathing her in. 'Livia, are you sure about this?'

'Yes,' she whispered, nodding, staring at his chest and up into his eyes. She reached for the waistband of his breeches and unfastened it, before tugging them down, setting him free.

And then she pushed him back gently onto the bed, so he was sitting on the edge, and she came to stand between his legs.

'You should be preparing for this afternoon,' he said. 'Getting ready.'

'This is preparing me,' she said. He was all she needed.

He placed his lips to her stomach, kissing her softly, his hand squeezing her bottom, pulling her closer, before his palm roamed up to carefully cup one breast, and she thrust towards him, her nipples hardening. Her hands gripped onto his shoulders and she wanted him to take her in his mouth, and as if he was answering her prayers, he drew one nipple between his lips, sucking down on her hard, and she raked her hands into his hair, gripping fistfuls of it, tight.

And then she released him, pulling his mouth away from her breast and she dropped to her knees. She ran her hands over his muscular thighs, looking up at him, and he watched her with heated interest, wondering what she was going to do next. He seemed to want her to take the lead.

She took his hard shaft in the palm of her hand before bending her head to caress the tip of him with her tongue. He swore, his muscles bunched, and she felt excitement rage through her. His reaction made her feel powerful. She took him further into her mouth, kissing and licking him, liking the taste of him, and he tipped his head back, giving in to all the sensations she was causing. Did it feel as good as it had for her last night?

'Livia,' he muttered, his fingers stealing into her hair, and she took him to the back of her throat.

'Livia,' he said more urgently. She didn't want to stop, but when he clamped his hand around her arm, tugging her upwards, she was forced to tear her mouth away from him.

'I want you,' he said, his voice desperate.

'Finally,' she whispered, smiling, but her legs trembled as she rose to her feet. The moment was huge.

'We'll have to be careful,' he said, and she nodded. She knew he would be. He had always been careful with her. It was why she had fallen in love with him.

He pulled her closer, bringing her on top of him, so she straddled his hips with her knees, sitting on his thighs. And she reached down and cradled his shaft in her hand again. He squeezed her bottom, drawing her closer, lifting her over the top of him, until she could feel the tip of him, straining against her moist folds. She hesitated. Looking down into his eyes, his big, muscular body sprawled out beneath her, she felt feverish and terrified all at once.

'Destin, I don't know how to do this,' she said, leaning over him.

He grinned against her mouth, pressing his forehead against hers. 'Neither do I, but I'm sure we can work it out together.'

And in one unexpected move he flipped her over, so he was lying on top of her, his large chest pressing against hers, his body between her legs, and he kissed her deeply, open-mouthed, as he pushed her legs wide apart with his knees. His hand stroked down between them, to where she wanted him to touch her most. He seemed to have reined in his fierce urgency from moments ago as he took his time with her, making her more excited, sliding his fingers in and out of her slick entrance, and she knew he was preparing her for what was to come. Her head tipped back on a wave of wonderment.

And then the hard, silky tip of him was right there, trailing down along her crease to her opening.

'Livia?' he asked, and she nodded. 'You're sure this is what you want?'

'Yes.'

He eased the tip inside her and she felt the rush of excitement, and burning need, and she wanted him to thrust hard, to claim her, so she lifted her legs up to wrap around his thighs, willing him to give just one nudge.

And as he held her hand with his above her head, entwining their fingers, he did.

But he thrust carefully, slowly impaling her body, and she gasped, tensing at the sudden invasion, and she was glad he'd been more gentle than she'd wanted him to be.

He stopped, her muscles clenched tight around him, preventing him from going any further, and his deep brown eyes looked down at her. 'Are you all right?'

'Yes,' she said, clamping her legs around his waist. 'Just…suddenly nervous.' She licked her lips, her mouth feeling dry.

'That makes two of us,' he smiled.

'I didn't think Norse warriors got nervous,' she said, raising an eyebrow.

'When you have something so precious in your hands, it's hard not to be. Are you sure you want to carry on?'

'Yes.' She nodded. And she thought she fell even more in love with him for asking.

He kissed her then, slowly, tenderly, her bruised lips barely even smarting, and she began to relax beneath him, allowing him to edge further inside her. When he gave another gentle thrust, this time he plunged all the way inside, breaching her inner wall, filling her up, and she cried out in unexpected pleasure.

He looked down at her in heated passion and amazement. 'You feel…so good,' he whispered.

She gripped his waist, his thighs, tugging him towards her, wanting more, wanting him to pin her down and possess her. 'So do you.'

But he continued to take it slow, finding his rhythm, ruthlessly rocking inside her, unhurriedly, as if he wanted to make it last. As if he'd waited a lifetime for this. He made each surge count, storming her, discovering what she liked as he slid in and out, pressing deeper, as if he couldn't get enough of her, as if he never wanted her to forget this moment and his thorough taking of her. His hand released hers to come down and curl around her bottom, pressing her closer, bringing her right up against him and she didn't know how much more she could take. The pleasure was too great. He was so much more than she could ever have dreamed of. She felt overwhelmed. Hot. Feverish. And she began to thrash about wildly beneath him, their bodies slick with sweat, and it only took one more torturous thrust for her to come apart. She screamed out her climax into his shoulder just as he pulled out of her and spilled the rush of his own pleasure on the furs, her name tumbling from his lips.

Livia's eyes flickered open. It had been…wow. All she had hoped it would be, and she lay there, sated, unwilling and unable to move. Destin lay heavily on top of her, breathing hard, and she liked the weight of him, his skin on hers. It felt intimate. Comforting, reminding her of when he'd saved her life on the journey to Rome. She felt protected. She wanted to stay like this for ever.

Once he'd recovered, Destin rolled off her onto his back and pulled her into his chest, kissing her forehead.

She knew this moment was significant, not just for her, but for him too. They had both taken something from each other, and given a whole lot in return. She knew that this would change them both. She already felt different. She felt like she was glowing from the inside out. She no longer felt like a girl, but a woman. As if her eyes had been opened to new wonders. And she felt loved. Complete.

'That was incredible,' she said, holding on to his jaw and reaching up to place a kiss against his lips. 'Thank you.' She felt so close to him.

He looked down at her, offering her a grin. Her stomach flipped.

'You're thanking me?' he asked, raising his eyebrows, incredulous. 'For finally giving in to your seduction? You're determined, I'll give you that.'

She laughed lightly. 'I just know what I want.' And she did. She hadn't made the decision to sleep with him lightly. She knew she wanted him in her future, even if the path wasn't clear-cut. 'But no, I was thanking you for being you. The best man I have ever met. I can't imagine it ever feeling more perfect than that.'

He nodded, his hand stroking her hip. His eyes shone down into hers and he kissed the tip of her nose. 'Neither can I.'

Chapter Ten

Destin and Alexios galloped down the street on horse-back, heading for the Lateran Palace, which was host-ing the German princes of the Electoral College for the first time. Approaching the impressive building, it was a symbol of the Holy Roman Empire's power if ever he saw one. It reminded Destin of the stunning stone palaces back in Constantinople, and he surprised himself by realising he wasn't missing home. But why would he, when there was such treasure—everything he needed—right here?

After leaving their horses, they climbed the steps and entered the palace, heading to the great hall, and he looked around in awe—the walls were lined with ornate mosaics, frescoes adorned the apses and there was an impressive indoor fountain spurting water in each and every direction. Yet despite the imposing surroundings, it was the stern looks on the princes' faces that caused his stomach to tighten in apprehension. He wondered how Livia would fare, making her speech in this mag-nificent place, to these formidable men. It was notably different to the hall in which she'd first received him in Harzburg and he was reminded of how far they'd come.

Matthias and his men had advised her it would be unwise to arrive with Emperor Alexios and his body-guard for the election. They'd felt it might sway the decision one way or another. Even though he knew they were right, he didn't like it. He hadn't wanted to let her out of his sight, not when she had to travel through the excited crowds of the city and Lothair was still at large. And especially after he had made love to her, branding her with his taste and touch, making her his. Or had she made him hers? Either way, he didn't want to be parted from her. He wanted to be the one taking care of her.

He kept glancing towards the door, hoping every new arrival would be her.

His lover. The woman he loved.

She had felt glorious when he had thrust inside her, like a silken, tight embrace. A spasm of pain had crossed her face, and he'd prepared himself to stop, but then she had slowly relaxed around him, holding him close, allowing him to sink deeper, and he'd never wanted it to end.

He was distracted from his thoughts when he heard the announcement marking Lothair's arrival and his beastly men entered the room and took up their positions on one side of the hall. The prince looked arrogant, as if he was assured of his success today, despite already suffering one defeat this morning, and Destin wanted to throw himself over the seats between them and pick up where they'd left off.

He was worried how Livia would react when she saw

her uncle again. Would she be intimidated? Or scared?
He glanced at the electors, wondering if they had already come to a decision in their minds, before the
College had even taken place. He hoped not. He hoped
they'd come here willing to listen.

The hall was overflowing, cloying with people, and
he knew the streets were just as bad. He pushed his hand
through his hair. Where was she?

'Relax,' Alexios whispered from beside him. 'Anyone would think you care.'

He opened his mouth, went to retort, when finally,
the doors swung open and Livia's name was announced,
marking her arrival, and everyone stood and turned
around to watch her enter.

He felt the breath leave him.

Livia stood, tall and proud, dressed in an exquisite,
refined black and gold mourning gown, her dark hair
swept up elegantly with several braids framing her face.
It was as if she had blossomed since this morning. She
looked the part—she'd bloomed into a true Roman
queen, and an awed hush settled around the room as
everyone was dazzled by her grace and beauty. Destin
swallowed, riveted. This was what she was born for, he
thought. To be on show, to be looked at. She was perfection. He needn't have worried, she made the great
hall look lacklustre.

Something was different about her. She seemed…
ready. As if she had transformed into a woman before
his eyes. Was he and the things they'd done together
somehow responsible for that? She looked like a woman

every man would want to worship. And of all the men in the room, he couldn't believe she'd allowed him to do so.

It had been glorious, considering it was both their first times. They had fitted together perfectly, as if they were made for each other, and it had felt so intense, so right. There had been a little blood on the furs, proof of him taking her innocence, and that was when the reality of what had happened between them hit him. The enormity of it. But he'd been powerless to stop it. And he couldn't bring himself to regret it. It had been too incredible. He'd wanted to make her his since the moment he'd first seen her, and now he had. He should be satisfied now. But looking across at her, he was starting to think he never would be. Not unless he was at her side, always.

She began to walk up the aisle, slow and steady, as they'd discussed, holding her head up high, her shoulders back, her eyes coolly assessing the crowd, nodding in acknowledgement to some of the nobles. As she walked past him, part of him hoped she'd glance his way, that their eyes would meet, but she did not. Rationally, he knew that was wise, in case either of them gave anything away, but still he clenched his jaw, feeling foolishly disappointed.

When she reached her seat and sat down on the opposite side of the hall to Lothair, it was as if the whole room took a collective breath, and the electors began. First, they commemorated the late king, talking a little of his achievements, before introducing the proceedings. Then they welcomed Prince Lothair up to address the room.

Bile rose in Destin's throat as he watched and listened to Lothair stand and make his speech as to why he should be the next Holy Roman Emperor, stating he had the greater claim as he was a man. His tactic was to quote his accolades of war and glory, and his plans to expand their empire further if he should come into power, through continuing the king's bloody campaign in southern Italy. Destin felt Alexios tense beside him.

Finally, Lothair put Livia down for her age and for being a woman, and Destin made a fist with his hand to try to curb his anger. But despite Lothair's debasement of her in front of everyone, she didn't flinch. Destin would have noticed if she had, for he couldn't take his eyes off her.

Next, it was Livia's turn. She stood gracefully and began to speak clearly. She didn't fidget once. And Destin's heart was in his mouth.

She addressed the electors, lords and ladies in the room, first stating she was the rightful heir—the direct descendant of her father and chosen by God. 'I intend to keep our empire in power and prosperity. But not through war, like my father, and like my uncle is proposing. In fact, I have already recalled my father's troops in southern Italy. We will never be a great power by focusing on lands outside our empire. We need to focus on what is within our already great realm.'

Whispers rustled around the room.

'And no man or woman shall live in fear here, as my uncle wishes it,' she said, turning to look him in the eye. 'I should like to tell you of his recent plot to displace me.' She didn't falter—or tremble—as she spoke of what he had done in Harzburg, and this morning, making sure the College knew what he was capable of. 'But I should like to call a few others up to speak for me,' and she nodded to the guard at the door. As he opened it, a line of injured, bloodied and broken men, women and children filed in. Destin stopped breathing. Among them were some of his men.

Gasps of horror and outrage rumbled around the room. 'These are some of my people from Harzburg, who arrived just this afternoon. Lothair razed my late mother's castle to the ground. Many are still wounded or recuperating in the hospice in the city, but some were determined to come today to show you all what Lothair did. So take a good look. These are the people he wishes to rule over. They're not his enemies, but this is how he treated them.'

Destin felt his rage spike at what Lothair had done, and looked around, hoping the other lords and ladies of Rome felt the same. He admired Livia's courage, and yet he wondered why she hadn't shared their arrival with him. He had been worried for hers and his men's safety too. But he was pleased she had given the councillors a reason to mistrust Lothair for his atrocious actions.

'Is this the kind of monarch we want ruling our empire?' she asked the room. 'Our realm won't thrive through war and bloodshed, but through peace. And alliances. Before our meeting here today, I visited the Pope, to ask him to pray for these people, and he offered me his full support and blessing.'

The murmurs turned to mutterings and a mixture of excitement and outrage in the hall.

The electors had to hammer on the tables for silence.

Destin had to hand it to her, it was a clever move. Besides the king, the Pope was the most powerful man in Rome. Whoever ruled here would need his approval.

'I also have the allegiance of the Byzantine emperor,' she said, turning to Alexios and offering him a smile. Her gaze still didn't stretch his way and Destin felt the burn of jealousy in his chest.

'What about foreign influence? We don't want our empire being taken over by Byzantium,' someone shouted out from the crowd.

'No, neither do I,' she said calmly. 'I am well aware my people don't want a foreign ruler, and I do not need one either. I have spoken with Emperor Alexios and we have agreed that he will release me from my father's marriage agreement.' She continued to look at Alexios while she was speaking to him. Her gaze didn't falter. 'In return, I am willing to give him the lands in southern Italy that my father has ravaged for the past few winters.'

He felt the shock, then the relief, that she was offering Alexios what he wanted, ripple through his ruler's body. She was trying to keep everyone happy.

'Ultimately, they have always belonged to Byzantium. And I wish for us to remain friends, Alexios, for our two great empires to remain as allies, as my father and your father always were.'

She turned to look at the council, as if she was ready to make her final and most poignant statement. 'If the College accepts me as their queen, I vow I will never marry a man unless you wish it, unless we find a man you deem worthy to be my husband. Until then, no man will rule over me or my country. I will be wedded to my empire instead.'

A hush now descended on the room, as everyone took on board the significance—and sacrifice—of what she was saying.

Destin struggled to rake in another breath. He felt as if he'd been punched in the gut.

It was a bold move. Admirable. But if they accepted her vow, it meant she could never be with him. They could never be together. And he felt like a fool. After the intimate things they had done together today, he had thought they would find a way…

But she was putting her empire, her duty, before him. Yet he of all people could understand that. Duty had always come first for him too. Until he'd met her.

He had always known, right from the start, that he would have to hand her over to someone else. That she could never be his. She was a princess, he was a soldier. So why did her statement, pronouncing that she would never take any man as her husband, unless the council approved him, now hurt so much? Why did her sacrifice feel as if she was ripping open his chest, like she was sacrificing him too? Was it because he knew they'd never choose him? A pagan, a Northman soldier, with a broken body. She must know that too.

When had she decided all this? While she'd been lying in his arms today, or when he'd been moving deep inside her? Had she been planning it all along and not thought to share it with him? Just like she hadn't told him of the arrival of his men? Rejection cut through him.

As Livia sat down, for the first time since her arrival,

he saw her hand tremble and she reached out to grip the arm of her seat to steady herself. He tried to tear his eyes away from her beautiful fingers as they reminded him of how they had trembled when they had touched him earlier. He wanted to go to her, to shake her, to ask her why, and yet, he already knew the answer. She had done what was necessary. For her people and her empire. Her throne was more important than him. He was both proud of her and furious with her all at once.

The College adjourned and the people in the room erupted into speculative chatter, giving their own thoughts on the speeches, anxiously awaiting what the verdict would be. But they didn't have to wait long— the electors returned with their unanimous decision in no time.

Livia was to be the new Holy Roman Empress.

On the morrow, she was to be taken to Saint Peter's Basilica and crowned by the Pope.

The hall went wild, clapping and cheering. And she stood, with her hand across her heart, in surprised disbelief, smiling, as people rushed forward to congratulate her, all wanting to speak with her, and offer their allegiance and service. And he felt as if she'd passed beyond his reach.

Alexios seemed to be in a state of elated shock beside him. He clapped Destin on the shoulder. 'Well, I never thought that would happen. Perhaps I should have come to Harzburg to fetch her myself. Then I might have been the ruler of two empires,' he said lightly.

'Perhaps you should have,' Destin said tightly. And then none of this would ever have come to pass. He wouldn't have nearly got himself killed, broken his oath of loyalty or had his heart damaged beyond repair.

'So neither of us gets the princess… But at least I have southern Italy, and my freedom,' the emperor grinned. 'And you still have your title, and me. A good result, I think.'

Yes, it was. So why then, did Destin not feel like celebrating?

Livia's eyes looked heavenward and she sent up a silent word of thanks. She was so glad it was over. She was overwhelmed the College had named her as their empress. She hoped her father was smiling down on her and he would now be at peace. He would be livid with her if he knew what she'd done about the lands in southern Italy, but he had said a great ruler would decide their own destiny, and this was what she felt was right.

As her guards ushered her out of the hall, there was a five-thousand-strong crowd waiting for her outside, lining the streets, wanting to catch a glimpse of her. Their new Holy Roman Empress. The soldiers surrounded her in a protective wall, trying to keep her safe.

She glanced all around, looking for Destin. She was desperate to see his face, to share the excitement of the incredible verdict with him. He was the only one she wanted at her side right now.

Finally, she saw him, as he stooped, coming out of the door, leaving the building. Standing at the top of the steps, taking in the crowds before him, he frowned, his hand coming up to shield his eyes from the sun. He looked deep in thought, his jaw tense, his eyes scanning the masses. He was still on alert, protecting her and Alexios, she thought. She willed his eyes to meet hers, but she was being swept up in the convoy, bustled along the road to her carriage.

A soldier held the door open for her and she lifted her skirts and climbed in, and then she was off to make a processional tour of the city. She looked back at Destin over her shoulder and he finally met her gaze, but she couldn't read his dark eyes as he watched her leave. He just stared after her as the distance grew between them.

Livia felt an enormous sense of relief when the carriage entered the palace gates later on that afternoon. It had taken what seemed like an age to travel down the streets, waving to all the crowds. She knew the hard task of ruling was only just beginning, but today had felt like a test. She'd had to prove herself worthy. She just hoped she could live up to all that she had promised her people. She would do her best.

As the carriage pulled up in the courtyard, she caught sight of Destin leading his horse back towards the stables and she rushed to get out, clambering down the steps.

She nodded her thanks to the footman and then picked up her skirts and, as quickly as she could, as gracefully as she could, without breaking into a run, raced across the courtyard. She had always been taught that a princess should never run. What about a queen?

'Commander,' she called.

He gave her a cursory glance over his shoulder, before continuing to stride on.

She felt a prickling sensation all over her, and was

uncomfortable that the other soldiers in the courtyard had witnessed that. But it didn't stop her. She charged after him, determined to speak to him. She tore after him up the steps into the stables, calling after him.

'Commander…'

Catching up to him as he secured the horses, she tugged his arm. 'Are you ignoring your queen?' she bit out, suddenly angry and terribly hurt. All she wanted was his support right now. To hear a few words of praise from the person she cared about most of all. Was that too much to ask?

'You forget, I answer to another sovereign, Highness. But congratulations on your success. It seems everything has worked out perfectly for you,' he spat, pulling off the saddles and hanging them up.

She felt wounded. This wasn't the Destin she knew, who had made love to her so tenderly earlier. Who had taken her virginity. This man was a cold, unfeeling stranger, like the man she had first met in Harzburg.

'What's wrong?' she asked.

'I'm busy. So if you'll excuse me, I need to ready my belongings. The emperor plans for us to leave for Constantinople before the day is out.'

Pain lanced her chest. He was leaving her? The hurt was so great she couldn't breathe. She shook her head. Had he got what he wanted from her and now decided that was it? That it was over?

He stole past her, exiting the stables, and she felt an anger tear through her like never before. She didn't deserve this. She charged after him, following him down the corridor towards the soldiers' barracks.

'Commander,' she shouted at his back. 'Destin.'

Past caring if anyone saw, she charged after him, determined to speak to him, pulling his arm and getting in the way of his path. He tried to sweep her aside as he reached for the handle to his door, but she pressed her back against the wood, blocking his entrance.

'What the hell are you doing? Have you lost your mind?' he bore down on her, suddenly furious. 'If anyone sees you here...'

'I don't care if they see...' she threw at him, reckless. 'You won't talk to me! Did today mean nothing to you?'

His neck was corded and he flexed his hand by his side. He glanced around furtively, to check if anyone was watching. He tried to move her aside again as he wrestled with the handle.

'Livia, move.'

'No.'

The door flew open and he stormed past her inside, and she followed him in.

'Meant nothing to me?' he asked, incredulous, rounding on her, his eyes burning with fire. 'You're the one who just swore to an entire empire never to be with a man for the rest of your life. But perhaps I'm just the foolish one, to have started to hope of having any kind of future with you. I'm not sure when or why! Maybe it was when you opened your robe and spread your legs, enticing me to kiss you there. Or perhaps it was when you bathed in front of me, then welcomed me into your arms and your body.'

Anger was rolling off him in waves, and she felt the full force of it crashing over her.

She slammed the door shut behind her, resting her back against it. 'What did you expect me to do—tell the council all about us and ask for permission? To confess I'd slept with you and hope they'd understand? Somehow, I don't think they'd deem our relationship appropriate, do you? You're a Northman and I was born into royalty. I said what I needed to say to make them listen. I had to put my own desires aside for the good of the empire.'

Pain slashed across his face and he turned away from her again.

In a blaze of fury, she pushed herself away from the wood.

'I said what I had to say to make them want me as their queen. They would never have elected me if they'd known I'd just lost my virginity to a Norseman. But it doesn't mean I can't stop thinking about it. It doesn't mean I don't want you. It doesn't mean I don't want to do it again.'

He cursed, raking his hand through his hair, and then in two strides he'd reached her, capturing her between his body and the door, her back hitting the wood, his hand coming round her neck to haul her to him. And it was all that she wanted. His mouth came down onto hers, hard and possessive, kissing her more furiously than ever before, his anger stirring his passion. And she kissed him back, not caring that her tender lips were stinging, her hands gripping his shoulders, pressing herself against him with the same desperate urgency, wanting to have him touch her again, wanting to feel skin against skin, wanting to become one.

She began to peel off his sling and leather vest, ruthlessly wrenching the fastenings open, before slipping them off his shoulders. And then she was bunching up his tunic, wanting to see his beautiful chest again. It had been too long since the last time. It was gone, discarded on the floor in an instant, and the way he was rucking up her skirts, she knew he was just as eager.

She felt the hard ridge of him pressing into her belly, holding her in place against the wood as he continued lifting her skirts, as if there was no time to undress her. As if he just needed to be inside her, now, and she whimpered, wanting the same. She raised her leg to hook over his hip, wanting to feel him right there. He pushed his hand down between their bodies to touch her as she clung on, his fingers stealing inside her body, making her gasp and her legs buckle. But his hips pinned her in place.

'I want you,' he whispered. 'So badly.'

'Then have me.'

He undid his breeches and freed himself, moving his shaft to her entrance. She curled her leg tighter around his hip, giving him better access, and he stroked her with the tip, and she groaned. She couldn't wait any longer, she thought she might come apart with him just touching her like this. She bucked against him and he thrust inside her, all the way, making her cry out in pleasure. She clung on. She couldn't do anything but.

He brought his hand up, no longer needing it to hold himself in place now that he was buried so deeply inside her, and he gripped her bottom tighter, tugging her closer, lifting her off the floor, with his one arm tucked beneath her, and she wrapped her legs around his waist, holding on. She looked up into his face, so focused, so intent on giving them both pleasure, and she gripped his jaw with both hands, kissing him as he surged inside her again, impaling her, her back pinned against the door. They were good at this, she thought.

Her head tipped back and his lips dragged down her throat, his hand coming up to fumble with the neckline of her tunic, pulling at the restrictive material, his lips pressing against the top of her breasts. He ruthlessly surged inside her again, slamming her against the door, and she'd barely caught her breath before he did it again, and again, the sensations intensifying. She buried her face in his neck, holding on as he plunged inside her one more time and when he hit home, she screamed with the insane pleasure of her release. He pulled out of her and bit out his climax as he erupted over her thigh.

His forehead pressed against hers, his breathing ragged, he continued to hold her in place against the door. 'Sorry,' he said. 'I'll clean it up.'

She laughed lightly. 'Don't be.' She felt off balance. Moved by the intensity of what had just happened.

He set her trembling body down, his hand coming up to cup her face.

'Are you all right?'

His face was stern from the fervour of their lovemaking, and her legs were shaking, her heart pounding. She nodded. She felt a lump grow in her throat. She loved him. So much.

He fastened up his breeches and disentangled himself from her arms, walking across the room to get a cloth, and came back to her to wipe her clean, stroking the material over her thigh.

'I was going to ask you what your first task as queen was going to be, but now I know,' he said, but his lips couldn't quite make a smile. And she realised she'd hurt him today. It hadn't been her intention.

He discarded the cloth and came back to her, gathering her in his arm. He pulled her into his chest. 'I was proud of you today, Livia,' he said, looking down at her, stroking her back. 'Your mother and father would have been proud of you too.'

'Really?' she asked. It was all she'd wanted to hear.

'Yes, you were everything I knew you could be,' he said.

'I can't believe they voted me queen.'

'I can. You deserved it. And you will make a wonderful ruler.' He stroked his knuckles down her cheek. 'This day will be memorable for a lot of reasons.'

'I already miss the freedom of being in Harzburg. All those people watching today were overwhelming. That giant hall…' She shook her head.

'I was worried about you, wanting to be at your side but knowing I'd been told to stay away, that it wasn't my place to protect you.'

He had grown more and more impatient, waiting for her carriage to return to the palace. He'd visited the hospice and his men, discovering what had happened back in Saxony, checking up on them, while she'd been on her procession of the city. He'd felt such a mixed-up jumble of emotions, that she had done it, she'd won

over the electors and they'd announced her as queen...
but at what cost? He had felt massively hurt at the same
time—that she had sacrificed him. An old fear had
reared its ugly head. That if his own parents had been
ashamed of him, hadn't wanted him, why would he
think anyone else would? Now she was empress, she
certainly couldn't attach herself to him. When she'd got
into that carriage, surrounded by a wall of soldiers, of
people baying for her, he'd had a glimpse of what the
future would be like. Him wanting to be with her all
the time, but unable to even get close to her.

When she'd returned after her procession, relief had
quickly given way to his underlying, simmering anger,
as she'd run across the courtyard to speak to him, and
then he'd needed her so badly, he'd made love to her
again, so passionately, so fiercely, it had taken his breath
away. He wondered how he could soar between feeling
so high and low when he was with her. Was this what
love felt like?

'I wanted to talk to you about that...' she said, looking up into his eyes.

He took a step back, taking her hand in his, pulling her
over towards the bed. They both sat down on the edge.

'Destin, now that my future has been decided, I
wanted to talk to you about yours,' she said, tracing
her other hand over his bare chest, her fingers following the ink. 'Now I'm queen, I can make decisions for
myself. And I've decided... I want you at my side, Destin, not because you have to be, because you were sent
to fetch me, because I'm a duty you have to fulfil, but
because you want to be here,' she said.

He leaned in closer, his thumb smoothing over the top of her hand.

'I was hoping you would talk to Alexios. Or I could. I could tell him that I want you to stay…'

He stared down into her golden eyes. His heart lifted just a little… She really wanted him?

'I want you to be my personal bodyguard, instead of his.'

His hope came tumbling down around him. His fingers stilled in hers. 'Your bodyguard?' A sentinel standing guard in the shadows.

'Yes. Whatever land or titles or gold he was going to give you, I will give you instead.'

He reeled, hurt and disappointment washing over him. He didn't want her to buy him! To give him coin to be with her. 'You're offering me a position in your Queen's Guard?' he said, pulling away from her.

'Yes. It would mean we could always be together.'

She leaned back into him and her hand flattened against his chest, smoothing her fingers over him. But he gripped her wrist and gently lifted her away, moving to get off the bed. He shook his head. 'I can't,' he said, his voice sounding strange, not like his own.

He got to his feet, and it took a lot of effort for him to start picking up his clothes and pulling them back on.

'Why not?' she said, tucking her knees beneath her on the bed, kneeling up.

Because, he realised, he didn't want to just be her bodyguard. He didn't want to be kept a secret, like she was ashamed of him—hidden away, as if he didn't exist. Silenced, as if he didn't mean anything to her. He didn't want to watch from afar as she made important decisions about her empire and then came looking for him for sex at the end of the day. He wanted to be the man at her side. The man who made decisions with her. The man she loved. The man she told the world she loved.

But she couldn't do that because she was the empress. And especially not now she'd made her vow.

She had found her place, become the woman she wanted to be. And yet he still didn't even know who he was or where he'd come from. He wanted to be the man she was proud of. But who was that man? *He* didn't even know who he was.

Deep down, he had known this would happen—that things would have to come to an end, and he was enraged with himself for getting attached. She belonged here and he was needed in Byzantium.

'My life is back in Constantinople.'

'But *I'm* here,' she said, wounded. 'You could make a new home here. Or in Germany. We could move back there, together. You could create a new role in my guard and have your own contingent of men,' she blurted. 'You could have me.'

He paused, midway through putting his sling back on, and breathed out a long unsteady breath.

'You? When would I have you?'

'Whenever you want!' she said, coming forward, stepping off the bed, moving towards him.

'Really?' It was a tempting offer. He had half hoped that when he took her to bed, his desire for her would be sated. But now he knew that would never be the case. It had been moments since he'd pulled out of her body and he already wanted her again. It would never be enough with Livia…he would always want more. 'You mean whenever I want in between your royal duties, when you can fit me in, and in secret.'

She frowned. 'It wouldn't be like that.'

'No? What would it be like? Are you really willing to keep risking your crown, to do this? To have a snatched moment here or there? Because people will find out… look how recklessly we behaved today.'

'I was mad at you.'

'And people saw.' He stepped towards her. 'We can't carry on like this after the vow you have made to your people. They see you as some kind of vestal virgin, who will continue the power of Rome and be chaste. You can't disappoint them. You can't break your promise.'

'But—'

'And what about your body? Aren't you worried about putting it at risk?'

The crease in her forehead deepened, as if she didn't understand.

'Because every time I make love to you, Livia, I have to pull out, so as not to plant a seed in your body, so we don't risk you becoming with child.' He raked a hand through his hair. 'Do you know how hard that is for me to do?'

She shook her head 'You didn't enjoy it?'

'Of course I did,' he said, softening a little. 'But don't you see it's dangerous? What if there's a time when I can't stop? What if I lose control? What if you get with child? There would be uproar in your empire. And we've discussed this. Neither of us wants a baby.'

She swallowed. 'So what? That's it? You're just going

to leave me?' Her beautiful eyes pooled with tears. She slumped back down on the edge of the bed.

He sat down next to her and cupped her chin in his hand, turning her to face him. 'I don't want to. You know I don't. This past week, with you, has been incredible. I will treasure it for ever. But I really think that I must go now, for both our sakes, don't you?'

Livia had thought Destin had made love to her to make her his, but instead he had made love to her to make a memory. He was leaving her, and the pain was too great. She had tried to convince him to stay, but she had always known he was a man unable to be swayed when he'd made up his mind. She might have been persuasive, coercive, once or twice, but this time he was resolute. And it felt as if someone was reaching into her chest and ripping out her heart. He had told her he would always be around to protect her, but now she knew that wasn't true. He was returning to Constantinople to go back to protecting the emperor instead.

She felt distraught, her legs heavy, as she made her way down from her room that evening. She wasn't sure how she was going to say goodbye to him. The thought of never seeing his handsome face again was too much to bear.

She had tried to distract herself by welcoming some of her people from Harzburg into the palace, hearing about the battle that had taken place, and how Destin's soldiers had saved many of them from the fire that had ravaged the building. After being under siege for days and realising Lothair was not going to stop until he'd razed the castle to the ground, with them inside, they had taken the same tunnel she and Destin had and escaped. Now some of them were planning to return to Saxony, others were thinking about staying with Livia, wherever she made her home. Others, she noticed, had fallen in love and were contemplating going with their soldiers to Constantinople. And her heart burned fiercely with jealously. She was pleased for them, but she couldn't deny she wanted what they had. She wanted him. The man she loved.

She forced herself to make her way out to the courtyard, where Alexios and Destin were readying their horses and their men to leave. Her chest ached, and her eyes and throat burned from holding in the tears. She was even sore between her legs, a reminder of where he'd been and what they'd done together, but she didn't mind. In fact, she never wanted the feeling to leave her. She didn't want him to leave her.

'It's been a fascinating trip,' Emperor Alexios said, turning to greet her. 'Not a wasted one after all. I feel we're parting ways stronger allies than ever before.'

She nodded. 'I'm glad that you came.'

'I am too. And I'm sorry again about…you know.'

She waved her hand in the air. 'It's all forgotten.'

'I do believe the right person got the crown,' he said.

'Thank you. That means a lot.'

'And I think things have turned out for the best, between you and me. I'm sure our friendship will last a lot longer than our marriage would have.' He winked, and she smiled. 'Do come and see us in Constantinople some time. We have some fantastic entertainment and I know our people would love a visit from the Holy Roman Empress.'

'I might just do that,' she rasped.

Alexios nodded and ascended his horse, moving the animal away to allow Destin to speak with her too.

She approached him, cautiously, steeling herself for the agony of having to say goodbye to him, knowing she couldn't reach out to him, touch him, or make a scene here.

'Will the trip take you very long?' she asked politely.

'No more than a few days by boat.'

'At least you won't be being pursued by anyone on this journey.'

'Thank goodness.'

'Or suffer intense torrents of rain and no sleep.'

'Small mercies.' He grimaced, his hand holding the horse's reins. But he inclined his head, lowering his voice. 'I'd suffer it all again to get to know you, Livia. I have no regrets.'

She nodded, but she could feel her chin begin to wobble from the strain of holding in her emotions. 'Neither do I.' She ran her gaze all over him, wanting to commit his molten ebony eyes, his long, wild hair, each scar, expression, every part of him, to her memory.

'Promise me you'll take care of yourself, so I don't have to worry.'

She nodded. 'I promise.' Though she could barely talk, her throat was raw. Her whole world was shattering and she had to stand there, pretending that it wasn't.

'Goodbye, Livia,' he said, ascending his horse. 'If you ever need anything, remember, we're only a sea away.'

Chapter Eleven

Putting duty over desire had been a terrible idea. Livia had been suffering ever since.

After Destin left, she threw herself into her new role, keeping busy. They had held the most splendid funeral for her father, giving him the magnificent send-off he deserved. And she had been crowned queen and empress by the Pope in an equally elaborate ceremony. But somehow, even with all those thousands of people in attendance, it had felt almost hollow without Destin at her side.

She'd tried to stay occupied, setting to work on rebuilding her mother's castle in Saxony from afar and improving the mountain pass in the Alps so her people could more readily get between the lands of their empire, improving trade. Livia had also discreetly sent some coin and horses to the monks up at the hospice, to make the place more hospitable for them and for the weary travellers they took in. The busier she was, the less time she had to think about Destin, she realised. And yet still the summer dragged on and on.

She couldn't regret the vow she had made to the College that day, as she knew it was what they'd needed to hear to make her queen. And this was what she wanted. It was her rightful place. But she had really thought Destin might stay. That he would want to be with her anyway. Yet he hadn't, and her heart had been fractured ever since. He had been her greatest sacrifice and he was always on her mind. She felt the absence of him everywhere she went.

Every night, when she lay awake in the bed where he had first made love to her, she pulled her chronicles open on her lap and found the little edelweiss flower he'd given her in the mountains. She had pressed it between the pages, to keep it safe, and took it out to study it, running her fingers over the petals. 'It can withstand most storms. A symbol of resilience…' he'd told her, and remembering his words helped to keep her strong.

She'd invited farmer Charles and his wife to visit soon, and she was looking forward to seeing how they were, and thought she could ask them to bring a few of these flowers from the mountainside and try to grow them here, in the palace gardens. Perhaps it wouldn't be the right conditions, like it hadn't been for her and Destin's relationship, but she thought she would try anyway.

The project she was most excited about and had thrown herself into fully was creating an orphanage in one of the monasteries in Rome. It was for families who didn't think they could raise their child. If they were struggling, instead of leaving the child out to die in the wilderness, or on the streets, parents could anonymously leave their unwanted child in a foundling wheel and the infant would be looked after by the church until they could be taken in by a loving household. Livia really hoped it would make a difference to children who had been abandoned, children like Destin.

Having decided to stay in Rome and rule from here, she was starting to grow into her position and she felt supported by her councillors. She had made just one error during her time in power so far. She should have seized her uncle in the palace that day, after the election had taken place. First, they had heard accounts of Lothair and his men having gone to France. Now, there were increasing rumours he had won support from the nobles there and was raising an army to attack Rome and usurp the throne, naming him the 'true sovereign' of the Holy Roman Empire. While free and alive, he was still very much a threat to her. A black cloud constantly hovering above her.

Lothair was yet to step foot back on the empire's soil, and she prayed an invasion would never come to pass, but if he did, it would be a direct act of opposition and Livia knew she would have to send troops to fight for her, to safeguard her lands and power. She had promised her people that her reign would be one free of conflict, so she would have to deal with an attack swiftly and effectively, so a battle didn't escalate into a war.

When the light of the city began to mellow, and the leaves on the trees began to change colour and fall to the ground, farmer Charles and Marta arrived for their visit. Livia was delighted to see them. She had met them at a dramatic time in her life, and their help had meant such a lot to her. She held a feast in their honour, thanking them for their assistance, and the following day, she and Marta took a stroll around the grounds and the woman helped her to plant the edelweiss flowers in a small rock garden. Marta had lifted the roots from the plants in the mountains and divided them, bringing them here as Livia had requested.

'Forgive me, Your Highness, I hope you do not mind me saying, but you do not seem as content as you were when we met you in the mountains, despite the danger you were in. You must miss your home in Saxony?' Marta queried.

Livia shrugged. 'Sometimes. But not as much as I thought I would.'

'You miss the commander more.'

Livia's head whipped round. 'What?' she gasped, halting digging a hole in the soil, looking up at the woman in disbelief.

'Oh, ignore me, I'm probably speaking out of turn...' she said, bustling about, handing out one of the plants for Livia to take.

Livia glanced all around her to check no one was about. A guard stood at the corner of the garden, watching them, but fortunately, he was out of hearing distance.

'No, it's all right,' she said, lowering her voice. She hadn't mentioned Destin to anyone in weeks, and it felt good to be able to speak of him with someone who knew him. 'Go on...'

'I saw you kissing,' the woman admitted.

Livia's eyes widened and she felt a flush sweep over her cheeks.

'By the lake, that day. I think you must have liked him,' the woman said conspiratorially.

Livia's throat constricted, the memories hitting her with force. It had been a glorious moment. Her first kiss. Destin had made her toes curl. She had loved him, even then. But she hadn't known they were being watched. And she realised Destin was right, they would have been found out eventually. She wouldn't have been able to keep her feelings hidden. They were irrepressible, much too strong.

Her eyes filled with tears and she tried to blink them away. 'Yes. I did. Very much. But I wish to thank you for not telling anyone about it. For being discreet.'

Marta's brow furrowed. 'Oh, I would never.'

'He gave me one of these,' Livia said, nodding to the little star-shaped plants. 'I love them.'

'People say an edelweiss is a sign of devotion, you know.'

'Do they?' She wondered if Destin had known that.

Marta nodded. 'He was a very handsome man. And one who was willing to die for you too. There's not too many of those about, I can tell you. What he did out there when those men attacked the cart...'

Livia nodded, still unable to comprehend it herself. 'I know.' She shuddered.

'He must have liked you too, I think!' she said, raising her eyebrow.

'Not enough to stay,' she said miserably, rising to her feet to look Marta in the eyes. 'When I became queen, I asked him to be my chief commander in my Queen's

Guard, so we could still be together. So I could see him every day. He refused.'

Marta looked at her thoughtfully, tipping her head to one side. 'I expect he wanted more than that, no?'

Did he?

'Perhaps. But that would have been impossible. I had just been made empress.'

'And he's just a soldier? A Northman…?'

Livia frowned. 'I didn't mean that… I didn't mean he's beneath me.'

'No, I don't think that man could ever be described as *just* anything,' the woman said.

But a sudden feeling of unease began to prickle along Livia's skin. Had she made him feel like he was lacking? Had she made him think he wasn't worthy? She had offered him a position in her Guard, telling him she'd give him all that the emperor gave him…but had that insulted him?

'Did you get the chance to tell him what he meant to you?' Marta asked. 'Before he left?'

'He knew.'

But *did* he?

She began to silently berate her words and actions on that final day, a tight knot forming in her stomach.

She had asked him to stay, saying she wanted to be with him, but she hadn't told him she loved him. She had shown him with her body, over and over again, she had given herself to him completely, but she'd never said the words. And then a thought lanced her, so swift and brutal, it made her gasp. When she'd suggested they could be together, but keep their relationship secret, had that been the worst thing she could have done? He would have thought she was ashamed of him, as his parents had been, but she wasn't at all. She just couldn't see another way around it, how they could be together, and she would have rather had him in secret than not at all.

But now she realised, with blinding obviousness, that a man such as he wouldn't have wanted to be kept hidden, out of sight, as if he wasn't significant. He'd suffered that his whole life. Especially as he was important.

She felt the emotion rise, thick in her throat. He was the one person she could depend on and trust more than anyone else. He was the man who had made her the woman she was today. He was the key to her happiness.

News of an imminent invasion came one night, a few weeks later, when Livia had just retired to bed. The beacons had been lit throughout the empire, warning them of the impending attack. Livia had wrapped herself in her robe and raced down to the hall, where all her councillors had gathered.

'Lothair has landed in Italy and is marching north,' Matthias told her, filling her in immediately. 'There have been skirmishes as his army has made its way through the lands in the south. Your people are standing up to him, putting up a fight, but his army is making incursions, heading this way.'

So he had come. Her uncle intended to invade Rome and try to secure his position as king. He would never give up unless he was put down.

Livia's stomach roiled and she clutched her arms to her chest as she attempted to swallow down her fear.

'How many of them are there?'

'They came by a fleet of a hundred ships. Combined with reinforcements picked up in southern Italy, our scouts tell us there are over a thousand men. That is, if he isn't joined by any other forces on the way north.'

The breath left her.

'What do you advise we do?'

'Meet him on our border, near to Naples, and stop him proceeding.'

'How many men will we need?'

'All that we have. At least enough to match his army.'

'Very well.' She nodded. 'I shall lead them.'

'Your Highness. I cannot allow...'

She held up her hand to silence him. 'I will not send my men into a battle I'm not prepared to fight myself. I'm going, Matthias, and nothing you can say will stop me from doing so.'

Perhaps he saw how adamant she was, how vital her presence might be for the morale of the soldiers, as he clamped his lips together and didn't fight it further, and later that day, they set off for the south.

The scale of her army was impressive—how many men were willing to fight for her and their empire— and more joined them along the way. Livia was humbled. But she hated that they were in this position. She didn't want to take fathers and husbands away from their homes and families. Still, she hoped they had a big enough force to fight Lothair and his foreign army.

It was a long trip down to Naples, especially in her heavy, restrictive armour, which she wasn't used to wearing, and carrying her father's sword. But she knew she had to remain stoic for her men. They would be looking up to her to set an example, and so she was determined to show no fear. She desperately wanted to be a queen they could believe in.

After what seemed like an immense journey, they heard they were nearing Lothair's army, and the battle site was picked—one which would give them the most advantage. The men erected tents and they sat around sharing stories by the fires, and she tried to gather her strength. She went around speaking to each group, hoping to remind them what they were fighting for, and in return, their tales of glory kept her spirits up. Still, the tension in the camp was high. Everyone knew that by morning, they would be in the throes of a great battle that would determine their future.

'You should get some rest now, Your Highness,' Matthias suggested.

'The same goes for all of you.' She nodded. 'We will all need our strength on the morrow.'

If it were to be her last night to live, she thought, retiring to her tent, this wasn't how she would choose to spend it. Given the option, she would want to be with Destin. She would want to die in his arms, like she had thought she was going to that day in the cart at the border. Or as an old lady, having lived a lifetime of happiness at his side. And she decided, if she was to survive this battle, afterwards, she would visit him in Constantinople. After all, the emperor had invited her. She needed to see his face again, to look into his eyes and tell him how she felt, to know she'd done everything she could for them to be together.

Morning came much too quickly. The autumn sun struggled to break through the clouds, an encroaching storm hovering overhead in the east, and the men began preparing themselves for what lay ahead. They sharpened their weapons in heavy silence, before forming a formidable line along the ridge above the expanse of meadow. The hilltop site offered them a good defensive position, and they stood awaiting their enemy.

Sitting atop her horse, Livia's heart was pounding in her chest. Since Lothair had been a threat, she had begun practising sword fighting again with her soldiers at home. She was competent, but she would not consider herself a warrior. She had no experience of ever fighting in a battle. She was afraid, but she could never let her men know that—she was determined to do her best, for them and her empire.

They knew Lothair's army was drawing near when the ground began to shudder beneath their feet. And as her uncle's army finally came into view on the horizon, her blood ran cold. There were many of them. And the noise was deafening, as they chanted and roared, trying to strike fear into the hearts of her men. Her soldiers' horses began to nicker and paw their hooves, agitated, and the men began to jostle for space, nervous now. Only the air was still.

A lone rider crossed the field towards them and Livia and Matthias pressed their ankles into their horses' sides, urging them forward to greet the man halfway.

'Your Highness. Prince Lothair demands you lay down your throne and your weapons and he will stop this fight.'

'Never. He is a traitor to his crown and empire. Tell my uncle that if he doesn't lay down his *own* weapons, we will not stop until he is defeated. This ends today.'

'Then you should prepare for the worst, Your Highness,' the stranger sneered.

As they galloped back towards her men, she gave a nod for them to get ready, with her leading the charge. Despite her whole body trembling, she would show them her courage, that she was worthy of their loyalty and swords.

Lothair's men began chanting faster, louder, and then they were charging towards them, swarming across the grass, waving their weapons. It was the most frightening sight she had ever seen.

But all of a sudden, out of nowhere, an enormous body of men appeared from out of the trees on the left, startling both sides, cutting into the flank of Lothair's men, and the whole of the field descended into chaos.

It took a moment for Livia to register what was happening. That these men wore the burgundy cloak of the Byzantine Varangians, the dragons' eyes on their tunics mocking their opponents. And there, leading them on his horse, was their commander, Destin.

Destin was here.

Momentarily, she forgot all else. The battle. The enemy. Where she was. She could only focus on him and how magnificent he looked, galloping towards her across the meadow, his brow forming a dark line. He looked almost godlike, in burnished armour, his muscled arm bare, his chest covered in chain-mail, the breeze ruffling his long tied-back hair. He wore a helmet, but his visor was up, and his dark, reprimanding eyes were focused on her. He had grown a full beard, she realised, as she openly stared at him, devouring him, forgetting to blink, and her mouth hung open in wonderment.

His cavalry were keeping the enemy occupied, taking them by surprise, cutting them down, while his infantry fearlessly lined up in formation in front of Livia's soldiers, putting themselves between her men and the enemy, protecting them.

He galloped towards her, before drawing his horse to a halt next to hers.

'You're here!' she gasped, breathless, verbalising her shock. Her eyes raked over him. She'd missed his handsome face. His ebony eyes. The curve of his generous smile. His incredible body. Their conversations. She'd missed everything about him.

'So are you,' he said, and she realised he wasn't pleased to see her, he was angry. 'You should not be! The battlefield is no place for a woman.' He turned to Matthias, unleashing his irritation on her councillor. 'What were you thinking?' he raged.

'I tried to dissuade her. She insisted,' he said.

'I don't want you fighting. It's much too dangerous,' Destin barked, his brittle gaze boring into her. 'Hold back in reserve, behind your infantry.'

She shook her head. 'No, I need to fight with my men.'

A muscle worked in his cheek, just visible under his armour. 'There's no time to argue with me.'

'What are *you* doing here?' she asked, her voice cracking with emotion. She needed to know, now, even though they were in the midst of a battle. 'Why did you come? How did you know we'd be here?'

Destin surveyed the scene before them, the bloody fight drawing closer. 'Shield wall!' he shouted. And all his men locked shields, forming a tight line. They looked formidable, as did he. Then he turned back to her, giving her his attention again. 'I told you, if you needed me, I would be here. We heard of Lothair leaving France. Alexios allowed me to come with my men. That's what allies do, right?'

She swallowed. *What about lovers?*

But she nodded, her eyes filling with grateful tears. She furiously blinked them away.

'I came as quickly as we could, Your Highness.'

She bristled at the formality of him using her title. And yet, she was elated he had come here for her. To protect her, again. To defend her title, even though it was the cause of their separation. He was still on her side, and it gave her hope...

'And we are very glad you're here, Chief Commander,' Matthias said.

'Chief?' Livia asked. The emperor must have raised his rank. Was that because he had done his duty, with her? She had been starved of news of him... How had Matthias not shared this information with her?

Destin turned his focus back to the fight. To commanding his men. And she wondered...reinforced by his troops, might they stand a chance?

She watched in awe as he unsheathed his sword and raised it in the air before leading his infantry into battle, fighting, at the heart of the action, striking the enemy down one by one. He rained down brutal blows on his opponents, as his men fought well by his side. He was a force to be reckoned with, incredible to watch.

His soldiers maintained their shield wall even as they met the enemy's onslaught. And then Livia lifted her own sword, commanding her own army, and they joined the fray, swords clashing, shields splintering, but she no longer felt afraid. Now Destin was here, she felt invincible.

The first strike of metal against her own shield winded her, but Livia quickly gathered herself together and fought back, trying to push one brute away, then the next. She saw Destin jump down from his horse, before disposing of a man who was bearing down on her, fighting without fear, and he protected her from the spears and axes flying in all directions. They fought back-to-back, and it was working, despite the carnage, soldiers falling wherever she looked, but she dug deep and pushed on, trying to make a difference.

The battle raged, and she was beginning to tire under the weight of her heavy weapon and armour, but she didn't dare stop, until finally, Lothair's army began to fragment and fracture. They were outflanked. Men began retreating, fleeing the battlefield, but Destin pressed on, seeking out Lothair, heading directly for his enemy, unwilling to allow him to escape this time.

'Ah, the one-armed warrior. Come to *single-handedly* defeat me,' Lothair mocked, and he gave a brutal swipe of his sword and they began to fight.

Livia's heart was in her mouth. She couldn't bear it if something were to happen to Destin. Not now. Especially after he'd come to the rescue of her and her men, putting himself at risk to save her again. Lothair bore down on him, but Destin ducked, just missing the swinging blade, before bringing his own sword down on his opponent. Lothair managed to raise his shield to prevent the blow from doing any damage.

They both fought savagely, and she felt every blow Lothair rained down on Destin as if she was suffering it herself, wincing at each jab. But Destin was quick on his feet, faster than Lothair, and a much more skilful warrior. He was relentless, ruthless, and finally, he managed to knock the weapon out of Lothair's hand and push him down, onto his back, into the muddy ground. He put his boot on his chest, just as he had done back in Rome, his breathing ragged.

'It seems we're here again,' he said, wiping his brow with the back of his arm, having lost his helmet during the battle. His long hair had come loose and he looked incredible. Powerful. All man. 'The second time I've beaten you. Only this time, you're not going free. I should kill you right here and now...'

'Please. Don't,' Lothair whimpered, like the coward he was, his eyes wide with fear, the remainder of his men dispersing, deserting him and his cause, not wanting to stick around to see what happened next.

Destin's and Livia's men watched on, waiting for the chief commander to run Lothair through. It was his right. But instead, as controlled as ever, Destin turned to look at Livia over his shoulder, his gaze seeking out hers.

'What do you want me to do with him, Your Highness?'

She swallowed, walking over to him on unsteady feet. 'The rebellion is defeated. The battle is over. Let us not spill any more blood. I want my reign to be one of mercy, not marked by bloodshed.'

Destin nodded. 'Get me some rope,' he ordered one of his men.

When they returned with it, they quickly bound Lothair's wrists and Destin dragged the traitor to his feet.

'You will be imprisoned for your crimes against your queen and the empire, Uncle,' Livia told him, looking her defeated enemy in the eye. 'You should be ashamed of yourself for all you have done. I never want to see you again.'

'Take him,' Destin said to his men. 'Guard him.' And the men bundled him away.

Destin sheathed his sword, before turning to look at her.

She stared back at him, her eyes glowing with admiration. It was over. He had saved them. He was alive…

She wanted to throw herself into his arms and collapse against him, to have him pull her close, for him to hold her again and whisper words of comfort into her ear, but she knew he could not with all the soldiers watching. She didn't even know if he wanted to. So instead, she settled on taking a step closer towards him.

'Thank you, Destin. For coming to help us. I can't tell you how much it means to me.'

He nodded, his gaze roaming over her. 'Are you hurt? I told you not to fight!' he said.

'No. Not a scratch,' she said, and she could see the tension ease from his face.

'Commander,' Matthias said, coming over, interrupting them, and Livia felt the crushing disappointment that they were no longer alone. 'How will we ever thank you? I hope you know how much we appreciate what you did today.'

'I will always come to your aid.'

Livia hadn't seen Destin all summer and she wanted to speak to him. Properly. There was so much she wanted to say to him. She wanted to ask him how he'd been. She wanted to know how he'd spent the past few months, and whether he'd missed her. She wanted to touch him, to press her hand against his handsome face again, to rest it over his solid chest. But instead, he turned to talk with her councillor about how word had reached them of Lothair's plan, the battle, and what now needed to be done to clear the field.

The men walked off, making a start, barking out orders, and she felt bereft. She wanted him to herself. She needed him. But it was clear everyone else did too. They were all in awe of him, at last. Finally, they all saw what she had seen in him from the start. All the men wanted to thank him and praise him, offering their words of appreciation, and they held him responsible for their success here today, for saving her throne and the empire. He was a hero to be admired. But she wanted to be the one to worship him, not them.

It took the rest of the day to bury the bodies. They had suffered far too many losses and it was a depressing task. By the time nightfall came and they'd set up camp, everyone was exhausted.

She tried to speak to Destin when they were sitting

around the campfire, but they got interrupted, and finally, when Matthias showed her to her tent and put a soldier on guard outside, she felt desperate. Would she ever get to be alone with him again?

She couldn't help but think he wasn't helping the situation, as if he was avoiding her, trying to keep her at a distance. Had he forgotten her, or moved on with his life? She hoped not, for she hadn't forgotten anything about him. And now she'd seen him again, she wanted him more than ever. She wanted him to come to her tent, to hold her, kiss her and make love to her again. And she lay down on the makeshift bed feeling frustrated.

She wanted to ask him what would happen in the morning. Now that he had come to their aid, that he'd done what he'd come here to achieve, would he be leaving again, returning to Constantinople? She didn't think she could bear to say goodbye to him for a second time, not now that she knew how bad it felt and how much she missed him. She didn't want to live without him any more. She wanted him in her future, and this time, she would do whatever it took to make that happen.

They rode all morning, the soldiers in high spirits despite their injuries and lack of sleep. Matthias had announced they would host a celebratory feast in Destin's honour back in Rome, and Destin had agreed to see them back to the city safely, before returning to Constantinople, but he was finding being back in Livia's company harder than he'd thought.

Last night, he'd been unable to sleep, knowing she was in a tent a few feet away from him, knowing he was unable to go to her. Seeing her again was a torment. When his gaze had fallen on her on the battlefield, his body had contracted in shock. Not for one moment had he thought she'd be here, on the frontline of the fight. He had hoped she would be safely at home in Rome, and she would never have to witness the brutal battle that had taken place yesterday. His heart had frozen over in fear for her safety.

When he and Alexios had heard of Lothair's fleet leaving France, they had known they had to help. Destin had headed straight here. But he'd never thought he would be fighting alongside her, just protecting her from afar. He had thought she wouldn't need to know about his intervention until it was all over.

Instead, she had surprised him by being competent with a sword. But she had been a distraction too. He hadn't been able to take his eyes off her for a moment. He'd never been so afraid when fighting. He'd been terrified of her getting hurt. What the hell had she been thinking? And yet, he had to admire her bravery. She was certainly an empress the men were ready to fight and die for. He knew he was.

He hadn't been prepared to see her again. And the force of his emotions came back like a landslide. It had taken him months to learn to cope with the misery of being without her. He had tried to forget her, just like Áki had done with Gerdur, all those years before. But he hadn't been able to set his mind to anything either, his thoughts were consumed by her, and in one moment, one meeting of their eyes, he was right back to where he'd started, wanting her, all over again.

When he'd ridden out of her life before, he'd felt like a broken man. He'd returned with Alexios to Constantinople and had been made chief commander in his Varangian Guard. He'd been rewarded with riches and a home of his own. He'd got everything he'd ever strived to achieve, and yet it had felt empty somehow without her. He was like the fruit trees he could see from his window in the Great City, lost without their sweet bounty.

He'd felt as if he didn't know who he was any more, and so, with Alexios's permission, he'd decided it was time to find out. It was why he'd returned to Norway to try to find his birth family.

He'd come so far. He'd thought he'd moved on. But now, riding behind her on this journey, watching her bottom sway from side to side as her horse trotted in front of him, he knew he wasn't over her. He had just tried to bury his feelings, pushing them down, trying not to acknowledge them. Now they had sprung forth once more like the water in the fountain in the palace that day, and he knew one thing was vital. He had to protect himself. He had to build a shield wall around his heart. He had to make sure they were never alone. He would see them safely back to Rome for the celebrations they were putting on in his honour, and then leave and never look back, before he did something foolish. Before he destroyed them both.

As they reached a wider track, Livia slowed her horse so they were riding side by side. 'How have you been?' she asked quietly.

'Well, thank you, Your Highness,' he lied.

Her jaw clenched. He knew she wouldn't like him calling her by her title, but they were surrounded by her men, what did she expect? Besides, she was the one who had wanted to keep up the pretence of them not being intimate.

'And you?'

'Yes, very well. How is the emperor? You will have to pass on my sincerest gratitude to him for sending men to support us.'

'I will be sure to do that.' He glanced across at her; she sat atop her horse, riding astride as she had the night they'd first met and had escaped the castle. She was still just as beautiful as she'd looked the first time he'd seen her, despite the dark shadows beneath her eyes. Yet she carried herself proudly, regardless of the weight of responsibility that he knew she must carry around with her for her empire. He wanted to ease her burden. 'How are you settling into your new role?'

'It has been busy, but I have learned so much. Something new every day, I think.'

He nodded. It felt good to talk to her again. He wanted to hear how she'd spent every moment of her time since they'd been apart, and he gave himself a silent talking to. He must not allow himself to care.

'We heard you have not long returned from Norway,' Matthias said, interrupting them.

Her head flipped round to look at her councillor, her eyes wide. Matthias obviously hadn't shared that information with her. Just like his title.

'Norway?' she asked Destin, incredulous, and he could see the questions burning behind her eyes.

He nodded. 'Visiting family. I'll tell you about it sometime,' he said, inclining his head. 'But right now, let's focus on the ride and getting back to Rome. I imagine your people will be eager to see you.'

And he was right. They were. A messenger had been sent ahead to tell the council of their success on the battlefield and when they finally arrived home, the whole of the city had turned out to celebrate their return. But he was shocked to discover they weren't just cheering for their empress and the soldiers, but for him, as well. It seemed he was the man of the moment. The warrior who had heroically made a stand against Lothair's forces, protecting their empress, their men and their realm. He bowed his head graciously. He wasn't used to the attention.

A huge celebration was held across the city to mark their win in Naples and the defeat of Lothair, and it culminated in a lively feast that night. He was surprised to be named the champion of the people and seated next to Livia as her guest of honour. It was quite a turnaround. Everyone wanted to speak to him, to hear his version of how the battle had gone. And yet, all he really wanted was to get her on her own, to have their own celebration. And he chastised himself for his thoughts.

When their knees brushed under the table, he hated that excitement hardened his groin, and when their arms collided, heat rippled through him, and he had to steel himself against it. Her floral scent drifted under his nose, causing a pang in his chest, but he was determined to deny the attraction that still burned between them, even though the feelings he felt for her were as intense as ever.

'I saw the farmer and his wife a few weeks ago,' Livia told him.

'How were they?' he asked, pouring her some ale from a jug.

'They are well. They're considering selling the farm and moving to the city. They're finding it a lot of work, and too remote. I offered Marta a position at the palace.'

'Did she accept?'

'She's thinking about it.'

He nodded, wondering what it would have been like if he'd accepted her proposition. Perhaps he would be retiring to a warm bed rather than a cold one. Had he made a huge mistake? Surely it would be better to have her in his life in some capacity, rather than not at all?

'We planted some edelweiss flowers in the palace gardens while she was here. I don't know if they'll put down roots and bloom, but I'm hoping so. Did you know they're a symbol of devotion?' she asked him, looking up into his eyes.

'I did know that, yes.'

She swallowed.

He was pleased when finally the meal came to an end and the entertainment began so he could excuse himself to get back to the safety of his barracks. When he pushed out his chair and stood, he saw her face fall, but he was determined to put himself far, far away from temptation.

He thought he had been successful. But as he crossed the courtyard to the soldier's barracks, he heard her softly call his name. Had he imagined it? Was it just wishful thinking? He halted, even though he knew he should keep walking. But the pull of her voice was too much. When he turned round he saw her coming towards him, her beautiful golden eyes glittering in the moonlight.

'Go back inside, Livia. We can't be seen out here.'

'I just wanted to ask you about Norway,' she said, and he knew he'd hurt her with his sharp words. She began wringing her hands. 'Will you tell me about it? Please?'

He was touched she was interested and his heart jammed in his chest. Did she still care? He raked his hand over his hair. 'I'll tell you about it if you promise to go back inside afterwards.'

She nodded. 'All right… What made you go back there?'

'You,' he said simply, shrugging. And he sat down on the courtyard steps.

Her eyes widened. 'Me?'

'Yes. Watching you become the woman you were born to be made me look at myself. It made me realise I still didn't know who I was or where I'd come from. I didn't know what kind of blood flowed through my veins. After I left here, for the first time in my life, I wanted to find out.'

'And did you find out?' she asked, coming to sit down beside him. 'Did you manage to find your family?'

The hall erupted into clapping and cheering inside, but he was only focused on her. *Helvete!* How did she have this hold over him?

'Yes. It took a while. I went back to the woods where Áki found me, and began asking questions of all the villagers in the settlements around there. I was getting nowhere, I was losing hope, when I was sitting in an alehouse and a woman approached me. She'd heard I'd been asking questions and hadn't known whether to speak out. It turned out she was my mother. And she was both shocked and delighted to find me alive. She told me not a day had passed when she hadn't thought about me, or regretted her decision. It was like I'd thought, they'd been worried about my future and had decided it would be more merciful to put me out to die.'

'It still shocks me to hear it, even now,' Livia said with a shudder.

'They are simple farmers. She couldn't believe it when I told her I was a commander in the Emperor's Guard.'

'*Chief* Commander,' she corrected him. 'I notice you have been raised to a higher rank. Congratulations.'

He inclined his head in acknowledgement. 'Thank you. She took me to meet my father. And I have two brothers, both younger than me. I looked into their faces and saw myself. They looked just like me, only they had no impairments.' He shook his head as he was reminiscing. 'It was…good, to finally know where I'd come from.'

'I can imagine.'

He'd finally felt free. As if he could return to Constantinople, knowing himself better. 'They welcomed me back, said I could stay, but I told them it wasn't where I belonged.'

But moving back to Constantinople, he hadn't felt as if he belonged there either. Not any more. He was unable to settle, finding it difficult to live without Livia.

He finally understood how Áki had felt when Gerdur had died, needing to travel, to see new places and make new memories to try to stamp out the pain of thinking about the old ones. Now that he was back here, with her, he didn't want to be parted from her. All he wanted to do was reach out and touch her. He so desperately wanted to stay. But their circumstances hadn't changed, and he knew he couldn't.

'Thank you, for telling me,' she said.

He gave a brief nod. 'Go back inside now. You promised.'

'What are you worried about? What do you think is going to happen?' she asked him, tipping her head to one side to study him. 'Don't you trust yourself around me?'

His eyes narrowed on her. 'Truthfully? No.'

He saw her eyes widen just a little, shocked at his searing honesty, that he'd admitted it. And then she smiled.

'Destin, I'd like to show you something on the morrow. Will you meet me here, at the gates, before we break our fast in the morning?'

'You know I'm leaving tomorrow, don't you? I'm returning to Constantinople.'

'Yes,' she said sadly. 'So will you do this one thing for me, before you go?'

He got to his feet and drew his hand over his beard. 'You know I can't deny you anything, Livia,' he said wryly. It's what he was so afraid of. Why he had to get away. 'I'll see you on the morrow then,' he said, and he turned his back on her, leaving her sitting there on the steps of her palace in the moonlight.

* * *

'Where are we going?' he asked.

'You'll see.'

The carriage took them along the streets of her capital to the monastery and when they arrived outside, he raised an eyebrow. 'You've brought me to church?'

She rolled her eyes at him as they got out. 'No, not quite. I wanted to share with you a project that's become close to my heart this summer,' she said, stepping out, waiting for him to follow her, stooping his head as he curled his big body out of the cabin. 'I've brought you to my orphanage.'

He swung to look at her and she met his gaze.

'Orphanage?' he pressed.

'Yes. We have turned one of the monasteries into an orphanage,' she explained. 'For families who don't feel able to raise a child, for whatever reason…'

He stared at her, incredulous. 'That is an admirable thing to do,' he rasped. 'What inspired that?'

'You.'

His throat closed in shock.

'Which is why I've called it Hospice Destiny. After you. You, and the children here, have proven that out of trauma and tragedy, true greatness can appear.'

Is that what she thought? He was incredibly moved.

'Will you come inside and meet some of the children? They are amazing,' she said, tugging his arm. 'They have so much potential.'

He allowed her to lead him through the doors and they spent the next few hours walking around the orphanage, talking to the children, and seeing the work the bishops were doing with them. And he was astounded. Of her. Of what they had achieved. He looked over at her, as she was cradling one of the babies, and their eyes met. His heart swelled.

He couldn't believe that he had had such an impact on her that she would create such a place for children like him. He was astounded. Perhaps he wasn't quite as insignificant to her as he'd thought.

'It's incredible, Livia. Really. I'm proud of you. You really are an empress to look up to.'

As they stepped back out onto the street, the afternoon sun shining down on them, he ran his hand round the back of his neck. The silence stretched between them.

'Shall we walk a little?' she asked.

He knew it was time to go, to leave her, so why was it that he couldn't bring himself to do so? He gave a short nod.

They began to walk down a leafy lane, her guards following behind them at a distance, but after a few strides, she stopped, turning towards him. 'Destin, I'm so glad you're here. I have thought of nothing but you all summer long. I have missed you, terribly. I've been miserable without you,' she said. 'I should never have made that vow to the College that day. It was wrong of me.'

He stared down at her, his throat choked with emotion. 'You said what you needed to say to make you empress. It was the right thing to do, Livia.'

'No, it wasn't,' she said, shaking her head adamantly. 'Because I was lying to my people and myself. And I wasn't fair to you. I hurt you. And nothing has felt right since, with you being gone. You say I've become the woman I was born to be, but you made me that woman, Destin. And I am only half of the woman I know I could be with you by my side.'

His dark gaze studied her. 'What are you saying?'

She reached down and took his hand in hers, looking up at him. 'I realise now, I made you feel as if you weren't good enough for me. That you weren't worthy of my love. But no one is more deserving of love than you, Destin. And I should have told everyone how I felt about you. That I couldn't live without you. I should have told you that I love you. Because I do. So much. And I want to make it up to you now, by telling you I love you every day, for the rest of our lives.'

He went very still, unable to believe what he was hearing. 'You love me?' Despite the fact he was a Northman? A pagan? His impairment? It was all he'd wanted to hear. 'I thought you just wanted to seduce me—I didn't realise you loved me,' he said, trying to jest, but he knew now was the time to be serious. What she was saying was very serious.

'I think I loved you from the moment you helped that horse in the stables that first night,' she said, her lips trying to form a smile, but it crumpled, the significance of what she was trying to tell him, getting to her. 'And every moment since then.'

'I don't think telling the College that would have helped you become empress, Livia,' Destin said, staring down into her eyes that were sparkling like yellow diamonds.

'No, but telling you might have changed your mind

about staying. I'm hoping it does now. I don't want you to leave again, Destin. I want you to stay. Always.'

His heart was overflowing with emotion. She loved him. But did that change anything? Could he now stay? He wanted to. And being the bodyguard of someone he loved, protecting someone he cared for was a good way to spend his time. He could live with that.

'Are you reiterating your offer, to be in your Queen's Guard, to be by your side and protect you every day?' He'd felt a fool for turning her down before, and had regretted it many a restless night since, longing to have her back in his embrace. If she asked him again now, he knew he would weaken and say yes.

'No,' she said, shaking her head. 'I don't need a bodyguard, Destin… But I do want a husband.'

When Livia saw how Destin had earned the respect and support of the people, how his name was revered around the city, she wondered if it was possible they might finally see in him what she did. She hoped so, because one thing had become very clear to her. She knew she had to have him in her future. She couldn't lose him again. And she was prepared to fight for him, as he had fought for her on the battlefield.

Last night, it was as if he'd returned to the man she'd first met in Harzburg, devoid of emotion. She'd seen a flicker of the real him return when he'd told her of finding his family, but apart from that, she knew he was shutting her out, trying to keep her at bay, even if it was a struggle. Because he was trying to do the right thing, as always. But seeing the flare of panic in his eyes as she'd approached him in the courtyard, she'd begun to hope. If he was so concerned something might happen between them if they were left alone, then perhaps he might still feel a little of what she felt for him.

Afraid now, she wrung her hands. 'I visited the electors at the palace this morning. I asked for their permission to marry you...'

His eyes widened. His brows rose. 'What?'

'I know it sounds absurd. I don't even know if you want to marry me, or how you feel about me any more. But I had to ask, just to know if there was even a possibility, a chance for us. You are the man who saved our empire, who saved me, after all, so I couldn't think of a better time to speak to them.'

His gaze raked over her and he stepped towards her. 'What did they say, Livia?'

Her eyes filled with tears. 'They asked me to wait outside while they discussed it. I paced the courtyard for a long while. But when they called me back in, they said yes.'

'They said yes?' he asked, repeating her words.

'Yes,' she smiled, her eyes filling with tears. 'But there are conditions attached, of course.' And she bit her lip, suddenly feeling nervous. She wasn't sure what he'd make of them.

'What are they?'

She shook her head. 'It is a big ask...'

'Tell me.'

'They would require you to renounce your nationality. And all titles. I know how hard you have worked to get to where you are now.' She knew it was too big a request, perhaps that's why the council had suggested it, to test him. But she hadn't wanted to give up her authority to a man. Why would he? 'And you would never be king here, but merely my husband. Perhaps a duke in time…' she continued. 'You could still command my Royal Guard, if you wanted… And…and they would expect you to convert to our religion. To be baptised…' She thought back to his comments about her religion in the chapel before they'd started out on the mountain pass, and how he would never convert to Christianity for Alexios, so she wondered if he might laugh at her, for even suggesting it. 'I know it is a lot to think about, that it is too much to ask…'

Suddenly, he pulled her close, wrapping his arm around her waist, bringing her right up against him, not caring they were in the middle of the lane, who saw, and she gasped.

'I don't need titles, Livia. Or riches or lands. All I want to be known as is the man who you love. That is enough for me. Because I love you so much and I cannot bear to be parted from you again either.'

She felt the breath leave her. She couldn't believe it. 'What about your religion? Your Norse gods.'

'I believe in you and our love far more than any faith… I will work around it.'

She frowned. 'So you're willing to do all those things, sacrifice them all, for me?'

'If it means I can be at your side for the rest of our lives, and not have to hide how I feel about you, then yes.'

He pressed a soft kiss to her temple to show her and

whoever was watching how much he loved her. 'Thank you, for fighting for me. And for the amazing legacy of the orphanage, Livia.'

'About that…' She bit her lip. 'Can I throw in another condition?'

He pulled her tighter, his lips a breath away from hers.

'Looking after the children at the orphanage, I was starting to think having a child of my own might be worth facing and dealing with my fear of childbirth. With the right person at my side to get me through it.'

He frowned, her statement sinking in. 'You want children?'

'*Your* children.'

'But…' He shook his head a little. 'What if they're like me? Look like me?'

She smiled then, wrapped her arms around him too. 'I really hope they do, Destin,' she laughed. 'Because you are the most beautiful man I have ever met. Inside and out. And they will be the most loved children in all the empire because I will love them as much as I love you.'

He drew her closer and pressed his lips against hers, kissing her tenderly.

'Is that a yes, then?' she said, when he ended the kiss, leaving her feeling warm and excited.

'If we can make a start on the having children part right now.'

Epilogue

Livia reached over to wake Destin in the middle of the night.

'The baby's coming,' she whispered, her breaths bursting in and out.

And he sat bolt upright, fully alert in an instant. He threw himself out of bed, pulling on his breeches. 'I'll go and get the maid.'

'No,' she said, gripping his arm. 'Don't leave me. I need you.'

'It's just for a moment, Livia.'

'No, please,' she said, gripping him hard, her eyes wide. The pains had been bearable until now, but they'd started to come thick and fast, and she was trying to control her fear. She knew the baby was imminent, she could feel the pressure down below, and she didn't want to let him out of her sight. She knew, if she had to, she could do this without him, but she didn't want to. She wanted him right here. Always.

He sat back down beside her on the bed and stroked her hair, tucking it behind her ear, before taking her hand in his. 'I'm just going to tell the guard down the corridor to fetch Marta and your servants. Perhaps they can run the bath… I promise I'll be back in just a moment.'

She nodded, and bravely she released him, letting him go. She was so desperate to meet her baby. So excited to hold it in her arms at last. Yet visions of her mother and baby brother kept entering her mind, and she couldn't shake them away.

But as he'd promised, Destin was back almost immediately. 'It will be all right, Livia. I'm here. You can do this. We can do this, together.' He sat on the bed, leaning against the wall, pulling her back against his chest, so she was sitting between his legs. 'Look how far we've come already,' he reminded her, kissing her on the forehead. And they really had.

When they had met in the mountains, she had been but a girl, on the cusp of being a woman and a queen. With Destin at her side, she had been able to achieve all that she had set out to do, and he told her every day that she had done the same for him. They were ruling this empire here together, successfully, and it had been the most glorious nine months of her life.

The wedding had been a dream come true, with all their friends around them. She had worn an exquisite gown and the ceremony had been magnificent, with the celebrations going on for weeks. But she had lived for the nights, where they had made every moment together count. They had made love whenever and wherever they could, not being able to get enough of each other. She had wanted him inside her, over and again, wanting him to show her how much he loved her, and her him in return. And she had fallen pregnant quickly.

She had worried he might not desire her as much as her belly had swollen, but the opposite was true. He had wanted her more, knowing she was growing his child inside her, finding her even more fascinating. And he'd been more protective of her than ever.

And now, it was as if they were facing their final fear together. The baby was coming and her maids were all there at her side, gathered around the bed, but it was her husband who was holding her in his arms, supporting her, encouraging her on with whispers of praise and love, and when she gave a final excruciating push and they heard their baby's first cry, she sank back against him as he planted proud kisses on her shoulders and cheeks.

Marta wrapped the child up and handed their child over to them, so they could cradle her in their arms. 'Congratulations,' she said. 'You have a beautiful, healthy daughter.'

And they both looked down on her in wonderment and love...

'Is she...?' Destin asked, his voice cracking.

'Healthy, my lord,' Marta told him, before ushering everyone out of the room, leaving them to be alone.

Livia curled her one arm around her daughter and brought her other hand up to hold her husband's tear-streaked face. 'Thank you,' she whispered, her own eyes overflowing. 'For being there for me.'

'Always,' he said, kissing her forehead. 'You never cease to amaze me, Livia. You were incredible. So brave.

I am in awe of you. I love you so much. Thank you, for making me the proudest, happiest man in the whole of the empire…' He stroked his hand down her arm, giving her a squeeze, before trailing his finger along his child's cheek, in awe of her too. 'She's perfect. Just like you.'

'And you,' Livia countered. 'I hope she grows up to be just like her father. The man I love.'

'A warrior? I'm not sure I could allow her to fight,' he said, already fiercely protective of her.

'If she would like. But certainly a protector of the realm, with the biggest heart I know.'

'What shall we call her?' he asked gently, his eyes shining down on her.

'I was thinking Edie,' Livia said, 'after the little edelweiss flower you gave me. So that she knows we and the empire will always be devoted to her.'

Like that little plant, blossoming out in the rock garden, she and Destin had been able to weather anything that had been thrown at them, and they'd thrived in spite of it all. Their devotion to one another had kept them strong, and she knew now, it always would.

* * * * *